MW01505409

Copyright © 2021 by S.Λ

All rights reserved. No part of this text may be reproduced, transmitted, downloaded, decompiled, reverse-engineered, or stored in, or introduced into any information storage and retrieval system, in any form or by any means, whether electronic or mechanical, now known, hereinafter invented, without express written permission of the publisher. For permission requests, write to the publisher, addressed "Attention: Permissions Coordinator," at the address below.

Typewriter Pub, an imprint of Blvnp Incorporated
A Nevada Corporation
1887 Whitney Mesa DR #2002
Henderson, NV 89014
www.typewriterpub.com/info@typewriterpub.com

ISBN: 978-1-64434-171-1

DISCLAIMER
This book is a work of fiction. The characters, incidents, and dialogue are drawn from the author's imagination and are not to be construed as real. While references might be made to actual historical events or existing locations, the names, characters, places, and incidents are either products of the author's imagination or are used fictitiously, and any resemblance to actual persons living or dead, business establishments, events or locales is entirely coincidental.

LOVED BY A DRAGON

Mate Me Series
BOOK ONE

S.M. MERRILL

type
writer
pub

*This book is dedicated to my husband, Jon,
who encouraged me to take a chance and write.*

CHAPTER ONE

"Roxie, you have to come with me to this new singles event!" her roommate, Evelyn, announced as she bounced into Roxie's bedroom. She pushed past several canvases and paint tubes left lying around. Roxie set down her paintbrush and sighed, reaching for a cloth to clean off her paint-covered hands. Ever since her divorce became official nine months ago, Evelyn had been pushing her to join the singles events that she frequented. Evelyn had rich brown hair, hazel eyes, and a sun-kissed tan. Roxie envied her skin tone. She, on the other hand, was pale, thanks to her Northern European heritage.

"No, I tried marriage once. I'm not interested in a new one." Roxie shook her head and went back to work on her landscape. Two weeks ago, she went on a trip to the Grand Canyon on a whim. Her mother had been asking her to quit painting since forever and just focus on her job as an executive assistant at her father's tax firm. The very thought made her sick. She loved her parents, but they were very traditional in their thinking.

Roxie always wore clothes with elbow-length sleeves to hide her intricate tattoos. She'd gotten one after her divorce to rebel against the ideals of her ex-husband, Mitchell. It snowballed from there, becoming a half sleeve on her left arm. Mitchell would frown every time they went past someone with tattoos, sucking his teeth in disapproval.

"It differs from the other events, Roxie. They seek us, curvy women. The company is called Mate Me. It's a social gathering hosted to bring together shifter forever mates. Just imagine an out-of-this-world large shifter devoted to you for life." Evelyn sighed. She gave a dreamy smile, and Roxie rolled her eyes. She and Evelyn were what the world deemed "plus-sized." They had extra all over, and in her experience, men moved on from her to a thinner younger model.

Roxie knew about shifters. Her half brother was one, but she had never spent time with one as an adult.

"I'm twenty-seven, Evvy, and divorced. Plus, I've never met a shifter aside from Anderson, my half brother, and he left when I was young," Roxie argued.

"Young and single! Come with me on Friday. Use this as an opportunity to meet new people. You don't know what you are missing with shifters. They don't play games with you. They are very take-it-or-leave-it when it comes to dating. These men are searching for their mates. They want a family and life with someone." Evelyn gave her puppy eyes, holding out the hot-pink flyer for Roxie to look over. Roxie took it, blinking at the brightness of the paper.

"Where will the event be?" She knew Evelyn wouldn't drop the issue until she caved.

"Club Cerulean. They've rented the place out. We pay a $30 cover, plus any food or drink we purchase."

"How long do I have to stay?"

"Two hours. I want you to at least try to meet people. No one is asking you to date. Just find a friend you can talk about art with, while I look for my mate." Evelyn's brown eyes danced with excitement as she spoke.

"I'll go for two hours. I can't promise to be much company."

"All I ask is you talk to anyone who speaks to you," Evelyn said with a laugh. Roxie tried to ignore her friend.

2

"Fine. Now let me get back to my painting."

"When are you going to show your portfolio to the Dragon Lore Art Gallery? I saw Xander Austin, the owner of the museum, checking out our newest exhibit." Evelyn worked as a tour guide for the local art museum and had been urging Roxie to show her work. Evelyn compared her art with the ones that were on display for the world to see, always telling Roxie she was in league with those on exhibit.

"Never. Mitchell constantly told me I was decent at best, and my art was not in the same caliber with the art he showed in the gallery." Roxie blinked back the tears that threatened to fill her eyes.

One reason she had fallen in love with Mitchell to begin with was his background in art. His parents were art dealers and ran their own gallery in New York. Mitchell was the current director. His job was to look for the newest artists and make them famous. He never thought much of Roxie's work and would tell her at any chance he got. She would show him a new piece and he would nitpick it apart, telling her everything she'd done wrong on the piece. This had happened too many times. Her heart would clench with pain, but she never let Mitchell know he got to her. She then would work late into the next night trying to create a piece he would be proud to show in the gallery. This had continued regularly in their relationship until she finally gave up six months before she caught him cheating on her.

"Screw him. He never wanted you to be successful and leave his ass first. He is a shallow man who never saw you as anything but a housewife who he couldn't make to stop working. Your landscapes are amazing and can even rival some at the museum." Evelyn looked at the painting on Roxie's easel. She then wrapped her arms around Roxie's shoulders.

"Thanks, sweetie, but I'm not ready for another rejection just yet. I don't know if my heart can handle being told I am terrible by someone so well respected as Xander Austin." Roxie put her earbuds as a signal that she was done with the conversation. She picked up her brush and added to the pink sunset over the Grand Canyon. Evelyn patted her shoulder and left her in peace. Roxie loved that about her roommate. She knew when to give her space. Roxie worked through the night, skipping dinner. Once she got in the zone with her art, nothing else mattered. In fact, during her time in college, the fire alarm went off in the art building. A classmate had to shake her to alert her of the noise.

CHAPTER TWO

Xander Austin groaned when his mother's name popped up on his caller ID. He quickly ran a hand through his sandy brown hair in frustration before he answered. He didn't have time to talk to his mother; he needed to find his next artist. Looking at his computer, he quickly put her on speaker while scanning through some potential artists's portfolios to showcase in his art gallery.

"Hello, Mother."

"Xander, I'm calling to remind you about attending Josie's event on Friday." His mother's melodic voice had a stern edge to it. Josie was his sister-in-law, and she'd started her own find-a-mate service.

"Friday at Club Cerulean. I know, Mother," Xander replied, busily sifting through the applicants that his assistant thought were promising.

"Eight o'clock, and I expect to hear that you spoke to some of the lovely young ladies at the event. This is Josie's launch, and I want it to go perfectly. I want your dragon to find a mate and be happy like Rhett and Josie. I noticed the last time we went flying as a family, your dragon's red scales were lacking their usual luster."

"Yes, Mother. My dragon is just fine. He hasn't lost his luster." His dragon had been pining after a mate ever since Rhett found Josie. Now he had a sad red dragon to deal with along with his mother pressuring him to find his mate. Xander was a hundred. It wasn't like he hadn't been looking; dragons were picky creatures.

He couldn't pick a woman who didn't make his dragon roar. Good thing dragons lived for hundreds of years; they were the only mythical shifter creatures left. Many of the others had gone extinct, refusing to mate with humans.

"Don't 'yes, Mother' me. Promise you will stay off your phone and interact!"

He sighed. Xander could see his mother's hazel eyes flashing with annoyance, the eyes he inherited. He felt happy Rhett had found Josie. She was the daughter his mother had always wanted. She was spunky and ambitious, the perfect mate for a dragon like Rhett's. Unfortunately, it made her think that Xander wasn't looking hard enough for his mate. Xander preferred a more quiet mate, one who would enjoy art and travel. His entire business revolved around art and traveling to find artists; he needed her to have an interest in his life. Most of the women he had gone out with wanted him because he was wealthy and handsome. He stood tall at six feet, shorter than many of his shifter friends, but he was trim.

"I promise to do my best to make the event go well." His eyes never left the multitude of portfolios he was looking through.

"Thank you. See you on Sunday for our family dinner."

"Bye, Mother." Xander hung up and pinched the bridge of his nose. He loved his family but sometimes he wanted the quiet, to be alone with his own thoughts. He closed the last portfolio on his computer screen. None of the ones he looked through were right. He needed a spark. He needed something that made him wonder what the artist was thinking as they painted, like in the art he showed the world. What was he supposed to do for his event showcase next week without a fresh sensation? *Damn*, he thought. He didn't want to advertise, but what could he do? He needed a new artist with actual talent, not some copycat.

"Hi, boss!" a perky redhead called into his office. He didn't remember her name; the temp agency sent her last week. His current assistant was on a month-long trip around the U.S. trying to find new artists for the gallery. To fill his vacancy, he had called the agency for a temp to help until his assistant came back.

"Hello, do we have any other artist portfolios to look through?" he asked, scrubbing his face in agitation.

"No, I gave you everything last night before I went home. Are none of them good enough?" She set his strong black coffee on his desk. She learned his habits quickly just within the week of temping, making his work easier.

"They are all talented but not quite what I am looking for. I need someone who speaks to your emotions and elicits more. I want spark!"

She gave him a thoughtful look. "I might have someone. We went to an art and design school together. I haven't spoken to her in six years, but I remember her art being amazing."

"Do you know where I can see a sample of her work?" He remembered from her résumé that she'd attended art school. Xander found it refreshing that she didn't push her own artwork on him.

"She has an online page where she showcases her completed works. She hasn't posted in quite a while, though." She pulled out her phone and tapped away with her manicured nails. Xander waited impatiently for her to find what she was searching for.

"Here." She handed him the phone, and he paused at the first picture. It was a painting of a geyser at Yellowstone National Park as it blew. Xander wondered how close the artist stood from the geyser as it exploded. He felt he could reach out and touch the water spraying out of the ground. The second was a scene with a black bear looking down as it climbed a tree. He was curious what the bear was looking at. In the painting, the forest floor was obscured by plants on the ground. The third was a picture of the sun setting over a beach. The reflection of the sun on the wet sand was so brilliantly painted that one could feel the warmth of the sand between their toes. Each painting captured a distinct moment, and all made him stare in amazement. He wanted to see the actual paintings and not just a picture on the internet. He needed to find this artist and convince her to let him show her work. He hoped she didn't already have a dealer helping her with her art. He knew she would be a sensation and take the world of art by storm.

"What's her name?" he asked, handing back her phone.

"Roxie Jones."

"Get in touch with her and tell her I'm interested in seeing her current work," he ordered. She nodded, settling at her desk, and Xander smiled. If Roxie Jones still had striking pieces, he wanted her in his gallery.

CHAPTER THREE

Roxie dragged herself home early Friday afternoon after her father saw how tired she was. He thought she was getting sick, but in reality, it was because she'd hit inspiration in her painting. It kept her awake most of the night, giving her only an hour of sleep before she needed to get up and go to work. She set her alarm for an hour from that moment to get a power nap. Roxie wanted to continue working on her Grand Canyon series. She lay down and let sleep take her.

Five minutes later, her phone rang. She groaned and hit "ignore." It rang again, and she hit "ignore" once more. This went on several times until she finally growled and hit silent, so she could get some sleep. She dreamed of hiking the Appalachian Trail, stopping to take photos of the mountain, forest, and animals.

"Roxie!" Evelyn shook her awake. Roxie shot up, rubbing her eyes. She looked out the window to see that it was dark outside. How long had she been asleep?

"What time is it?"

"Seven. We need to get ready for the club. I ordered pizza for us to eat while we get dressed." Evelyn sat on the edge of Roxie's full-sized bed.

"Damn, I wanted to get in some painting before we went. Why didn't my alarm go off?" She grabbed her phone and saw fifty missed calls and three voice mails.

"Whoa, who wanted to get a hold of you?" Evelyn asked. Roxie remembered she kept getting calls and silenced her phone so she could sleep.

"I don't recognize the numbers." She pressed play on her voice mail.

Roxie, you stupid bitch! If I ever see your lawyer poking around my gallery again, I'll sue you. I have your awful paintings hanging in the gallery. I can't do anything about them not selling because you are an awful artist.

Roxie quickly deleted the message from her horrid ex-husband, Mitchell.

"Ignore the jerk. What are the other messages?" Evelyn patted her gently on the arm.

Hi Roxie, it's Lauren Hurts. We went to art school together. I'm temping for the Dragon Lore Art Gallery, and my boss wants to—

Next message.

Sorry, Lauren again. My boss wants to see your current work. If it's the same as your work on your website, he might showcase you. Call me back at 5-5-5-2-8-9-6. Thanks, bye!

Roxie stared at her phone in shock. *Someone looked at my website and liked my work?* She'd only put it together to have a place to put up her finished pieces. Evelyn wrapped her arms around her and screamed.

"That's amazing!"

"I'm not calling her back." Roxie shook her head. The thought of showing her work in a gallery was nerve-wracking. Mitchell had told her enough times that he would never show her work in his gallery and that no gallery would ever want her. He constantly urged her to give up and be his stay-at-home wife.

"What? Why?" Evelyn pulled back and glared at her.

10

"I've told you why. I'm not interested in being rejected again." Roxie plugged her phone in to give it an extra charge. She didn't want to be without it at the club.

"Don't give Mitchell that control over you. You two divorced. Move on and let someone tell you how amazing you are! I say go for it. They are the ones seeking you out."

A knock sounded on their door.

"Pizza!" Evelyn raced to get the door, while Roxie stretched out her legs and back. She opened her closet and searched for something to wear to the club. Maybe Evelyn was right. Dragon Lore Gallery had reached out to her.

"One works pizza, no mushrooms from Luigi's."

"Evvy, what are you wearing tonight?" She pulled out a deep purple dress with cap sleeves from her closet to show her friend.

"I have my spaghetti strap black dress. I'm going to enjoy tonight and show off some skin. You should wear your turquoise dress with that super short skirt. It will show off the half sleeve tattoo you've been hiding from your parents," Evelyn said.

She put down the slice and pulled out the dress. Roxie held the dress at arm's length. She'd bought it for an event at Mitchell's work. She never got the chance to wear it, thanks to the divorce.

"I don't know. I bought it to wear with a sweater. My boobs pop out too much without one." Roxie pulled out the corresponding sweater.

"No covering up, Rox. Tonight, you will be the sexy mama I know you are. Embrace your curves and show off those tatas." Evelyn snatched the sweater away.

"Fine. How was work?" Roxie plopped on the bed and snagged her slice again.Evelyn proceeded to talk about her own boss. Roxie's thoughts went back to the voice mail from Lauren. Roxie hadn't heard from her in years, but she remembered her being a smart fiery girl with hair to match. She couldn't believe someone wanted to look at her work. Roxie posted nothing new

11

since the divorce. She wanted to put up her Grand Canyon pieces once she finished them.

She wouldn't be calling Lauren back; she knew the owner would reject her work. If the man who was supposed to love her for all time hated her work, what would a complete stranger think?

"Rox. Roxie! Are you even listening?" Evelyn said. "Stop thinking about painting and get dressed." She closed the pizza box and tossed Roxie her dress.

Roxie gave her a sheepish grin and dusted her hands off. She got ready to go out for the first time in over a year. Stepping into the bathroom, she changed into the dress and admired her tattoos. She loved how they looked on her shoulder. One of her rebellious moments from Mitchell and her parents had been getting a tattoo. She quickly curled her hair, braiding the front away from her eyes and pinning it behind one ear. Roxie did natural makeup. She put on foundation, a light dust of blush, brown eyeshadow, and a touch of lip gloss. She was never the one to go for the smokey eye. She always ended up looking like a raccoon by the end of the night. Tonight, she didn't feel like embarrassing herself.

CHAPTER FOUR

Xander parked his blue Maserati behind the club and climbed out. His day hadn't gone as planned. His temp named Lauren could not get a hold of Roxie Jones. She said she left messages and would try social media this weekend.

The last thing he wanted to do was to mingle with a bunch of women pretending he cared about anything they had to say. He wanted to be at home with a good book or on the phone to check up on the travels of his assistant, Anderson. He straightened his black polo, brushing any lint off his dark wash jeans. His plan for the night was to sit at the bar and chat with the women who came up to order drinks, nothing more. He walked in and heard Josie.

"Xander, you made it!" She launched herself into his arms. His sister-in-law had ebony skin, shining hazel eyes, and black hair that was kept in dozens of small braids.

"Of course, Josie, I couldn't let my favorite sister-in-law down." He hugged her back, smiling.

"I'm your only sister-in-law." She swatted his arm, making him laugh.

"This place looks pretty full. You sure you still need me?" he asked, looking around the bouncing club. There were shifters and beautiful curvy women all over. Some were chatting at low tables surrounded by couches, and others were dancing on the dance floor. The music boomed in his sensitive shifter ears. He had to fight the urge to wince when the speaker by his head changed to a pop song by Katy Perry.

"Of course, I do. I want you to find your mate. I think I met a young woman perfect for you. She is a tour guide at the art museum in Green Falls. Come, I'll introduce you." Josie took his hand and led him over to one of the low tables. Two women were talking to a few men. He sniffed; the men were wolf shifters. His eyes locked on one woman. She wore a blue-green dress that showed off her delectable bosom. He took her in, admiring her dark blonde hair that was curled, braided away from her face, and let loose. He noticed the almost half sleeve floral tattoo on her shoulder and how she seemed uncomfortable with the man seated next to her.

When she looked up at Josie coming over, she smiled and his heart stopped. She was beautiful and her deep blue, almost violet eyes held him captive. His dragon shook awake, taking notice. She smelled amazing; her light floral perfume mixed with something entirely hers.

Mate!

Xander mentally slammed his dragon back before it could take over. Josie would never forgive him if a thirty-foot fire-breathing red dragon appeared at her event.

"Xander, this is Evelyn Tate and her friend. I'm sorry, dear, I didn't catch your name." Josie motioned to the brunette-haired woman sitting next to his mate, then looked at his mate to ask her name. It hit him. Josie was introducing him to Evelyn, not his mate.

"I'm Roxie," she replied in a clear, warm tone. His dragon purred, and he couldn't stop staring.

"You wouldn't be Roxie Jones, would you?" he asked. Life couldn't be that funny. The one woman he wanted to get a hold of was at a club.

"Uh, um, yes, do I know you?" She cocked her head to the side, looking him up and down.

14

"I'm Xander Austin. My assistant, Lauren, called you about sending in your portfolio. She showed me some of your earlier art, and I wanted to see something more current." Xander walked over and gave the wolf shifter next to her a pointed look. He stood, giving Xander his seat.

"You own Dragon Lore Art Gallery?" she asked. He nodded and took one of her hands in his. His dragon rumbled with delight; he could tell that she heard it by the way her eyes opened wide.

CHAPTER FIVE

Roxie couldn't believe who had just been introduced to her. Xander Austin was well-known in the art community as being the most particular about the artists he showcased. Those he chose always sold everything and shot to stardom in the art world. "Yes, I do. It is a pleasure to meet you." Xander squeezed her hand, and another jolt went through her body. Xander had sandy brown hair, hazel eyes, broad shoulders, and very long legs. His shirt clung to his muscles, enough for her to know that he kept in good shape. When he came over, she had to look all the way up to see his face. If she had to guess, he was around 6'1, which put him six inches taller than her.

"No talking shop, Xander!" Josie warned. Roxie looked up at her with a smile. She didn't want to tell him no to showing her work just yet. Something about Xander pulled her to him, and she didn't want to disappoint him.

"Would you like a drink?" he asked, pointing to her empty wineglass. He had to raise his voice to be heard over the blaring music.

"Yes, I'm having chardonnay," Roxie replied. He nodded and went over to the bar. She admired him from behind. He walked with such grace, and his pants hugged his ass in the most delicious way.

She looked around the club and spotted Evelyn. She had gotten up to dance with a medium build shifter. Her friend looked relaxed. She knew Evelyn worried about her since she moved in with her as her roommate. Roxie hadn't been the most social person after the man who promised to love her forever dumped her for someone younger, thinner, and in her opinion not nearly as smart.

"Hello, beautiful. Tell me, how can I get you to come home with me tonight?" a man with slicked-back hair and beady eyes asked. He sat close enough for his leg to touch her. She had to suppress a shudder. He smelled heavily of expensive cologne. It made her sick to her stomach.

"I'm sorry. I already have a date who is sitting there. He went to get me a drink." She moved away from him.

"He shouldn't have left you alone. Tell me about your tattoo. Does it mean you get freaky in bed?" He tried to put an arm around her, and she stood up.

"That is disgusting. I'll ask you once to please leave me alone. I am not interested in doing anything with you." Roxie dusted off her dress and left to find Xander.

"Your loss!" the man shouted. She shuddered, feeling as if she needed a shower. Looking around, she spotted Xander and noticed a sexy brunette had cornered him. She was dressed in a crop top and miniskirt. The woman leaned in, and Xander shifted back.

"I'm sorry, but I have a date for the night," Xander announced. It warmed her heart to see him rejecting a woman ten times more beautiful than she felt.

"You should leave her. I saw the cow you were with. Don't you want someone you can lift?" She put a hand on his arm, and he jerked away.

"There you are!" Roxie slid in next to Xander, wrapping her arms around his waist. He put an arm over her shoulders, pulling her close.

"Hello, mate." Xander dropped a kiss on her temple. She came up to his shoulder, loving how he made her feel small. The kiss sent tingles all over her body.

"Thank you for keeping Xander company while he fetched our drinks." She flashed the brunette a sickly-sweet smile. Xander handed Roxie her wineglass and picked up his own.

"Where should we sit?" Xander asked once the woman left in a huff. Roxie went to move away from him, but he squeezed her close.

"I don't know. There isn't a place to talk without shouting," Roxie replied. She looked around to see most of the seating areas were full of chatting men and women. In some cases, there were couples making out.

"I know the owner. Come on." Xander took her hand and walked over to a door marked "Employees Only."

"How do you know the owner?" she asked.

"He is my brother, and his wife is the creator of this whole shindig." She sighed and released his hand. It really was too good to be true to find a man who wanted to talk to her.

"So you are only here to help? You don't want a mate?" She stopped, turning around to walk back the way she came. What she didn't expect was him grabbing her, tossing her over his shoulder, and carrying her away from the exit.

"Xander!" she shrieked. Her glass slipped from her hand, shattering into thousands of pieces on the tile floor. Xander said nothing, shouldering through the door and taking confident strides down the hallway. He took her to a room that looked like the main office. He placed her on a leather wingback chair and locked the door. She looked around the room. There was a desk in the center. Hanging on the walls were quite a few pictures of Josie and a man who looked a lot like Xander. The furniture were all black leather to accent the cream-colored walls.

"You are scaring me. Why won't you just let me go?" she demanded, jumping up from the chair. She was angry and aroused

18

at the display of his dominant nature. She walked back to where he stood, leaning against the door and glaring with her arms crossed. "Move."

"No," he replied, keeping a blank expression on his face. He was so good looking, but acting like a jerk wouldn't get him anywhere with her.

"What? You can't keep me here," she demanded, maintaining eye contact. She noticed flecks of gold in his hazel eyes, which fascinated her.

"Yes, I can. You are my mate," he replied calmly.

"I am not! You just said that to get rid of the other girl." She waved a hand dismissively. How could he know they were mates?

"It made her go away, but that doesn't mean it isn't true."

"Impossible. You know nothing about me." She paced the compact room. She hated being played with. The three years she spent with Mitchell sprang to mind. He would always give her a sweet smile and make her feel like she was being paranoid about his behavior. Turned out, she was right to suspect her now ex-husband. In the last year of their marriage, he was sneaking around with his secretary.

"We, shifters, know the instant we meet our mate. I knew the second your eyes met mine." He reached out and put his hands on her shoulders. She stopped pacing and looked up at him. His hazel eyes were sincere, and they flashed with desire when they stopped at her lips. She nervously darted her tongue out to wet her lips. His grip tightened and his head lowered slowly. He was giving her a chance to back away from the kiss. She didn't pull away. She wanted to know what his sculpted lips would feel like.

His soft, warm lips collided with her own, making her close her eyes. He felt right, as if he was made just for her. She opened her mouth when she felt his tongue run along the seam of her lips. Roxie let him in, and he took control. She wrapped her arms around his waist, pressing her curves against his hard body. She felt

19

her belly tighten with desire as his hands slid up to cup her face, holding her gently as if she were made of glass. He nipped at her bottom lip and she moaned. She wanted him to touch her so badly that she ached.

CHAPTER SIX

Xander couldn't get enough of her through the kiss. He moved down her neck, nipping gently until he reached the swell of her breasts. He bit and sucked until he left a blooming mark.

"Xander." Roxie's voice was breathless, and her hands clung to the back of his shirt.

"Roxie, I want you," he murmured, kissing across her chest and up to her ear. His body tightened as his erection pushed against his jeans.

"Touch me please," she moaned and he did, cupping her ample breasts in both hands. He rubbed her nipples through the fabric, making them strain for contact.

"You can touch me too." He pulled the fabric of her dress down, revealing two perfect globes, a little more than a handful each. Her skin was creamy pale and her nipples, rosy red. He couldn't control himself and slipped one round nipple into his mouth. Xander's voice seemed to break her trance. Her hands dove under his shirt to run her fingers across his abs. Her fingers moved up to rake down his chest until they hooked into the waistband of his jeans. He sucked in a breath and groaned in pleasure. Her dainty hands were driving him and his dragon to the edge.

"Roxie, I need you?" He had to ask. He didn't want to push too fast.

"I . . ."

A loud knock banged on the door.

"Yo, Xander, Josie wants to know when you will reappear and mingle," his brother, Rhett, called through the door. Xander sighed and watched her pull her dress back up to cover her perfect breasts. Her eyes looked frantic at the thought of his brother possibly opening the door to see what they were doing. Her hair was mussed, and her lipstick smeared around the edges of her lips. There was no mistaking they had just engaged in a steamy make out session. He almost lost his resolve, watching her fix her disheveled appearance.

"Give me five minutes," he growled. His younger brother had the worst timing.

"I'll start the timer," Rhett threatened.

"Do I have to bring Mom into this?" Xander countered.

"Touché. See you and your hook up soon." Rhett walked away with purposefully heavy footsteps.

"Hook up? I'm just a hook up to you?" She flung open the office door, running down the hall and over to her friend.

F*cking Rhett!

"Roxie, no, that isn't what this is," he called but it was too late. She grabbed her friend and ran off. Xander punched the wall next to him, leaving a sizable divot.

"Hey, don't break my club," Rhett yelled. Xander glared at his younger brother, his face heating in anger.

"It's your fault," he seethed.

"What did I do?"

"You called my mate a hook up! Right now, she took her friend and ran away from me," Xander explained.

"Your mate?" Rhett stood with his hands on his hips, a frown on his face.

"The second I saw her, my dragon roared for his mate." Xander walked over to the bar and motioned the young bartender to give him a shot of whiskey.

"Shit, I'm sorry. What are you going to do?" Rhett ran a hand through his hair. Rhett took after their father, with black hair

22

and bright blue eyes. Xander looked like their mother, with sandy brown hair and hazel eyes.

"I will find her and explain." Xander downed his shot and found Josie.

"Josie, do you get any information about the participants of your Mate Me business?" Xander asked.

"I get their phone numbers and addresses to charge for the activities. Why?" She gave him a suspicious look.

"I found my mate, Roxie Jones. I need her address, so I can fix what your husband screwed up," Xander explained.

"What did Rhett do?" She glared at her husband, one of the many reasons he liked his sister-in-law. She knew her husband wasn't perfect.

"I was spending some time with Roxie and Rhett came to find me. He told me he'd see me and my 'hook up' in a few. Roxie took it the wrong way and ran off. I need to find her and explain that she is my mate."

"Rhett, how could you!" Josie yelled. Rhett had the smart sense to look remorseful.

"I didn't know she was his mate!" he defended.

"We never use the words 'hook up' with my business. Yes, some couplings tonight will be just that, a hook up, but some will be genuine matches. Xander, I am so happy you found your mate. Come to the office. I will get you her information." Josie walked off. Xander quickly followed, eager to fix things.

CHAPTER SEVEN

A hook up? How could she be so stupid? Someone as hot as Xander couldn't possibly be interested in her for anything more. He only pulled the mate card to have sex with her. Thank goodness for his brother, Rhett, or she might have had sex with him.

"What happened?" Evelyn asked once they were back home. She had changed out of her dress into a pair of soft shorts and a tank top. When Roxie had begged to leave, she went without asking questions. Now she wanted an answer.

"You know that guy Xander Austin?"

"Yeah, what about him?"

"He told me we were mates just to get me to have sex with him in the manager's office." Roxie stripped off her dress, tossing it into a heap on the floor. She slipped into a pair of black leggings and an extra large t-shirt.

"How do you know?" Evelyn asked.

"His brother interrupted. He wanted Xander to come back and mingle with other people. His brother specifically said, 'see you and your hookup soon.'" Roxie stormed into the kitchen and pulled out a pint of her favorite mint chocolate chip ice cream and dropped onto the couch.

"Maybe his brother was wrong? Maybe you are mates. Is there something about him you feel?" Evelyn took a spoon to her own pint of ice cream.

"There was this pull when we made eye contact. I felt at peace, as if he was the one I was meant to be with. When he touched me, my body tingled. And the kiss we shared? Best. Kiss. Ever!" Roxie gushed. She thought back to the twenty minutes she'd spent in the office with Xander. When she was with Mitchell, she never felt the same desire rage through her body like when she'd been with Xander. Xander made her heart race and her body heat up with lust. She wanted to let him make love to her.

"Sounds like there might be something between you two? Why not find out? It could be the start of something amazing," Evelyn pointed out, licking her spoon.

"No, I told you, I don't want another husband who will pass me up when he tires of me." Roxie shook her head and stood up. "I'm going to paint and sleep all day tomorrow."

"Paint well. See you around dinner time. Put your phone on silent, so no one can disturb you." Evelyn gave her a comforting hug.

"Night, Evvy." Roxie disappeared into her room, put her phone on silent, and took out her paints. Once set up, she put her headphones on and connected to her music player through Bluetooth. She closed her eyes, took a deep breath, and let her imagination take her away. Tonight, she was starting a fresh piece of the Grand Canyon on a cloudy day. She felt gloomy after a disappointing night and threw herself into her work, painting well into the morning.

By the time she surfaced from her work, the clock on her nightstand read 9 AM. She'd worked for ten hours straight. Setting her brushes aside, she inspected her work. The sky was dark and stormy with grayish purple colors casting down onto the burnt orange rocks. She'd added several burrows with packs attached descending into the canyon, their riders unseen. She would add more details once her base had dried completely. She looked down at her hands, which were covered in paint along with her tank top. She tried to wear an apron but found it got in her way more than helped protect her clothing. She had a specific set of tops and bottoms in which to paint.

"Roxie, I don't want to disturb you, but you have a visitor," Evelyn's voice carried through the door. She never bothered her unless it was important, so she stretched and padded out of her room. She knew she must look like a mess, with paint everywhere and her hair piled on top of her head. Stopping short, she caught sight of Xander holding two coffee cups and a pastry bag.

"No." Roxie turned to go back to her room. She did not want to see him, to feel things for him, and to cave if he asked her out.

"Please, just give me a chance to explain." Xander chased her down the hall, his footsteps heavy.

"How did you find me? What is there to explain? You are a hot model, while I'm a fat cow. We both know I would have just been another notch on your belt. There is no future here with me and you." She marched into her room, gathering brushes to clean.

"You are not a fat cow! You are an amazing, sexy woman with a body that drives me insane. I couldn't sleep after the way we left things last night. I found you because Josie believes in mates. Please let me take you on a true date, one where we can get to know each other," he said.

Holding dirty brushes, she walked around her easel, using it as a barrier. "How do I know this isn't just to make me think you aren't an ass?" She planted a hand on her hip and huffed. He looked so good in another tight-fitting shirt, this time with a superhero on the front. He wore a pair of faded jeans torn at one knee and his hair had been left disheveled as if he had been running his hands through it.

"That is part of it, but you are my mate and I want you." Xander set the cups and bag down on her dresser and strode across the room. She stared at him, her body warming with desire. He was almost half a foot taller than her, which made her feel short, not something she'd experienced often.

"What are you doing?" she whispered. He plucked the brushes from her hands.

"Proving what a desirable woman you are." He pulled her flush against him and kissed her. He didn't wait for permission but pushed his tongue into her mouth. She clung to his chest, bunching his shirt in her fists. He was overwhelming her senses; she could only hold on and enjoy the sensations coursing through her. Her arms moved up to wrap around his neck, her fingers slipping into the hair at the nape of his neck. She dueled tongues with him, heating the kiss. His scent filled her nostrils, making her panties wet. He pulled back and pressed her against the wall, his chest flush against hers.

"Can you feel what you do to me?" Xander said. She felt the pounding of his heart and the long bar of his erection against her belly.

"I did that?"

How could she not know what she did to him? All he wanted to do was to push her onto the bed and make love to her.

"Yes, I want to strip you down, put my face between your legs, and taste you. I want to hear you scream out my name when you orgasm, your juices on my tongue." He kissed her once more, pushing himself against her again. He hooked his hands under her thighs and lifted her effortlessly. She wrapped her legs around his waist, his erection pushing at her entrance. He kissed down to the sensitive spot on her collarbone, drawing out a deep moan from her plump lips.

"You feel amazing, Roxie." His dragon pushed for him to mate her before she got away again.

"Roxie?" Evelyn called, throwing a mental bucket of ice water on their make-out session. He groaned at the interruption, placing his forehead against hers, his breathing uneven.

"Your parents are here!" Evelyn hissed through the door and Roxie froze in his arms. He lowered her to the floor.

27

"Stay here, please! My parents are very conservative and will balk at me if they see you," she asked as she threw on a robe, hiding her tattoos. Something in her panicked voice had him nodding in agreement. She rushed past Evelyn, out to the living room.

"Just a warning, her ex-husband did a number on her. She is going to take some time being convinced that she is good enough." Evelyn walked away, leaving him to listen to Roxie talk to her parents and mull over the fact that she had an ex-husband.

CHAPTER EIGHT

"Mom, Dad! What are you doing here?" Roxie asked, tying her robe, making sure it hid her tattoos.

"You haven't answered our calls all week, and it worried us," her mother said. Her mother was a thin woman with shapely hips and fine skin. She had the same blonde hair and blue eyes as Roxie but now dyed it to keep it the same shade as when she was younger. She'd always worried about Roxie being a plus-sized girl. Today, she was wearing a fifties housewife dress of white with bright red flowers splashed all over. Her hair had been curled to perfection; her makeup, flawless. Another reason her mother was disappointed in her all the time was that Roxie did not take as much pride in her appearance as her mother thought she should.

"I've been seeing Dad every day this week. Why do I have to answer your calls?" Roxie huffed. She kept herself between the back hallway and her parents, trying to hide any sign of Xander.

"We wanted to talk about your art. We think it is time you put it aside and focus on another career," her mom continued, undeterred by Roxie's callous response.

"What? Why?" She was shocked. Her mother had taken little interest in her choice of a career, unlike what she did with Elizabeth, her older sister.

"It's why Mitch left you," her mother commented. She felt punched in the gut. Leave it to Mitch to ruin her life even after their divorce.

"Where did you get that idea?" She was furious that her mother always took Mitch's side.

"We spoke at his engagement party last week. He said he'd found a woman who would put his needs first and care for him." Her mother looked at her as if Mitch's words were law.

"Get out," Roxie growled. Her mother gave her a surprised look.

"Excuse me? Roxanne Leigh Jones. Did you say to get out?" Her mother tried to puff up, but at five foot two, she wasn't imposing.

"You heard me. Mitch is not your family. I am! He cheated on me with that woman because she was thinner and younger. I will not stop painting, and I quit, Dad. I do not need to work for you if this is how Mom will treat me." She held open her apartment door, waiting for them to leave. Her heart raced a mile a minute. She'd never lost her temper on her parents.

"You will never make it as an artist. You were told by Mitch, and he is a renowned art dealer," her mother hissed and marched out of the apartment.

"I'm sorry, sweetheart," her dad whispered, patting her on the shoulder. He followed her mom out. She slammed the door and pressed her head against it, biting back tears. Her mom never understood her need to paint. This just proved how much Mitch had influenced her family. She remembered the day she found out he was cheating on her.

She had just gotten off work as a secretary for a local law firm. Usually, her boss made her stay late, but today he had a date with a famous heiress. She parked her car under her apartment building and walked into the lobby.

"Good evening, Mrs. Jones. Good to see you're home early for a change," Sal, the front doorman, called.

"It is nice to come home during daylight hours, Sal. Has Mitch come through?" she asked, pressing the elevator button.

30

"He did, with his secretary. I heard him say something about giving her a contract that needed to be sent to a new artist," Sal replied. She nodded. It was common for Barbie to come over and collect work from Mitch. For the past few months, she had been coming in when Barbie was leaving. It never sat right with her that Barbie and Mitch were alone a lot in their apartment, but he was her husband. He loved her, didn't he? She went up to her apartment and pushed her key into the lock. She heard soft music playing, the music she knew to be Mitch's make love playlist. Maybe he was finally doing something romantic for her and was waiting for her to come home. She pushed open the door and stopped dead. On the coffee table were two glasses of red wine, one had red lipstick around the rim. A pair of sky-high heels were lying on the floor, and a flimsy dress was draped over the couch. She followed the trail of clothes, picking each one until she made it to their bedroom door.

She was afraid of what she would see on the other side. She knew in her heart that Mitch had cheated; she knew this wasn't the first time. Roxie bet it was every time she came home and Barbie was leaving the apartment. Furious with her husband for breaking his vows, she slammed the door open. A scream came from Barbie's throat as Roxie threw her shoes at her head. Mitchell was lying on the bed; Barbie had been riding him. His eyes went round with shock when he saw who was standing by the door.

"Get out!" Roxie roared at Barbie. Grabbing her by the hair, she pulled her off of Mitch, not caring when he cried out from the pain of her being pulled off his cock awkwardly. She shoved Barbie's clothes into her hands and dragged her down the hallway and out the door. Pushing her into the hallway naked, she slammed and locked the door, then went to deal with Mitch.

"Roxie," he began, his hands out in a gesture of surrender.

"How dare you!" She picked up the book she kept on the nightstand and threw it at Mitchell's head. "If you didn't want to be with me anymore, you could have just asked for a divorce. I never want to see your lying, cheating ass ever again!" She grabbed a suitcase and quickly threw her clothing into it, not caring about the mess she was making. She went into the bathroom and gathered all her items. Every time Mitch tried to talk to her, she would shove past him.

"Fine, get your way, but know I will never be out of your life, Roxie. Ever. Your mother loves me more than you," he hissed and stormed out of the apartment. She had dropped to the bed and cried. Her one relationship had shattered around her, and she had caught none of the telltale signs of cheating. She felt humiliated and needed to go home. She called up Evelyn and planned to go home that very night.

"She is wrong, you know," Xander's soft voice came before he enveloped her in a tight hug.

"No, she is right." Roxie turned in his arms to rest her head against his chest.

"No, I may have peeked at your painting while trying not to listen in on your conversation. It is beautiful, and I can tell you are not done yet. Let me take you to brunch on a date. I won't push you into letting me show your work, but know this, I think we can sell anything you show." Xander rubbed her back, and she sighed.

"Could we do dinner? I've pulled an all-nighter doing that painting." She looked up, worried it would upset him.

"Sure thing, beautiful. I can always do laundry and clean my home." He kissed her nose and she giggled, her body slowly fighting her to get some sleep.

"Come on." He picked her up in a princess hold, walking her to bed.

"I can walk." She yawned and felt his chest rumble with laughter.

"I enjoy being able to hold you." He dropped a kiss on her lips and shot her a smile. Her panties instantly went wet. She didn't want to sleep now; she wanted him in her bed making her feel good.

"I can smell how turned on you are, but you need sleep and I want to sweep you off your feet on our date. Where have you always wanted to go? Anywhere in the world." He set her down carefully, laying her among the many colorful blankets she kept to stay warm.

"Uh, um, Rome. I've never been able to travel internationally, but I have my passport. I keep it in hopes I'll earn enough to go one day." She lay her head down and felt a soft kiss on her temple.

"Good night, my princess. I'll be back at seven to take you out."

CHAPTER NINE

Xander busied himself all day, making plans for a week-long trip. If Roxie wanted to go to Rome, he would take her. He postponed his showcase in hopes he could convince Roxie to let him show her work. Before he left her apartment, he had stopped at Evelyn's room and had convinced her to pack a carry-on of Roxie's belongings. He would take care of her clothes when they landed.

His phone rang. Looking down, he saw it was from his assistant, Anderson, traveling around the U.S.

"Hello."

"Xander, I've found our next resident artist." Anderson's voice was excited on the other end.

"Same here. She lives in Green Falls, Virginia."

"Who did you find?" Anderson's interest was piqued.

"I'm still working on getting her to agree. Her parents and an ex-husband stand in my way." Xander grimaced, thinking about how awful Roxie's mother was that morning.

"I found a painting by an artist, but the gallery I found it in was being very cagey about selling the piece."

"Do you know the artist's name?"

"Only the initials R.J.," Anderson explained. Xander could sense his frustration.

"Who is the gallery owner?" Xander knew he could try as a fellow art dealer to get the information.

"The Wright family. Their son, Mitchell, is the current director."

"What is the name of the gallery?"

"The Golden Painting."

"Ugh, what an awful name." Xander immediately pulled the gallery up on his computer. He wrinkled his nose at the gaudy golden statues standing outside the entrance.

"True. They had an entire wing devoted to R.J., but none of the pieces were available for sale. I am thinking something is not right with the paintings."

"I'll look into him. I'm taking a week off to spend time with my mate."

"You found a mate for your prickly dragon?" Anderson laughed. Xander rolled his eyes. Anderson had pushed for Xander to find a mate and settle after being alive for a hundred years.

"Yes, I'm taking her to Rome to convince her she truly is my mate."

"Of course, you'd find a woman who won't just fall in your arms." Anderson laughed louder.

"Enough, Anderson. I'll get on the R.J. situation when I come back." Xander hung up and got onto his computer to do some recon on The Golden Painting and the Wright family. He spent the better part of the afternoon digging into the gallery and their owners. What he found worried him. Many artists were unhappy with the exorbitant hanging fee. Other not so legal things popped up in his research. He would have to be careful when speaking to Mitchell. He remembered him vaguely from a conference they both attended. Mitchell seemed to want to show him up at every turn. Having been in the art game for a very long time, Xander had ignored the young man. He jotted down the office number and put it aside to call after he convinced Roxie to be with him forever.

She was the only one for him. He had been with plenty of women, but none of them sent his dragon into a frenzy like Roxie.

Her beautiful curves, dark blonde hair, and mesmerizing blue-violet eyes had him willing to do whatever it took to make her his.

CHAPTER TEN

Roxie awoke from her sleep, blinking away the blur from her eyes. She had a date with Xander in two hours. She couldn't wait. He made her happy. Just being around him lifted her spirits. He had told her that her mom was wrong, and so was Mitch. He wanted to showcase her work!

However, you heard Mitch. He said your work was mediocre and wouldn't sell, a grim voice told her. She shook her head and groaned. Xander had to be wrong. The Wright family had been trading and dealing art for generations. Why would Mitch steer her wrong? They loved each other at one time.

She got up. Looking at the clock, she decided she had time to work on her painting. It was the only thing that calmed her down when she was worried. She had an hour before she needed to get ready. Settling at her canvas, she dove in, not bothering to change or fix her hair. When the urge to paint flared, she couldn't stop. She added another layer to the clouds, working to match her photograph. Lost in her own world, she'd forgotten to set an alarm and jumped when Xander spoke.

"You are amazing." She dropped her brush with a squeak. Xander, with his quick reflexes, caught it before it hit her unprotected carpet. She looked at the clock, which read six-thirty.

"You are early," she accused and he smiled.

"I had a hunch you would dive into your painting. One thing I find fascinating about you is your focus. I was in the

37

doorway for ten minutes and you had no idea." Xander swooped in and kissed her. She paused in surprise; he was acting so familiar around her.

"Sorry, one of my many faults as an artist. Since my parents had already brought it up, it was part of the reason my ex Mitch left me." Roxie took her brush from his hand and put it down. She stood, looking up at Xander. She realized she only came up to his shoulder. Taking the time to admire him, she noticed he was in jeans and a different t-shirt from that morning.

"Mitch was an idiot. You are an artist. It comes with dating one and being married. You know they need their time to paint and focus." Xander leaned down and kissed her gently. She melted into his touch. His words made her feel as if he wanted her long term. He understood what it was like to date an artist. Releasing him, she turned away to hide her rising blush.

"How should I dress for our date?" Heading for her closet, she needed a moment to collect herself.

"Same as me. Something you'll be comfortable sitting in for a long time." She looked over her shoulder and lifted an eyebrow.

"Pardon?"

"Just want you to be comfortable." He broke eye contact, which made her even more suspicious.

"Going to tell me where we are heading?" She grabbed her most comfortable jeans and a t-shirt. She walked over to her bathroom to shower, purposefully leaving the door ajar. She wanted to see if he would be tempted to sneak a peek.

"Are you okay if I neaten up your paints?" Xander asked. Why did her paints need storing? She would only be gone for a few hours. Maybe he was a neat freak like Mitch?

Roxie remembered when they had moved in together after the wedding. She was up all night painting after satisfying Mitch's needs. She then crawled into bed twenty minutes before his alarm went off. She had the day off and planned to go back to sleep. That was until Mitch stormed back into the room raving about her studio being a disaster.

"Roxie, get your ass up and clean your studio! You left the paints open and dirty brushes in a cup of water on our brand new desk, not to mention the drop cloth under your easel. I expect it to be clean when you are done painting. This is our home, and you will take pride in the way it looks," Mitch roared.

It took her a whole minute to process what had just happened. To make her new husband happy, she got up and cleaned. He stood at the doorway, watching her clean and pointing out places she missed until the place was up to his standards.

Stepping out of the shower, she dried off, dressed, and did her makeup.

"Xander, do you . . ." she trailed off when she saw all her work placed carefully around the room.

"These are amazing, but I thought you'd have more. I only see a dozen or so." He was standing by the first one that she did post-divorce. It was a lightning storm she'd witnessed the night they filed the papers.

"My ex-husband got some. Well, most during the divorce. In exchange for not asking for alimony, Mitchell was supposed to sell my art at his gallery. I am getting ninety-five percent of the sale." She hadn't seen a penny yet from the paintings, which only confirmed her inadequacies.

"From that look, I can tell he has sold none. Do you know if he has them up at a gallery?" Xander wrapped her in a comforting hug. She breathed in his scent. It was like a fall evening when campfires were lit.

"Not one, and my lawyer checked on him a month ago. The paintings are displayed. Just goes to show Mitch was right about my talent."

"Hmm, could we talk more about this on our way to our date?" Xander suggested, dropping a kiss on the top of her head.

"Sure, but wouldn't you rather talk about more interesting things?" She did not want to think about Mitch or her failure as an artist. "We can talk about anything you want." Xander looked at his watch. "We need to go or we'll be late." Xander smiled, holding out a hand. She took it without hesitation, letting him lead her out. "Bye, Evvy." Roxie waved to her friend. "See you later." Evelyn waved back and winked. Roxie grabbed her purse and left the apartment. Waiting outside was a black limo, the driver holding the door open. Xander led her over and let her get inside first. The inside had soft black leather seats with lowlights. Roxie smiled.

"All this for a first date?"

Xander grinned, leaned over, and kissed her. "I'm just getting started."

"Where are we going?" Roxie asked. Xander handed her a bottle of water and grabbed one for himself.

"Rome."

She gasped and choked on her water, coughing hard as she gaped at him.

CHAPTER ELEVEN

"Did you say Rome, as in Rome, Italy?"

"I did. I heard you quit your job at your dad's business. I hope I didn't overstep by assuming you could go," Xander said.

"No, of course not. I never expected this for a first date. Can you afford to take so much time off?" she asked. No one had ever taken her on a trip far away. Mitch had taken her to DC for their honeymoon to look at all the art museums. He had told her it would be educational for her growth as an artist. She had wanted to walk around all the Smithsonian museums, but Mitch had refused, saying he did not want to be around all the small kids and crowds.

"I have it handled. I don't have an artist to showcase yet. I am hoping it will be you, but I won't pressure you. I want to spend this week doing everything you want. I even bought a guidebook for you to look through on our flight." He held out the book, and Roxie grinned.

"But what about clothes?"

"Your roommate packed you some essentials, but I wanted to take you shopping."

"You are voluntarily going clothing shopping with me?" She shook her head in disbelief.

"Yes. You are my mate. I want to do everything with you." Xander leaned over and kissed her. She felt her body melt, and she pressed against his body.

"We are here, sir," the driver announced. Roxie reluctantly released Xander.

"We can continue on the plane." Xander's heated whisper made her shudder.

"Won't there be others?"

"It is my private jet. I mostly use it to fly in artists and their work for showcases. This week, I'll use it for pleasure." He kissed her sweetly and helped her out of the limo.

"Won't this be expensive?"

"Won't even make a dent in my bank account, I promise," he assured her. They went onto the plane and sat down side by side. She took a moment to look around the sleek jet. The chairs were tan leather. They were large enough to allow adequate legroom. She could sit cross-legged.

"Please buckle up. We will take off shortly," the pilot's voice announced. She buckled up and watched Xander do the same.

"How long have you been an art dealer?" Roxie asked once the flight attendant was done going over the safety procedures.

"About seventy-five years," he answered and she gasped.

"How old are you?" How could someone deal with art for seventy-five years? He didn't look a day over thirty.

"One hundred."

"No way! You look like you're thirty max." She couldn't believe he was one hundred years old. What shifter lived that long?

"My particular type of shifter doesn't age past thirty until I find my mate. Then I'll age along with her until we get to mid-fifties. After that, we stay around our mid-fifties for as long as we live," Xander explained.

"Would it be rude to ask what animal you shift into?" She looked up at him, hesitant to make eye contact.

"I'm a dragon," he answered, patting her hand.

"No freakin' way!"

"Yes way." He waggled his eyebrows, and she laughed.

42

"That is so awesome. What does your dragon look like? Do you breathe fire? Do you have a treasure trove? Am I being rude?" She clapped a hand over her mouth to stop her barrage of questions.

"No, you are not being rude. I'm a red fire-breathing dragon, and yes, I have treasure. I have been collecting paintings since I was very young." Xander leaned over and kissed her gently. She sighed into the kiss, opening her mouth to let in his tongue. When his tongue touched hers, she felt an inferno erupt in her pussy, which soaked her panties instantly. There was a faint ding. She barely registered Xander releasing her seat belt. Suddenly, she was straddling his lap, her hand buried deep in his silky hair. She moaned, pressing her chest against him. His unyielding muscles twitched when she rubbed her breasts back and forth. Her nipples tightened into peaks. The sensation of her nipples against the fabric of her bra turned her on even more. She gasped, breaking the kiss.

"Xander, I need more."

"My pleasure." Xander slipped his hands under her shirt and pulled it over her head. He buried his face between her double Ds, pushing them together and sucking on the top. It left a blooming red mark behind to match the one from last night. She moaned from the sensation of his tongue and teeth nipping and licking the tops of her breasts.

"Mmm," she moaned and held him against her. He reached behind and unclasped her bra, revealing her chest. Roxie let the straps slip down her arms, watching his eyes dilate when her breasts were completely revealed. She felt powerful just showing a small part of herself. She could see his control slipping.

"You are beautiful." He cupped them, bringing one to his mouth. He sucked on the nipple until it was a tight bud. Gripping his head, she held him to her breast. Her body burned as desire flared into a steady flame.

43

"That feels amazing," she whispered. He switched to the other, massaging the breast he'd just released. She tugged his shirt off, wrapping her arms around his neck. "I need more," she demanded, her hands roaming down his back.

"Are you sure?" he asked, looking up into her eyes.

"Very," Roxie stepped off his lap and slowly stripped out of her jeans. She undid the button and slid down the zipper. She could see the desire blazing in his eyes as she shimmed the jeans past her hips. Roxie felt amazing knowing what she could do to him. She let gravity pull them down to her ankles. Stepping out, she stood in her black lace panties. She played with her nipples, showing Xander just how much she wanted him.

"Come." Xander crooked his finger, and she walked over to him, stopping just before their toes touched.

"You are perfect, my love." He reached for her, but she shook her head.

"You are wearing too much. I want to feel my skin against yours." She gestured to his jeans, and he smirked.

"With pleasure." Standing, he unzipped and tugged both jeans and boxer briefs to his feet. Her eyes widened at the sight of his cock—thick and long. The veins showed how hard he was for her. There was no way it would fit. Mitch wasn't much smaller, and it had hurt every time. Hesitating, she took a slight step back, her eyes never leaving his erection.

"I can sense your fear. Don't worry, love, I'll be very gentle." He pulled her in for another kiss, driving away her fear. She let the kiss wash over her. She reached down and stroked. He felt like steel encased in velvet. A rumble filled his chest, and she looked up, surprised.

"My dragon likes you touching me," Xander explained, smiling. She smirked and stroked him, feeling bolder. Xander's eyes rolled back, and he moaned. "Come on." Xander took her hand

44

and led her to a room in the back of the plane. He opened the door to reveal a queen-sized, fully made bed.

He guided her to sit on the bed then knelt. "These have got to go." He tugged and her panties came off. "You smell amazing, fully aroused for me. I can't wait to taste your sweet honey." Xander placed kisses on both knees, alternating up her legs until he made it to the apex of her thighs.

"Open for me, love," he coaxed and she faltered.

"I've never . . ." she trailed off, and Xander gave a surprised look.

CHAPTER TWELVE

"You mean no man has ever pleasured you with his mouth?" It shocked him. Why wouldn't a man want his partner ready for him? He knew they needed proper lubrication to make his mate feel amazing. If not, it would just hurt and she wouldn't want to have sex ever.

"No," she whispered.

"Allow me to show you how amazing I can make you feel." He pushed her thighs apart and slipped her legs over his shoulders. He kissed the inside of each thigh up to the top of her curls covering her pussy. Using his fingers, he spread her lips and licked from slit to clit. Her cry of pleasure spurred him on. He sucked her clit gently using his tongue to dip into her opening. She tasted like heaven; he couldn't get enough. He slipped a finger in and her hips jerked. She was tight. Moaning, he added a second finger, scissoring to loosen her. His mouth continued to torture her clit until she screamed her release. Her thighs clamped around his head, and he pumped his fingers in and out through her orgasm. She smelled divine and tasted even better. He knew she was finally slick enough to take his entire length without pain.

He stood and slipped between her legs, his cock pushing at her entrance. He connected with her eyes and licked her juices from his fingers.

"You taste perfect." Leaning over, he captured her mouth and entered at the same time. She was more than ready to take him after her orgasm.

"Xander!" she moaned, wrapping her legs around his waist, making him go deeper. He nipped at her neck and groaned.

"You are so tight. You will make me spill my seed early." Her pussy clutched him tightly. He knew he filled her completely and was being as gentle as he could with her.

"Don't hold back." She kissed him and moved her hips to his rhythm, her hands cupping her breasts, tweaking her nipples. Taking her words to heart, he sped up and lifted her legs over his shoulders. He went deeper and harder, grunting and moaning his pleasure. His orgasm was coming quickly. Slowing his pace, he took deep breaths. He did not want to come too early. Xander wanted to prolong the intense sensations her tight, hot, wet pussy sent along his body. Leaning down, he captured her mouth with his, kissing her hard and slipping in his tongue. He could feel her getting close to her orgasm.

He reached down and stroked her clit once, twice, and on the third touch, she arched, gasping for breath, as her orgasm overtook her. Her pussy clenching his cock sent him soaring into his own. He grabbed her hips hard, moaning as his cock swelled and filled her with his seed. He held tightly until all his seed was spent and settled deep in her womb. He silently hoped she would get pregnant with his child. Xander waited so long to become a father, and with Roxie, he knew it would be perfect. He collapsed to her side and pulled her tight, their sweaty bodies tangled together. Her eyes were closed, and she was taking deep breaths to calm her body down. His breathing was slightly labored. He kissed her temple.

"Are you okay?"

"That was amazing," she whispered, her eyes dark with desire. He almost took her again, but he could see it exhausted her.

47

"Only because it was with you. Get some sleep. We will arrive in Rome in the morning." He kissed her gently and closed his eyes, pulling her tightly against his frame. She sighed and rolled until her face was resting on his chest.

He felt content. For the first time in a hundred years, he knew he found the one for him. Sleep slowly claimed him. He tried hard to keep his eyes open and watch his mate, but he couldn't fight the exhaustion.

CHAPTER THIRTEEN

Xander awoke to the pilot's announcement.

"We will arrive in Rome, Italy in ten minutes. Please return to your seats." Roxie stirred in his arms, her naked body rubbing against him. He was sorely tempted to take her again but knew they needed to get back to their seats.

"Mmm, where are we?" Roxie asked, her voice husky from sleep.

"Almost in Rome, love. We need to get dressed," he said, kissing her head, not interested in moving.

"We are almost in Rome?" She shot up, excitement shining in her eyes.

"Yes, ten minutes." Xander sat up as he enjoyed watching her unabashedly hopping out of bed to get dressed. She looked around the room and paused.

"How did my clothes get here?"

"Probably the flight attendant." Xander stood, walking over to his pile of clothes. Shaking out the wrinkles, he dressed. Every chance he got, he kissed or touched her until he was hard for her again. Roxie raised an eyebrow once her shirt was back on.

"We don't have enough time. Will you be alright?"

"Not the first time I've gone without," Xander assured her and led her back to their seats.

"What are we doing first?" she asked, as the plane began its descent.

"I thought we'd get settled in the penthouse suite of my parents's hotel, The Austin Luxury. After that, we can go shopping for some clothes. I didn't want Evelyn waking you while she was packing an entire week's worth of clothing."

"You are so sweet to me and you've only known me for twenty-four hours."

"That's what we, dragons, do when we meet our mates. It is instant wanting to care for you and always making you happy."

"So it is the honeymoon phase of any relationship?"

"One that will never end. Mates don't cheat or break up. They are for life." He brought her hand up, kissing her knuckles. He would spend the rest of his life devoted to Roxie, making her happy.

"That sounds too good to be true. Mitch promised me forever, and I got three years. One of which he spent cheating on me with his younger, thinner assistant." Roxie's pain was palpable. He wanted to take it away.

"There will never be another for me, Roxie. Let me spend this week proving how perfect we are for each other." He leaned over and placed a kiss on her lips.

"I hope you can. I don't want to be broken like this anymore. Since meeting you, my painting urge has exploded. I am happy. I cannot wait to go around Rome and find inspiration." Roxie kissed him and rested her head on his shoulder.

Xander was livid when she'd told him about her ex cheating on her. That was the lowest of the low. When you make a commitment, you stick with it. He was happy she divorced the idiot because if he had met her while married, he would have run off with her.

"What time will it be when we land?" Her question broke through his thoughts.

"Close to ten, by the time we get off and into the waiting car."

"Can I get a shower before we go shopping?"

"Anything you want. This entire week is about you and me making a connection." He kissed her again, this time adding tongue. They kissed until the plane landed.

CHAPTER FOURTEEN

Roxie walked into the penthouse suite of The Austin Luxury Hotel and stared in awe. There was a vast lounge area with a fireplace and a massive TV. The suite had four bedrooms and a compact kitchen with better appliances than her apartment.

"Come, the master bedroom is here," Xander said, pointing toward the left where only one door stood. "The nice shower with the waterfall head is through here."

She smiled. His hair looked so sexy tussled from their nap on the plane and the sex they'd had. She laughed, and Xander gave her a confused look.

"I just realized I've joined the mile high club, and it was the best sex I've ever had," Roxie explained, giggling as Xander smirked.

"Seems I've joined the club too, and the sex was the best I've ever had as well. You are truly my mate."

"It will only get better. You haven't seen all my talents yet." Roxie winked and walked into the bathroom. There was a spacious shower and a jacuzzi big enough for multiple people. All surfaces gleaned from the chrome fixtures and sparkling white counters.

"This is beautiful. How many hotels do your parents own?" she asked, stripping out of her clothes, feeling comfortable around him.

"Close to a hundred Austin Luxury hotels, but they own a ton more under different brand names." Xander joined her in taking off his clothes and turned on the shower.

"How come you didn't get into hotels?" She stepped into the shower and bit back a moan as the scalding water hit her aching muscles.

"Dragons can live hundreds of years, as long as they aren't killed or contracted with an incurable disease. There wasn't anything for me to inherit since they don't die out quickly. I went into something else entirely." Xander joined her under the spray, wrapping his arms around her.

"But I'm human. Won't I die long before you?" She turned around, worried about how he would be if they mated and she died.

"Part of the mating ritual is me biting you and then we make a blood pact."

"What is a blood pact?" She reached for the loofah and soaped it up, starting at his chest and working her way around his back.

"We each make a cut on our wrists and exchange blood. This will give you the ability to become a dragon and live alongside me eternally." She stopped and gaped at him.

"You mean, I can become a dragon if we mate?"

"Yes, dragons are rare, and to preserve our race, we've adapted to taking human mates. The downside is when one mate dies, the other will live a loveless life. There are no second mates. A dragon named Maximillian Da Vinci, no relation to Leonardo, discovered a way to change a mate. This change can only happen with a true mate, so people haven't tried to capture a dragon to change others," Xander explained.

"This is the oddest conversation I've had in a shower," Roxie laughed, leaning up to kiss him.

"I didn't plan on having this conversation here, but it came up." Xander shrugged and took the loofah from her. He put the unscented body wash on it and scrubbed her down.

"Well, you've given me a lot to think about this week." Roxie bit back a moan as his hands massaged her breasts. Did she want to become a dragon? How would that change her life? Was Xander worth the risk? These thoughts swirled around in her head. "I want to taste you again." He backed her against the cool shower wall, kneeling. He lifted one of her legs over his shoulder and went to work on her pussy. His tongue teased her clit, and she screamed from the jolt of desire racing through her.

"Xander!" She gripped his head with her hands hard. He slipped two fingers in, curling to find her sensitive spot. He pumped in and out, sucking on her clit. He scraped his teeth against her sensitive nub which shattered her. Her body tensed and exploded, her eyes seeing stars. Xander held her shaking legs, pumping his fingers in and out as her orgasm subsided.

"Your pussy tasted amazing, but I need more, my love." Xander lifted her up and slid home, pinning her to the wall.

"I don't know if I can be gentle this time." Xander bent his head and took one nipple in his teeth and bit. Roxie moaned. She'd barely recovered from one orgasm and Xander was building another. He filled her completely. It didn't hurt like with Mitch and she craved more. He was holding back.

"Don't be careful, Xander. Take me how you would normally. I won't break," she demanded and moaned her pleasure as he sped up.

"Are you sure?" he asked, looking down to stare into her eyes.

"I like it rough, please," she begged. Xander set her on her feet and turned her around to lean against the wall. He slid back in quickly, slamming his cock deep, his balls hitting her ass. He gripped her hips almost painfully and pounded in and out. Suddenly, a sting spread from the sharp slap he laid on her bottom.

"Oh!" she gasped. The sting spurred on her orgasm.

"Like that?" he groaned and hit her other ass cheek.

"Yes," she moaned. He spread her stinging cheeks and circled her tight hole. He reached down and brought some of her juices to lubricate her ass. He pushed one finger in and she moaned. No one had ever touched her there, but she'd been very curious how it would feel. His finger filled her. She felt pleasantly stretched from his one finger.

"When we have more time, I will take your ass. I will mark every hole as mine." Xander pushed a second finger in with the first and she moaned louder. She felt stretched, fuller than before. Her orgasm was building with a slow tension as Xander brought her to the edge but never let her go over with his measured strokes.

"Xander, please," she begged him to give her release. He sped up and touched her clit deftly. She shattered, seeing white as her orgasm shook her entire body. She was dimly aware of Xander stiffening behind her and spilling his scalding seed inside her. Her pussy clenched and squeezed every drop out of him.

Xander cleaned them both up quickly under the showerhead. Roxie barely had the strength to stand, so she let him take care of her. He turned off the water and grabbed two towels. He wrapped Roxie up, rubbing her dry. He slung one towel around his waist, letting it sit low. Scooping her up, he placed her on the king-sized bed. He slipped in with her, wrapping her up in his warm arms. She lay there, reveling in his warmth and strength.

"Tell me about your tattoos," Xander murmured, placing a kiss on the almost half sleeve of colorful flowers.

"I got my first one when I split from Mitch. We were in the process of separating long enough for the divorce to go through. You remember me saying my parents are very conservative?" she began, her fingers stroking his arm around her waist.

"Mmm hmm."

"Well, Mitch was worse. I mentioned wanting to get one flower in my wedding bouquet as a tattoo. He went into a rage about me marring my skin, and as his wife, I couldn't embarrass him. The day we split, I got a yellow rose to symbolize my freedom."

"Then how did you get the rest?" He kissed his way down her arm. She giggled at the ticklish feel of his stubble.

"Each time I went on a trip, I picked a flower to represent how I felt after I got home. Some of them are special to me in other ways. I have the flower that represents my birthday. I have one for my brother. He is why I painted. It has almost become an addiction for me. I just need to move where I put them to hide it from my parents," Roxie explained, rolling to face him.

"Your parents don't know?" Xander gave her a shocked look.

"No, can you imagine my mother's reaction? You heard her with my painting." Roxie smirked when Xander laughed.

"True. Do you have any other siblings?"

"I have one, an older sister who is a doctor two states away and the older brother I told you about. I have no clue where he is. He moved away at eighteen. We haven't heard from him since."

"Is his last name the same as yours?" Xander asked.

"Yes, but he was from my father's first marriage. My brother helped me find my love of painting. He saw me draw one day and suggested I try painting."

"How far apart are you two?"

"Six years. My sister is only two years older than me. She is my parents's golden child, doing exactly what my mother wants. She moved because of her job offer."

"What is her name?"

"Elizabeth and my brother, Anderson. My full name is Roxanne, but I've always preferred Roxie." Xander raised an eyebrow as she mentioned her brother's name, but her stomach rumbled. It made her smile and he laughed. "It's noon. Can we go out and get lunch, plus some clothes?" she asked, blushing.

"Of course, my love." Xander jumped out of bed and walked out naked to the living room. He came back with his suitcase and her carry on.

"You should have one change of clothes," he explained. She pulled the bag toward her and saw all matching sets of her sexiest underwear. Two spring dresses were tucked in the bottom— one was blue; the other, pink. Evvy knew she would want options. She chose the blue dress and got dressed.

"Beautiful," Xander complimented after she emerged from the bathroom, her hair tamed and makeup applied.

"Not bad yourself, hot stuff." She sauntered over and kissed him with just enough heat to feel his cock stiffen.

"Keep that up and we'll never get out of here," Xander groaned and she laughed.

"Feed me, let me shop and then you can have me again, dragon." She laughed again when his eyes darkened and took a reptilian quality. Xander took her hand, and they left the penthouse suite to enjoy Rome.

CHAPTER FIFTEEN

Xander took her to Via Del Corso to shop for her wardrobe. He wanted to dress her in the best; she deserved to see how special she was.

"Come here," he instructed, opening a door to a boutique. She looked up at the name and gasped. They were entering the store of her favorite brand for plus-sized women. She owned a few dresses from them when she needed to play the trophy wife for Mitchell.

"Why are we here?" she asked, looking up into his deep-set hazel eyes.

"To get you new clothes for our trek around Rome. We have a private showing in a few minutes," he explained. She pulled him in for a gentle kiss.

"I cannot believe you did this for me. I thought we'd hit up a few of the mainstream stores. I've heard it is nearly impossible to meet the designer," she remarked, fingering a beautiful sundress of sky blue.

"Do you like that one?" he whispered in her ear. He delighted in the slight shiver that went down her back.

"It is beautiful. I like solids with a fun print mixed in. I can't say I appreciate the way stripes or ugly floral are the only prints for plus-sized women. Who wants to wear stripes to make yourself look larger than you already are?" She ended her rant to see a petite, plus-sized woman laughing.

"I like a woman with firm opinions. I agree with you on the stripes. You won't see any in my collection. I'm Colleen Bianchi, and I own this shop." Colleen held out her hand and Roxie shook it, her eyes wide.

"I'm Xander Austin, and this is my girlfriend, Roxie Jones. I called yesterday about a private fitting," Xander explained.

"You are Koraline's son!" She held out her arms for a hug.

"Nice to meet you," he replied, giving her the obligatory hug.

"Koraline is the reason I became a household name. She wore one of my formal gowns to a hotel opening. Everyone wanted to know who her designer was. Well, let me tell you, I sold out overnight. I'm happy to do anything for the Austin family," Colleen shared, leading them to a closed-off area.

"Now tell me, Roxie, what do you do for a living?" Colleen pushed her down into a plush chair.

"I'm an assis—no, I'm an artist," she replied. She almost said she was an assistant, but she quit her job yesterday.

"Are you sure?" Colleen didn't look convinced.

"Yes, it is a recent career change for me," she admitted.

"More power to you, taking a chance on a passion. Tell me what you prefer to wear."

"Loose tops and dresses with empire waistlines. I find dresses with a natural waist cut me at an odd spot. I wear solid tops with patterned cardigans. I want to find a more relaxed style now that I don't work in an office. I enjoy wearing dresses and flowing tops," Roxie shared. Colleen was digging through the racks, pulling out clothes the entire time.

"I have the perfect look for you. Go in the changing room, and I'll bring you my top picks. Xander, you sit and get comfortable. This will take a while."

"Anything you say, Ms. Bianchi." He laughed. It made him feel good knowing Roxie would get a fresh one of a kind wardrobe.

59

Roxie tried on what felt like hundreds of outfits. The amazing thing was, all the clothes looked fantastic on her body. She didn't get the normal feeling of being too fat when she tried on clothes. Colleen was amazing; she made Roxie feel beautiful, something she hadn't felt in a long time.

"This is your best look yet. You look good in sleeveless swing dresses. Shows off that gorgeous tattoo you've got. Let's see what you look like in jeans." Roxie cringed. Jeans were very hard for her to find. Skinny jeans made her feel like an ice cream cone.

"Don't give me that look. I have the perfect pair for you. Your mate out there won't be able to keep his hands off you," Colleen promised. She handed her a pair of dark wash boot cut jeans. She slid them on, and like with everything else, they zipped without trouble. Stepping out of the dressing room, she silently thanked Colleen when Xander's jaw dropped open.

"You look hot!" he complimented her, and she blushed.

"Thanks. This entire thing has been a major boost to my confidence. Thank you, Colleen, and Xander, you've helped me find a new style. This is something I will never forget." She blinked back the happy tears threatening to fall.

"You deserve to be happy. You are beautiful, smart, creative, talented, and sweet. I wanted you to see how special you are to me. Pick your favorites and we'll take them with us," he told her and she gasped.

"Xander, I can't afford these," she began and he cut her off.

"I am paying. Now go choose," he ordered, waving her on.

"I can't accept something so expensive," she argued.

"Yes, you can and you will. We are mates and I want to spoil you," he demanded.

"Honey, take the man up on his offer. It's not every day you get to be spoiled. Enjoy the moment," Colleen chastised.

She finally dipped a nod and went to change back into her clothes. Roxie would pick only enough outfits for the week, nothing more. She didn't want to take advantage of Xander's generosity.

CHAPTER SIXTEEN

On their last night, Roxie and Xander visited the Trevi Fountain. She tossed a coin, wishing to be with Xander for a long time. The week had been eye-opening with how he treated her. Never once did they argue. When a disagreement arose, they talked through it and came to an agreement. Not once did he ask her to become his mate or about showcasing her artwork. She couldn't wait to get home and start on a new collection.

"Made a wish?" Xander asked, pulling her back to the present.

"Yes, but if I tell you, it won't come true," she joked, sitting on the edge of the fountain.

"True." He gave her a serious look.

"Come here and take a picture with me." She tugged him down and held out her phone, trying to get a wonderful shot of them and the fountain.

"Would you like help?" an older woman asked.

"Yes, thank you." Roxie handed her the phone and settled against Xander. He wrapped an arm around her waist and kissed her temple. She looked up at him and could see the love in his eyes.

"Oh, you two are so much in love. Are you on your honeymoon?" The woman's voice made them jump.

"Oh no, we are just dating," Xander answered.

"Mate her quick. You two are meant to be." She gave a wink and returned Roxie's phone, walking off. Roxie stared at Xander, afraid he might have been made uncomfortable.

"You know how I feel, Roxie. You are my mate, and I'll happily marry you any day. Roxie, you tell me when you are ready. I'll wait however long you need." Xander placed a chaste kiss on her lips.

"This week has been amazing, and you've shown me how a genuine man treats a woman. I'm just afraid I'm not good enough. I want to contribute to our relationship financially, and I can't see myself going back to being a secretary." Roxie leaned against him, listening to the fountain bubble behind her.

"Would you be willing to let me showcase your work? I'll treat you like all my other artists in residence, not as a mate. We can even get the paintings from your ex and sell them for your alimony," Xander offered.

"Can I think about it over dinner?" She wasn't sure she was ready for the world to see her work. Mitch's words continued to echo in her head. *You will never be more than mediocre at painting.*

"I won't push you." Xander took her hand and led her to the waiting car.

"To Chef Antonio's," Xander instructed.

"I haven't heard of that restaurant," Roxie commented as the car drove down several small streets.

"It's not. My friend Antonio invited us to dinner, and I thought you'd like to meet some other dragon shifters."

"That is awesome. I'd love to meet your friends. When do I get to meet your parents and Rhett?"

"Maybe at the next family dinner. It would be nice not to be the only one without a mate. Josie started her Mate Me service to find me a mate. Lucky for me, you showed on the first night." Xander pulled her close, kissing her temple.

"I know Josie was trying to introduce you to Evvy when we met."

"That she was, but Evvy doesn't hold a candle to you. The second I saw you, I wanted you."

"You practically had me at hello. I'm not sure we would have had sex in the office if your brother didn't knock."

"Poor timing and wording. I was worried I lost you when Rhett had called you my hook up."

"You almost did."

The car stopped at a small home with flower beds hanging from each window.

"This place is so cute!" She walked up the stone path, admiring the house.

"Why thank you," a tall man with black hair and green eyes said.

"Antonio!" Xander held out a hand, and they gave each other a half hug with a hearty slap on the back.

"Antonio, meet Roxie, my mate, although she hasn't agreed yet."

"Good for you, honey. Make him work for it," a tall woman with ample curves, black hair, brown eyes, and beautiful olive skin announced.

"Marta, good to see you. Roxie, Marta is Antonio's mate." Xander pulled her close.

"Uncle Xander!" came the cry of several children, all with ebony hair, olive skin, and an array of eye color between brown and green.

"Hello!" Xander knelt and was bombarded by three children around elementary age.

"Austin, Isabella, and Joseph, this is Roxie," Xander explained, hugging each one.

"Xand," came a small voice from behind Marta. Roxie could make out a three-year-old clutching a pink blanket and a small dragon.

"There is my Mary." Xander scooped her up and spun her around. She screamed in delight. Roxie had a flash of him holding

64

their own daughter, blonde curls and hazel eyes. Her ovaries clenched, wanting to give him a child. He'd waited a hundred years, she didn't want him to wait longer. *What about your art?* A small voice sounded in her head, and she paused. That was it. She would let him show her art, and if one piece sold, she would take him as her mate. Once they got home, she'd let her lawyer know she wanted her art returned. Mitch had had long enough to sell it, and he hadn't.

"Roxie, how did you and Xander meet?" Marta asked, breaking into her thoughts. They'd moved into the living room, and Antonio had poured everyone a glass of red wine.

"My roommate dragged me to a shifter event. She told me it was about time I moved on from my divorce. The woman running the event brought Xander over to meet Evvy, my roommate. She works for an art museum as a guide," Roxie explained.

"I took one look at my golden-haired goddess and knew she was my mate," Xander added, kissing her knuckles. She blushed and leaned into his side.

"He surprised me with this trip to help me see how a wonderful relationship can be. He even got my roommate to pack a bag for me while I slept off my all-nighter."

"Are you studying for a degree?" Antonio asked.

"No, I have a degree in art and creative design. I used to work as a secretary for my father's tax firm, and it bit into my ability to paint during the day," she explained, sipping her wine.

"What do you paint?" Marta asked from the kitchen.

"Mostly landscapes and architecture. I am decent at portraits."

"Have anything we can see? I'm opening a new restaurant and want to show new artists." Antonio drained his glass and stood for a refill.

65

"I have some. Most are not accessible at the moment." Roxie pulled out her phone and opened her file on the twelve she had at her apartment. Antonio scrolled through and smiled.

"Any not based in the U.S.?"

"No, this is my first trip abroad. As soon as I get home, I'm going to start a new series of paintings from my time here in Rome." Roxie took back her phone.

"Let me know when you do them. I can tell you are very talented and would be honored to hang one in my restaurant."

"Thank you! That means more than you know. My ex owns his own gallery, and he told me I'd never sell one." Roxie smiled and Xander rubbed her back. Antonio wanted one of her paintings! Did that mean she had a sale? She'd have to wait and see.

"Dinner!" Marta called and three pairs of footsteps thundered into the dining room. Mary toddled behind, trying to keep up. She paused at Roxie.

"Up, please." Roxie was shocked but picked her up.

"You have pretty eyes. Xand likes you." Mary held Roxie's cheeks in her small hands as she commented.

"I'll tell you a secret," Roxie whispered, giving her a sweet, sneaky smile.

"What?" Mary gasped.

"I like Uncle Xander too."

"Good. Mama says he needs to settle down and make some babies." Roxie laughed, knowing Mary had repeated in verbatim something her mother must say often.

"We are working on it," Roxie replied and carried her to the dining room.

CHAPTER SEVENTEEN

"Where do you sit?" Roxie asked and Xander had to do a double-take. She looked so natural holding Mary. He could see her being the mother to his children and had to hold back his grin. He watched Mary direct Roxie to her chair.

"Roxie, you sit with Xand," Mary declared.

"Yes, ma'am." Roxie winked and took her place on Xander's right. He reached over and slipped his hand up her thigh. She grabbed it and laced their fingers. He didn't remember ever feeling so content. They passed around the food and the conversation turned to their trip to Rome and what her favorite moment was.

"I think today at the Trevi Fountain. I know it is the first thing I will paint once we're back home."

"When are you going to have a show? I'll be in your neck of the woods next month for work," Marta informed them.

"Hopefully next month, if I can get my paintings out of Mitch's gallery," Roxie announced. Xander stared at her in shock.

"You'll let me show your work?"

"Yes, I can't go back to office work. I want to focus on my art." Xander couldn't resist. She made him so excited, he kissed her hard on the mouth.

"Eww, Uncle Xander!" Austin yelled, covering his eyes. All the adults laughed and his father said, "Give yourself a few years. Girls won't be yucky."

"True, I was twelve when I first developed a crush on Penelope Barker," Xander shared. Roxie looked at him with a gleam in her eyes.

"Sounds to me there is a story there?" Roxie said.

"Oh, there is. I was in what you would call seventh grade. She was a year older. I went up to her, and mind you, my growth spurt hadn't come yet. I told her she should be my girlfriend. She and all her friends laughed and walked away from me. The rest of the year, her group avoided me like the plague. Made making friends harder than necessary." Xander shook his head over the folly of middle school students.

"Middle school was rough for me but, I bet, very different," Roxie commented. He could see the ominous cloud of a bad experience pass through her eyes.

"Want to talk about it?" he offered.

"Hard pass. It happened fourteen years ago. All in the past." Roxie's smile came back but not as bright. The rest of the evening passed playing games with the kids until Marta announced bedtime. Roxie offered to help get the kids ready, leaving Xander to sip scotch with Antonio.

"She is perfect for you and an artist to boot," Antonio said with a smirk.

"I'm in love with her. This week has been amazing. I've learned so much about her and her family." Xander grimaced at the reminder of her family.

"What's up with her family?"

"More her mother. The day I had asked Roxie out, her parents showed up. Her mother demanded she stop painting, saying it was why her ex left her. He told Roxie she would be lucky to have one painting sold. They did a number to her self-esteem."

"What about siblings?"

"Her half-brother left as soon as he turned eighteen. Her sister is a doctor two states away and is apparently the golden child."

"Sounds to me, you'll have some interesting in-laws." Antonio laughed.

"Not helpful," Xander grumbled.

"All you need to do is love her with everything you have. You show her she is worth more than gold, and her self-esteem will come back. Plus, I want to purchase her first Rome painting," Antonio assured him and Xander nodded. It was sound advice, and he wouldn't ever make her feel less than amazing.

"Thanks, Antonio. I knew coming here tonight would be a magnificent idea." Xander threw back the last of his scotch just as Roxie came down the stairs.

"Ready to go home?" he asked, standing up. She nodded and they said their goodbyes to Antonio and Marta. Marta promised she would come to the show as long as she gets the details.

CHAPTER EIGHTEEN

"Back in Green Falls again." Roxie sighed as the plane touched down the private runway.

"Not happy to be home?" Xander asked, squeezing her hand.

"Not that. It means I need to face the real world. I can assure you my mother is livid. I just took off for a week. I also have to contact Mitch and try to get my art back." She shuddered at having to talk to Mitchell Wright again.

"I kept meaning to ask, did you take your ex's last name?"

"No, I wanted to keep my last name on my art. Mitch's last name is Wright."

"Does he own The Golden Painting in New York?"

"Yes, why?"

"What name do you sell your art under?"

"Roxie Jones, although Mitch had a dumb idea of putting R.J. to make me sound mysterious," Roxie grumbled over his stupidity.

"My assistant, Anderson, went to the gallery and called me about our next artist. The owner was being evasive about the artist R.J. and refused to sell any paintings," Xander explained.

"That jerk! I had my lawyer check that he'd hung my art, not if he was actively telling people no. I will have to figure out a way to get them all back. Knowing Mitch, he'll try to cite our divorce agreement for not giving them back." Roxie was seething with anger. Mitch wouldn't sell any. It would prove him wrong.

"Do you mind letting my lawyer look at your agreement? Maybe he can find a loophole," Xander offered and she paused.

"Yes, I want to prove to him and my parents all my art can be sold." She knew Xander would do everything possible to help her succeed. He never tried to put her down just to make himself feel better.

"I'll call him first thing in the morning," Xander told her and she smiled. Life was looking so much better with him by her side.

The week went by fast; Roxie spent most of her time in her bedroom working her way through paintings of her time in Rome. Her mother called and yelled at her for not showing up to work.

"How could you leave your father in such a lurch? Do you know how bad that makes our family look? I cannot believe you just quit! Where were you this past week?" her mother yelled into the phone. Roxie used every ounce of willpower to keep herself from hanging up.

"I went away. I needed to get away from Green Falls. I quit because it is time for me to focus on my work as an artist. Xander Austin asked me to show my art, and I told him yes," she told her mother.

"That is the worst idea I have ever heard. You can never make it financially on art. Don't you dare think about moving back in with your father and me either," her mother replied.

"Wouldn't dream of it, Mom. I've got to go. Bye." Roxie hung up and rubbed her temples. She needed Advil every time she spoke with her mother. She didn't get why she was so against her being an artist. Her mother never insulted her work when she was in high school. It was as if going to art school made her dream real to her mother and suddenly she was no longer good enough. It all began once she started dating Mitchell. Her mom kept encouraging her to quit and become a housewife.

71

"Hey, Rox, how was your day?" Evelyn stood in her doorway with a concerned look on her face.

"Just spoke with my mother," she replied and Evelyn came over to give her an enormous hug.

"So, you need a drink?" Evelyn asked and Roxie laughed.

"I could, or just some Advil. I want to get more done on my paintings of Rome," she answered.

"I can get you that. Mind if I look at your paintings?" Evelyn asked.

"Sure, I am almost done with my one of the colosseum." Roxie got up from her stool and grabbed her bottle of Advil.

"These are so good. I am jealous you got to go and on your first date to boot! You have the best boyfriend." Evelyn gently touched her painting of the Trevi Fountain and Roxie smiled.

"Xander is the most amazing man I've ever met. Our week in Rome was just what I needed to know he is the one for me. I wanted to wait until I sold a painting before I let him mate me, but I know Xander will love me no matter what. He won't care if I don't sell a single painting. He will continue to encourage me," Roxie shared, her eyes going soft at the thought of Xander.

"You love him," Evelyn accused her.

"I guess I do," Roxie agreed. She thought about everything Xander had done for her in the past two weeks. He loved her. Even if he hadn't said the words yet, his actions told her.

"You are so lucky. I want to find my mate." Evelyn pouted. Roxie walked over and hugged her.

"You will find him. I know you will."

"I hope so. Does Xander have any cute shifter friends?" Evelyn joked.

"I can ask. I haven't met his friends here yet. We are going to speak to his lawyer tomorrow about getting my art back from Mitchell. I'll let you know if he is cute," Roxie promised and Evelyn laughed harder.

"Deal. I am off to another Mate Me event. Don't wait up."
Evelyn waved goodbye and left Roxie to her art.

CHAPTER NINETEEN

Friday morning, Roxie was sitting in the law office of Howard, Peters and Greenway.

"Roxie, it looks like you must prove Mitch is purposely not selling your art. The agreement states he must sell, but there is no time limit," Jordan Howard explained, putting down her divorce agreement. He had dark blond hair and bright green eyes. She was curious what type of shifter he was; she'd ask Xander later.

"Can I ask to get them back and give his gallery the five percent owed?"

"Possibly. I take it, Xander has offered to host you?" Jordan asked, steepling his fingers.

"Yes, I have. I won't take commissions from any of the art prior to her divorce," Xander piped up and Roxie grinned. He was taking an enormous hit financially to let her take over his gallery.

"It might work. Call and offer that scenario. If it doesn't work, I have a judge friend who will help. She hates ex-husbands who take advantage of their ex-wives. She'll give us a court order to release the paintings. It will also cause a stir in the art world if he refuses and the police get involved." Jordan looked practically giddy at the idea.

"Let me call him now. I don't want to wait any longer for what is rightfully mine." She smiled in excitement. She pulled out her phone and dialed his office.

"The Golden Painting."

"Hi, Mitch. It's Roxie." She felt nervous talking to him after such a disastrous breakup.

"What do you want?" he snarled. Both men raised their eyebrows but kept silent.

"I want my art. Another gallery has asked me to show my work. You've had them for over a year and haven't sold one."

"You ungrateful bitch! I've been trying to sell your awful paintings. They are taking up space on my walls."

"Then it will be no hardship to give them back and open the space for other artists." She tried to remain calm. Xander clenched his chair hard enough, the wood groaned.

"No, our divorce agreement states I get five percent of each one sold." Xander held out his hand for the phone. She passed it over.

"Hello, Mr. Wright. This is Xander Austin, director for the Dragon Lore Gallery. Your ex-wife and I came to an agreement. I will try to sell her art and the ones you hold at your gallery. If they sell, you get your five percent commission."

"How did you even find her? She is an unknown artist." Mitch's voice changed to business polite.

"My temp assistant went to art school with Ms. Jones. My other assistant has been traveling the U.S. in search of unknown talents. He called to tell me about a whole wing of paintings by an artist with the initials R.J. He made some interesting comments about your unwillingness to sell any to him or give him the information to contact R.J." Xander kept his voice quiet, but his eyes blazed.

"She cannot have any of her paintings back! I'll destroy all of them before I let her make a dime!" Mitch hung up and Roxie gasped. She'd never heard such venom in his voice before.

"Court order it is. Did you record everything?" Xander asked, handing the phone back to Roxie.

"Got it. I'll talk to Sally. I'll ask for police presence because of his threat." Jordan picked up his notes, phone, and keys.

75

"I'll call the minute I get a court order. Where is the gallery located?"

"New York City. Mitch lives in New Jersey. I moved home after we split," Roxie explained.

"My gallery is in D.C. Makes sense to live away from the hustle and bustle of the city," Xander added. Roxie nodded and they left the office. She felt free. Finally, her art would be appreciated by the world.

"Mind telling me how you ended up married to Mitch?" Xander probed softly. She shook her head. The story no longer made her hurt.

"We met through our moms, actually. They were best friends while growing up in New Jersey. My mother came from money until a stock market venture went bad for my grandfather. He was a well-known politician, and the scandal broke when he was arrested for insider trading. My mom was in college to become a lawyer. With the money gone, she couldn't complete school without going into major debt. Long story short, she moved here and met my dad and Anderson. She married him and had Elizabeth and then me. Well, my mother always wanted to go back to her old life. She resented being stuck here where my father's firm lived."

"She introduced Elizabeth to Mitch first. They got along like oil and water, then she introduced me. I was nineteen and a naïve virgin. I let Mitch manipulate me into transferring schools to New Jersey. We married when I was twenty-three and divorced at twenty-six. He said my art was interfering with my ability to be his housewife, party planner, and sexual partner. He'd found all of those things in his twenty-year-old secretary. I moved back here with Evvy and he gets to marry Barbie." They had driven home and were inside her apartment by the time she was done telling her tale.

"Wow, that is awful. Didn't Mitch know what you were like before you were married?" Xander led the way back to her room. He reached to open the door, and she stopped him.

"Sort of. I don't think he understood what happens when I get into the zone for painting. Everything else disappears and I don't respond to anything. I am warning you, my room has become mostly an art studio and is a mess. I know last time you were here, you needed it cleaned up, but that's not who I am, and if we mate, it will be messy." She waited for him to get upset, but all he did was look at her confused.

"Why would I get upset? I know how artists are. They make a mess." Xander opened her door and smiled.

"Come, show me what you've done this week. I'm eager to see your work." Roxie had refused to let him see anything until she felt she had a series on their time in Rome. She painted throughout the day and went on dates and spent the night in Xander's luxurious bedroom. He owned a modest four-bedroom home with three full bathrooms. The outside made it look like a quaint cottage, but as soon as she stepped inside, it exuded money. All the furniture was top quality and the art, rare. It was the first time she'd been afraid to touch anything.

CHAPTER TWENTY

Xander waited on her bed. He didn't want to push her into showing him, but he was anxious.

"I did a day in Rome. The paintings start at the crack of dawn over the Colosseum and end at night with our stop at the Trevi Fountain. I've managed four so far. I'm working on sunset over the pantheon. I made the Trevi Fountain first. Our moment there was the moment I realized I loved you." Roxie blushed, turning around the four completed paintings. His words stuck in his throat, and he had to swallow to get his voice back.

"You love me?"

"Very much."

"I love you too. I've been afraid you'd think I was going too fast after only two weeks together." He stood and crushed her mouth in a searing kiss. He couldn't believe this beautiful curvy goddess loved him!

"I love you, and after my family dinner, I am going to make you mine," he whispered, loving her shiver at his words.

"I can't wait." She nipped at his bottom lip, and he almost lost his resolve to wait.

"Let me get a good look. How many more are you making?" He knelt and took in each one. He could see the long hours she put in.

"I have three more to go, but I am keeping the Trevi Fountain. It means too much to me."

"How many hours have you slept this week?" He looked at the dark circles under her eyes with worry.

"Every night I spent at your house in White Valley."

"So out of the seven days we've been back, you've slept four nights?" Xander sighed. Once the showcase was over, he knew she'd sleep more.

"Promise you'll keep to just painting during the days once we mate?" He knew he was asking a lot from her, but he knew he wouldn't sleep without her once mated.

"I have time during the day now that I don't have to work." She smiled and kissed his cheek.

"You are truly talented. I cannot wait to show you off. If you want, we have about an hour until dinner that you can use to paint." He saw the delight in her eyes.

"Come get me fifteen minutes before we go."

"Can do, my love." Xander gave her a kiss and went to work, answering emails on his phone in the kitchen area.

CHAPTER TWENTY-ONE

Roxie bounced one knee in Xander's sports car. She was nervous about officially meeting his family as his future mate. He put his hand on her knee.

"They will love you because I love you," Xander assured her, and she nodded. He didn't know that Mitch's family pretended to like her to her face but said nasty things behind her back. One of their biggest jabs at her was her weight. She knew she wasn't thin. She shopped in the plus-sized section of the stores. It didn't mean she didn't think she was beautiful. She knew she was, and to Xander, she was all that mattered.

"Trust me, I can smell your nervousness." Xander stroked her leg, the contact calming her down.

"I'm trying very hard not to let my past color my opinions."

"I understand. Your past made you who you are today. Just remember we aren't high society. My family loves living in our close-knit community of White Valley."

"I like White Valley. You have such cute shops. I never would have thought we had something so nice a town away." Roxie smiled up at him, and he grinned.

"I'm happy to hear that. I've been hoping that once we mate, you'll move in with me. I don't need an answer right away. I have something at the house to show you after dinner. No, I won't tell you. You will just have to wait and see," Xander teased. She crossed her arms over her chest and pouted.

"Please?" she asked, her curiosity piqued.

"Nope." Xander parked his car in front of a home twice the size of his.

"And I thought your house was big," Roxie mumbled, taking his hand and walking up the stone pathway to the door. She hoped his parents would enjoy the gift she brought.

"Don't let it intimidate you. My mother loves to throw parties and insisted on an enormous home to do so." Xander kissed her temple and rang the doorbell. Within a minute, a woman with the same hazel eyes and sandy hair answered the door. Hers was up in a twist with an intricate clip holding it in place. She wore a flowy maxi dress with flat sandals. She still stood taller than Roxie's five foot seven.

"Xander, and you must be Roxie. You are so beautiful! Let me get a good look at you." His mother pulled her away from Xander, taking both her hands.

"It is nice to meet you, Mrs. Austin," Roxie greeted her soon to be mother-in-law.

"To my eldest's mate, I am Mom or Koraline. Come sit. Xander's father is out back with his smoker working on dinner. Xander, go get your dad and tell him to come meet his newest daughter-in-law," Koraline ordered, taking Roxie into the adjoining room. Roxie looked over as Xander laughed quietly.

"Yes, Mother." He went into the kitchen and disappeared.

"Tell me, Roxie. Are you the one Xander found at Josie's Mate Me event?" Koraline handed her a glass of wine and sat on a delicate settee across from Roxie.

"I was there with my roommate, Evelyn. I almost didn't go because I wasn't in the market for a new husband," Roxie began.

"Aren't we all when we fall in love? It was the last thing on my mind when I met Rhett, but he just had to have me," Josie commented. Roxie recognized her from the party. She sat in the lap

81

of a man with black hair and blue eyes. She assumed he was Rhett, Xander's brother.

"So how did Xander grab you?" Koraline leaned forward eagerly.

"Josie was bringing him over to introduce him to Evelyn. She works at an art museum in Green Falls. The rest is history. We hit it off really well, and he whisked me off to Rome for a week. I was hesitant to believe in mates. Xander spent the week showing me how a genuine man treats his mate," Roxie finished just as Xander and his father came in.

"I cannot believe Xander took you away for the entire week! I've not seen him take any time off since I got with Rhett." Josie laughed; Roxie wasn't sure how she felt about Josie. Every time she spoke, it was about her being with Rhett.

"I finally found an excellent reason to slow down. Rhett was the same before he met you. He owns a dozen nightclubs across the U.S." Xander sat next to Roxie, snagging her wine glass and taking a sip. She blushed; it was an intimate gesture to drink from the same glass.

"Are all your clubs called Club Cerulean?" Roxie asked, looking at Rhett.

"No, each has its own color theme."

"Like what?"

"Well, Club Cerulean is water-themed. You have seen the Zen water features and themed food. In D.C., I have Club Scarlet. It is fire-themed," Rhett explained.

"Sounds exciting to come up with all those themes." Roxie smiled.

"What do you do?" Rhett asked, giving her a smile in return.

"I am an artist." She waited for all their kind expressions to drop.

"Do you have any work on your phone that you can show us?" Koraline asked, her eyes showing genuine interest.

"Well, actually, I have a gift for you and Mr. Austin. It's a thank-you present for welcoming me into the family." Roxie pulled a small eight-by-ten canvas out of her bag. She'd wrapped it in plain brown paper. She squeezed Xander's hand, nervous about their reaction.

"It is beautiful! Our very first hotel!" Koraline turned the canvas to reveal their very first Austin Luxury Hotel. She'd spent several days getting the details just right.

"You are very talented. I can see why Xander fell for you." His father gave her a soft smile.

"Thank you, sir." She gave a shy smile.

"Please call me James. Are you doing a show soon?"

"We are working on it. We've hit a snag with her ex refusing to give back her art. The Wright family has a gallery in New York called The Golden Painting," Xander explained, and she leaned onto his side. Naturally, his arm wrapped around her waist, holding her close. He made her feel safe knowing everything would work out.

"Why does he have your art?" James asked.

"In exchange for not asking for alimony, Mitchell is supposed to sell my art at his gallery, but the judge never set a time limit on selling my work." Roxie frowned. The judge was a friend of Mitch's. She fought for a new judge, but her lawyer was of little help.

"Did you get Jordan Howard on it yet?" James wanted to know.

"Yes, we went to his office earlier today. He went to a friend to get a court order," Xander answered, kissing her temple.

"Good. I bet by tomorrow Jordan will have the court order. Rhett and I will come and help gather your paintings too," James offered.

"Oh, I couldn't disrupt your lives and drag you to New York," Roxie objected. She didn't think Mitch would cause any major problems; he wouldn't want terrible publicity for his gallery.

His gallery meant more to him than any person ever could. She found that out the hard way. He would continually stand her up for dates when a crisis came up. He constantly spoke on his phone or checked emails if they got to dinner.

"Nonsense. You will be family. With three dragons on your side, nothing will happen to you or your art." James smiled. He looked like an older version of Xander. He had gray throughout his dark brown hair, giving himself a distinguished look. His blue eyes were kind as he looked over at her. He reminded her of her father before her mother decided her art was no longer a splendid idea.

"Thank you. It is nice to feel supported." She sighed. Xander ran a soothing hand up and down her back. Just then, James's phone dinged.

"Dinner is ready. Come, we are sitting outside to enjoy the last of summer before fall takes over." James stood. Xander took her glass.

"I will refill it and bring it out to you," he told her and kissed her, heading over to the sideboard where the wine sat. Roxie followed his family outside. The backyard had a large patio with a built-in grill, cooktop, and smoker. The center of the patio had an eight-person wooden table with elegant chairs covered in blue cushions. Under the umbrella were twinkle lights lighting up the patio.

"This is lovely," Roxie complimented Koraline, sitting on one side of the table.

"Thank you. We love eating out here when the weather is nice," she answered with a soft smile on her face.

"Dinner!" James placed a large platter of smoked ribs on the table. Behind him, Xander held bowls of potato salad and sautéed vegetables. Her mouth watered as the smell hit her nose.

"This looks delicious," Josie announced, reaching for the tongs on the rib tray. Roxie sat back and watched the family laugh and joke, passing around all the dishes.

"Are you okay?" Xander whispered in her ear as he placed some ribs on her plate.

"Yes, my family never gets along this well." She didn't remember them ever having family dinners, except on holidays. Roxie and her sister were always off doing after-school sports or clubs.

"We don't always get along so well." Xander laughed. She smiled and took a bite of her dinner. The food was delicious, and the company was delightful. Roxie couldn't wait to be a part of this family. All she needed was for Xander to ask her to marry him. She knew he wanted to mate her, but did that mean he wanted to marry her too? She bit her bottom lip until Xander's hand rubbed her leg. Looking up at him, she caught the concern in his eyes. She shook her head and gave him a smile.

CHAPTER TWENTY-TWO

Xander watched Roxie like a hawk throughout dinner. She was so quiet watching his family. His brother was regaling them with a tale about having to throw a bear shifter out of the club.

"Why not hire an extra bouncer with experience in handling other shifters?" Xander offered. He had quite a few shifters on his payroll to protect his art.

"Know anyone?" Rhett asked.

"Let me ask some of my security guys. I'm sure one of them has a friend, cousin, or brother who is looking for a job."

"Thanks. I appreciate the help. We will be busy come the winter months." Rhett reached over and grabbed Josie's hand, his eyes shining with love.

"We are expecting our first child come February," Josie announced. His mother jumped from her seat and hugged Josie tight. Xander shook Rhett's hand, along with his father.

"Congratulations! I can't wait to meet the little one."

"Congratulations." Roxie gave a slight smile, and Xander could sense her longing for children. The rest of dinner passed with the conversation centered on how Josie was feeling and their plans for the baby.

"Are you going to find out what gender your baby will be?" Roxie asked.

"No, we want it to be a surprise," Josie answered before Rhett could give his opinion. Xander knew Rhett liked to have a plan for everything, and Josie was more go with the flow.

"I'm impressed. I couldn't wait with either Xander nor Rhett. Unfortunately, in my day, ultrasounds weren't around," Koraline explained, laughing at the memory.

"What about you, Roxie?" Koraline turned her attention to him and his mate.

"Me what?" Roxie said. Xander could see the panic in her eyes.

"Ever thought about children?" Koraline asked. Xander wanted to shut his mother up. He and Roxie hadn't spoken about kids just yet.

"I'd like to have one someday," Roxie replied in a very neutral tone.

"Only one?" Josie asked with raised eyebrows.

"One to start. I have two older siblings, and I always felt it overwhelmed my mom having three of us," Roxie shared. Xander looked at her in surprise. He hadn't heard her say that before.

"All children are unique. Just look at these two," James commented, looking between Xander and Rhett.

"What were they like as boys?" Roxie asked. Dinner had ended, and they were all enjoying an evening cup of coffee. Xander cringed. He knew he didn't make life easy for his parents. His dad laughed.

"Xander was forever getting into trouble. He liked to sneak out at night and shift to scare the crap out of the local boys. He was sixteen when the local sheriff caught wind of his ability. We had to move here to keep him hidden. Shifters have only been publicly known for almost sixty years. We came out in the sixties when peace and love were being promoted," his dad explained. Roxie was smiling over at him.

"What?" he asked, feeling the warmth of her smile down to his toes.

87

"Just trying to picture you as a rebellious teen."

"And?" He was curious about her answer.

"I can sort of see it, especially when you were around Antonio."

"You met Antonio?" His mom gave a surprised look.

"Yes, he took me the last night we were in Rome," Roxie shared. She gave him a confused look.

Sighing, he answered, "Antonio is my best friend. I've never taken a girlfriend to meet him or his family."

"How often do you visit?" Roxie asked.

"Every other month. Rome is a second home for me." Xander felt oddly at ease, sharing such an important part of him with her in front of his family.

"Marta is such a gracious person. We had a lovely chat while I was helping get the kids to sleep." Roxie smirked. It made him wonder just what they had talked about.

"Marta is an amazing clothing designer. She has a show in New York's fashion week every year. She caters toward plus-sized women," his mom explained to Josie. Josie hasn't met her yet.

"What clothing line does she own?" Josie asked.

"Blessed," Roxie answered.

"I love that line! She knows a plus-sized body. I'm in love with her maternity line and can't wait to try them on," Josie gushed, leaning back on her chair. Xander caught the wistful look in Roxie's eye when Josie spoke.

"We should head home," he said, looking at his watch. It was almost ten, and he wanted Roxie to be well-rested for any news from Jordan.

"True. We all have things to do tomorrow, and Josie has an event tomorrow night," Rhett added. He gave Josie a worried look, and Xander could tell he wanted to get her to bed.

"Thank you for dinner and dessert. It was delicious." Roxie stood with Xander. He took her hand, kissing her knuckles.

"Any time, my dear. Thank you for the painting." His mother gave her a hug and a kiss on the cheek. They left, Xander happily taking Roxie back to what he was considering their home.

CHAPTER TWENTY-THREE

Roxie fidgeted the entire drive back to the house. She was dying to know what surprise Xander had for her.

"Can you give me a hint of what the surprise is?" she begged, running her hand up to his thigh, close to his cock.

"No . . . hints," he groaned out. He knew he was trying to hold back his moan. She moved her hand to the top button of his pants and got it undone.

"Roxie," he warned. She gave a smirk and dipped a finger in to stroke him through his boxers.

"What?" she asked, pushing his boxers aside, letting his hard cock spring free.

"We will be home in five minutes," Xander groaned, gripping the steering wheel hard enough that the leather creaked.

"I'll make it quick then." Roxie stroked up and down, gripping him tight. She changed the tension at which she held him and her speed. She brought him to the edge just as they pulled into the driveway. Throwing the car into park, Xander grabbed her and yanked. He pulled her onto his lap.

"I need to be inside you now!" He reached down and ripped her panties off.

"That is so hot," she moaned, rubbing against his exposed cock. She'd been turned on by the power she wielded over him the entire car ride. More than ready, she lifted herself until he was poised at her entrance.

"Roxie, you are so sexy." Xander gripped her hips and helped her lower onto his cock, an inch at a time. She felt branded by his slow entrance. He was thick, long, and incredibly hard. Once fully seated on him, she rocked, gasping when his cock hit her most sensitive spot. Her eyes rolled back, and she rocked again. Xander's hands helped her bounce up and down on him.

"Xander," she moaned, burying her face in the crook of his neck.

"Roxie, I love you," he gasped and sped up, hitting her G-spot harder.

"Please," she begged, so close to her own release. She slipped a hand down and pressed her clit, moaning her pleasure.

"I'm so close," she gasped and then her world went white as her orgasm overtook her. She felt Xander shout and pumped his seed deep inside, filling her until some dripped down her legs. She laid her head on his shoulder for a long moment, enjoying the sweet moment after they made love. To her surprise, Xander's cock remained hard inside her.

"I need more," he whispered, and she nodded. Her orgasm only spurred on her need for more of him.

"Get me inside," she demanded, and he laughed.

"As my mate commands me." Reluctantly, she eased off his lap and exited the car. Xander moved faster than she did and met her at her car door. She noticed his pants weren't buttoned, and it only took a second for her to wrap around him, thick cock buried in her pussy once again. He carried them to the door, each step shifting him in and out of her.

"Hurry," she moaned. Xander chuckled and kissed her quickly before opening his front door. He pinned her to the closed door, growling as he pumped hard and fast. Roxie gripped his hair, demanding his lips to stay on hers. She shoved her tongue in to possess his mouth. She couldn't get enough of the spicy taste.

"Will you become my mate forever?" Xander stopped moving inside her and held her gaze.

91

"Yes, I want to be yours forever." Roxie gave him a small kiss on the lips. She was burning for him to move inside her again, and she knew her eyes said it all.

"To make you mine, I have to take you from behind and leave my mark," he explained in a tight voice. She could tell he was holding back to speak about what would happen.

"Xander, take me." She kissed him with all the passion built up within her. He didn't need to be told twice. He carried her up to his bed, dropping her in the middle. The soft mattress absorbed most of her impact, so she only bounced a little. She watched Xander strip, revealing his chiseled body. Staring, she couldn't help but marvel at the fact that he was all hers. She would never have to share him and knew he'd never leave her. She'd found her happy beginning and never wanted their time together to end.

"What?" Xander asked, his hands hooked into the waistband of his boxers. He looked sexy enough to be in an underwear ad.

"Nothing. Just happy." She smirked and leaned on her elbows, motioning for him to continue.

"I think you are wearing too many clothes." Xander paused in pulling down his boxers and arched an eyebrow. She laughed and pulled her dress over her head. She was only left in a blush pink bra; he'd destroyed her panties in the car.

"Now you," she prompted. He obeyed and pulled his boxers down, revealing his monumental cock. Her mouth watered, wanting to suck him deep and make him groan and moan his pleasure.

"Your turn," his voice came out deep. She slowly removed her bra. Xander knelt and took each breast in his hand and kissed her hard nipples. She gasped when he sucked one into his mouth. He used his teeth to gently tug, and she shrieked with pleasure. He moved to her other one and repeated the action. Reaching down, she grabbed his cock.

"No, no. You pleasured me in the car, now I get to make you feel good." Xander kissed down her waist, dipping his tongue in her belly button before kissing the top of her curls.

"Baby," she moaned, and his tongue dove in to lick from slit to clit. She arched off the bed as lightning shot through her body.

"That's right, my love," Xander's voice vibrated in her pussy, adding to the powerful sensations building within her. He slipped two fingers into her pussy and fucked her, sucking on her clit. He bit down and she screamed, her vision covered in stars as her orgasm rocked her body.

Xander gave her no time to recover before slipping onto her stomach and entering her swiftly.

"Are you ready, my love?" Xander whispered, leaning over her completely, nipping at the back of her neck.

"Yes, make me yours, Xander Austin," she cried and let him take full control. His hips pounded away while slipping one finger into her ass. He pushed in gently, and she moaned.

"Xander!"

"It will feel even better this way, baby," he promised, pumping in and out, alternating his finger and cock. She couldn't contain the moan. She felt fuller than ever and loved it.

"I am going to add a toy. Is that okay?" he asked. She nodded, unable to use her voice. She felt the coldness of lube slipping down her asshole. Gently, Xander worked a plug into her ass. It was bigger than his finger, and a stinging pain spread through her ass. Finally, the plug slid home in her ass, and when Xander moved, she forgot how to breathe.

"I'm going to make you mine." Xander slammed into her, his hips bumping her ass, pushing the plug deeper. She gripped the sheets and screamed her pleasure. She felt so full with the plug and his cock filling her. When her orgasm hit, she couldn't hold herself up and fell face first into the mattress, her ass high in the air. Xander dove deeper. He gripped her hips tightly, shouting with his own release. His claws raked across each of her hips, sending a stinging sensation through her body. It caused another orgasm to rack her body. His teeth sunk into her right shoulder. Her insides burned with his seed and her hips stung from his mark, but she felt powerful with his marking.

CHAPTER TWENTY-FOUR

Xander collapsed next to Roxie, breathing heavily. He'd never orgasmed so hard in his life. Reaching for her, he gently eased the plug from her ass and laid it on a waiting towel.

"Are you okay?" he asked. Never had he felt such a deep connection after having sex with someone.

"That was wild. I never knew I would like anal play. I feel connected to you, as if I can feel your emotions. I don't know how else to explain how I feel." She snuggled close in his arms, and he felt complete. All was right in the world with Roxie by his side.

"Oh!" She shot up in bed, letting the sheet slip away from her body. "What was my surprise?" she asked, bouncing up and down. His eyes strayed to her breasts, and he couldn't help but lean down and nip. Her eyes clouded with desire, and he caught her in a passionate kiss.

"No." She pulled back, her blue eyes dancing with laughter. "Tell me," she demanded, putting distance between them by shifting to the far side of the bed.

"We have to get out of bed for your surprise," he said, watching her weigh her options. She laughed and jumped out of bed, pulling on his discarded shirt. He chuckled at her enthusiasm and grabbed his discarded boxer briefs.

"Come, it is down the hall." He held out his hand and loved how right she felt in his home, by his side.

"What is it?" she asked, giving him a curious look.

"Open the last door at the end." He gave her a gentle push, wanting to see her reaction. As she opened the door, his heart stopped. He prayed she would love her surprise.

"Oh my god! Xander, is this?" She turned and he saw the tears in her eyes.

"Your own studio, so you can paint in your own space." He'd left the walls blank for her to hang her artwork.

"I bought you every color made in your favorite paint brand. I have new canvases ready and all your brushes." Xander walked around and showed her everything.

"This is amazing! Are you sure I can use this room? I can't guarantee it will stay clean." She gave him a worried look.

"Baby, this is your space. I expect it to get messy. You need a space where you can be creative. Why would I get upset?" Xander looked at her, confused.

"Past experience. Sorry." Her eyes dropped, and he quickly pulled her in for a kiss.

"You are an artist. You will have a mess. Want to tell me what happened?" Xander hugged her close and felt her body relax.

"Mitchell would get angry whenever I left my studio in a mess. He would tell me I wasn't taking pride in our house by leaving my room messy. If I didn't clean it up, he'd yell at me and would wake me from my sleep to clean it," she shared.

"I love you, and that includes the messy parts." He wanted to reassure her he loved everything about her.

"Are we officially mated now?" Roxie asked, and he paused.

"The only thing left is the blood pact."

"Let's do it now." Roxie looked up at him with her bright eyes. He could read the readiness there and knew she wouldn't regret her choice.

"Come, there is a special blade we must use." Xander took her to his office.

"You keep it in your office?"

"Yes, it hangs above my doorway. I use it as a reminder to always be the best mate I can be," he explained, pulling her into his side.

"That is so sweet." Roxie kissed his cheek. "Go get it," she whispered. He stepped away and reached above his doorway. The knife was six inches from tip to tip with a red ruby inlaid on the hilt.

"It's beautiful." Roxie stood waiting in the center of the room. Her hair was tousled from their lovemaking. His shirt hit just above her knees, and her eyes were alight with her love for him.

"Ready?" he asked. She nodded, taking a deep breath.

"Roxanne Leigh Jones, do you take me, Xander Richard Austin, as your true dragon mate? Will you take on being a dragon and spend the rest of our days together?" Xander asked, holding the blade parallel with his wrist.

"I will." Her voice came out husky and deep.

"I, Xander Richard Austin, take you, Roxanne Leigh Jones, as my one true mate." He cut a thin line on each of their wrists, just deep enough for a negligible amount of blood to show. Xander pressed their wrists together, letting the blood mix. He watched Roxie glow a gentle gold. It was proof of her accepting his shifter power.

"Whoa," she gasped and held onto him, her legs going weak.

"The power might feel intense, but it will subside."

"When can I shift? I really want to see you as a dragon too," Roxie asked.

"Now, if you want," he offered and laughed when she nodded and squealed in excitement.

CHAPTER TWENTY-FIVE

Roxie couldn't believe she was a dragon. When her blood mixed with Xander's, warmth flooded her body. She could tell her dragon had awakened. Nothing changed outwardly, but her confidence inside grew. She was no longer Roxie, a disappointment to her family. She was Roxie—a painter, a dragon, and Xander's mate.

"Let's go!" she demanded, pulling Xander outside into the large backyard.

"Is Josie a dragon?" she asked, thinking about her soon-to-be sister-in-law.

"Yes. She made Rhett wait until after they were married. I think she was nervous to become a dragon and live for several centuries. You need to shift the night of the transformation to get your dragon. If you don't, it is deadly," Xander explained, and she gasped in surprise.

"We need to make me shift now! I don't want to die." Panic set in. Why was he being so calm? What if her dragon refused to come and she died anyway?

"Roxie, breathe. We will shift together." Xander held her face between his enormous hands. She focused on his hazel eyes and nodded.

"Good. Shifting is easy. You take a deep breath and let your dragon take over." Xander showed her. He took a deep breath and closed his eyes. He then started to shift. Now standing in front of her was a massive scarlet dragon. The dragon had varying shades of red throughout its scales. It was at least thirty feet without the whip of a tail. The dragon had Xander's hazel eyes, which made her frantically beating heart slow down. She knew she was safe with him. He unfurled his wings, and she gasped in awe. His wings were bat-like with a thin layer of scales. She could see the moonlight filter through.

"Okay, dragon, do your thing." She took a deep breath, closed her eyes, and waited. Slowly, she felt a feminine sigh. *"As you wish."* Suddenly, she was looking down at two large legs with killer claws attached. She looked around, noticing she was much higher from the ground. Her scales were a mirage of colors: orange, red, pink, purple, and yellow—all in varying shades. It reminded her of the sunset she painted from her time in Rome. Unfurling her wings, she crouched and sprang into the air. It took her a minute to let her dragon have full control over their flight. She was a little nervous. She watched Xander take flight after her. He easily caught up. From what she could tell, he was much larger than her and his dragon had sharper claws. She felt powerful and free from all worldly constraints while up in the sky.

Xander flew ahead and led her on a night flight around White Valley. She could identify his parents's home, the grocery store, and their home. She knew with Xander's family around, no one would think twice about a dragon flying overhead. Her town of Green Falls did not have a high shifter population and therefore did not accept shifters as easily. Xander banked right and landed smoothly in his backyard. She took a little longer to feel comfortable at landing and not running into Xander. She watched him shift back into his human form and paused, unsure how to turn back.

"Just think of yourself and your dragon will let you back in control," he explained. She thought about what she felt as Roxie the human. Slowly she slipped back into her own skin and shivered when the cool air touched her bare skin.

"Here." Xander handed her a fresh shirt. "Usually, I try to strip before I change, so I don't rip through my clothing. I also keep an extra set in the kitchen for after my flights."

"How often do you need to shift?" She was curious about shifting needs.

"Once a week. I go out at night when I won't attract as much attention. You are a beautiful dragon, just like the sunset." Xander wrapped her up in a tight hug.

"So are you. You look like fire." Roxie closed her eyes, recalling the image of Xander's dragon.

"I didn't frighten you?"

"No, it felt like I finally met the missing piece of you. Everything is perfect, and I cannot believe I am so lucky to have you. After the fiasco with Mitch, I never thought I would be good enough. He told me my art wouldn't sell, and I believed him. Now I have you, and soon I'll have my very first art show. I originally wanted to wait until I sold a painting to become your mate, but after talking with Evvy, it doesn't matter. I want to prove I could help financially, but I love you too much to make you wait." She knew in her heart Xander loved her no matter if she ever sold a painting.

"I have complete faith we will sell everything you choose next month. I have many buyers interested in the paintings we have on the web as treasures." Xander carried her to their bedroom and laid her down. Her body felt exhausted from the number of times they'd made love and her first shift.

"How long do you think it will take for Jordan to get a court order?" she asked sleepily, curling up in his arms. Her eyes were heavy, and she couldn't keep them open.

"Probably by Monday. Most judges don't work on the weekends," Xander answered, pulling her leg to hook over his hip.

"Mmm good," she murmured and fell fast asleep.

CHAPTER TWENTY-SIX

The weekend went by quickly as Xander helped Roxie move into his place. She'd laughed when he dropped a tube of paint, getting it all over his hands.

"I will miss having you here," Evvy said, hugging her tightly.

"I won't ever be able to thank you enough for making me go to the Mate Me event. The past two weeks have been a whirlwind, and I never would have had it without you." Roxie cried, sad she was leaving Evvy but happy to be with Xander.

"Oh please, you won't get rid of me that easily. I expect to be the maid of honor at your wedding. That is when Xander gets around to asking!" Evvy yelled the last part and Roxie winced. It took time getting used to hearing every little sound. Her senses were in overdrive since she'd woken up. Xander told her she would get used to everything soon enough.

"You are really a dragon now?" The news had shocked Evvy at first, then ecstatic for her best friend.

"Yep, Xander and I mated last night, and we made our blood pact. We are together forever." Roxie taped shut a box of clothes, looking up to see Evvy holding back tears.

"Evvy, I promise regular girl nights. Xander is happy to let me paint away my days, so my nights are free. Plus, next month or really in two weeks I have my art show. We will see plenty of each other." Roxie pulled her in for a tight hug of her own.

"I know and I know Xander is perfect for you. I just don't like change. I need order and routine in my life. This disrupts it, and I feel bad for being selfish," Evvy murmured, wiping away her tears.

"I know, sweetie. It's what I love about you. Want to schedule our weekly time? This way you are on my calendar," Roxie offered. She knew Evvy had a type A personality and needed the time scheduled.

"Yes," Evvy hiccupped and Roxie pulled out her phone.

"How about Wednesday nights at seven? We can trade off towns each week so one of us isn't doing all the driving."

"I like that. Let's start in your town because it's new to us," Evvy suggested.

"Perfect! Now help me get these to the door, and Xander can take them to the truck. I am going to leave my bed, desk, and dresser since I won't need them. That should help you find a roommate quickly. Xander will cover my half of the rent until you find a roommate." Roxie and Xander had talked it over and would pay rent because Roxie was moving out on such short notice. Roxie took one last look around the room that had been her home for almost two years. The walls were painted a pale cream color with marks from the art she had hung up. Never did she think her art would be good enough, but with Xander at her side, she was brave enough to show it to the world. Evelyn had been the very best friend, and she couldn't imagine getting through her divorce without her.

"I should argue, but I hated working two jobs just to pay for my place."

"I don't want you to ever feel that way." Roxie hugged her again, and the two women moved the last of the boxes to the front door.

"Thank you for being my best friend." Roxie smiled, and Evvy laughed.

"We will always be besties," Evvy replied, and Xander came in to pick up the last boxes with ease.

"Now, I am jealous of his strength. It would have taken us three times as long to load up all your things. Promise me you will be happy and please talk to your parents. I'm tired of your mom calling me," Evvy joked and Roxie grimaced.

"I sent them an invitation to my show, but I'll call my dad and let him know I moved." Roxie hugged her one last time and left when Xander came back up for her.

CHAPTER TWENTY-SEVEN

"What should we make for dinner?" Xander asked. They were lying in bed after a blissful day of lovemaking. He couldn't believe how lucky he was, a mate and fiancé all in one weekend. Roxie was perfect for him in every way. When he saw her in dragon form, he almost pounced on her. A sunset dragon was very rare. Most dragons were a solid color with varying shades of that color throughout their scales.

"Want to make Mexican food? I love making fajitas, and I have a killer Mexican rice recipe." Roxie sat up, brushing her hair over her shoulder. He kissed her bare shoulder and nipped.

"Sounds perfect. Come, let's see if we have the ingredients." He pulled her out of bed and down to the kitchen. "What do we need?" he asked, opening the refrigerator.

"Bell peppers, onions, chicken, black beans or refried beans, cumin, garlic, salt, tomato sauce, and tortillas," she rattled off the list of ingredients, touching her fingers as she listed them.

"Sounds like a trip to the grocery store is in order. I don't have all of that," Xander answered.

"Just means we need to get dressed," Roxie sighed, and he laughed. Getting dressed seemed like a lot of work, and he was enjoying knowing she was naked underneath his t-shirt.

"Don't hide your tattoos," he requested.

"What?"

"I enjoy seeing them. They make me happy." He leaned over and kissed her neck where the low neckline revealed several flower petals. He felt her shiver, and he gently sucked to leave his own mark on her body.

"Xander," she moaned his name, and he forgot all about going to the grocery store. He lifted her to sit on the counter, sliding his hands under her shirt to cup her soft round breasts. Her stomach ruined the moment by rumbling loudly. Xander laughed and let Roxie down from the counter.

"Looks like we need dinner first, then I can have you for dessert," Xander whispered. Roxie nodded, blushing as she led the way up to their room. She tossed on a bra, panties, a tank top, and shorts. Feeling slightly self-conscious, she grabbed a zip-up hoodie.

"No covering up, Roxie. You look beautiful with your half sleeve." Xander kissed her sweetly on the lips, tugging the hoodie from her hands.

"Fine, you win. It's just weird for me to go out without covering them. I love them and am proud of myself. I'm just afraid that word will get back to my mother," she answered, looking down at her feet.

"Hey, you are your own woman. Your mother doesn't control you. You showed that the day you quit, so you could focus on your art," he assured her, lifting her chin to look him in the eyes.

"You're right. It is still warm enough to wear a tank top." She agreed to let him keep the hoodie. He smiled and quickly got dressed in shorts and a t-shirt.

"Mmm, I enjoy looking at you," she admitted, and he laughed.

"I like you best naked and moaning while I make love to you," he replied. She blushed and looked away. He always knew what to say to fluster her.

"Come on, I'm hungry and we still have to cook." She walked out of their bedroom and down to their bowl of keys.

"Who's driving?" she asked, putting on her shoes.

"I can. We should do a real grocery run, so you have food here. I don't want you going hungry while I'm at work," he said while walking out to the car.

"I need quick items to heat then. When I get in a painting zone, I'm known to skip a meal," Roxie admitted.

"I know, love. Why don't we meal prep on Sundays? This way we both have lunch available when we need it," Xander suggested.

"I like that idea. When it gets colder, I like to make soups and stews. They freeze-dry well and are quick to heat," she shared, and he smiled.

"Sounds good. I can't wait to try them." He parked, and they walked into the grocery store hand in hand.

"I'll grab a cart. You pick out what you want. Do you have any foods you like the most?" Xander asked, walking over to the carts.

"I am a sucker for mint chocolate chip ice cream. Other than that, I try to eat healthily. Painting isn't exactly an active lifestyle," she shared, and he laughed.

"You are a dragon now. You can eat pretty much anything you want, and when you shift, it will all burn off."

"What? No way!" she shot back, and he nodded.

"Yes, shifting takes a lot of energy."

"That is so cool, but I don't want to kill myself with all the fatty foods I want to eat. This just means I can indulge a little more," she replied with a bright smile.

"Indulge away." Xander motioned her onward, and they made their way around the grocery store.

In the checkout line, Roxie caught sight of her mother's best friend in town, Frieda Poppelton. She tried not to let her presence freak her out. Frieda was the biggest busybody in Great Falls. What she was doing in White Valley, Roxie didn't want to know. Freida was wearing her traditional neon pink outfit. Her shirt too tight for her plump body and her track pants rolled at the ankles. Her hair had recently been dyed a coppery red and her makeup over the top.

"Why are you all jittery?" Xander asked as he was placing items on the conveyor belt.

"Frieda Poppelton, my mom's best friend," she hissed.

"And?" he prompted.

"If she sees me, she will tell my mom. I really don't want her to call me," Roxie admitted.

"You've got a new phone number. Unless your dad tells her, how is she supposed to call?" he pointed out. She stopped and looked at him in surprise.

"I'm an idiot," she huffed.

"No, you are not. You are just not used to being free of her," he explained, and she kissed him.

"I love you."

"I love you too. Now help me with the groceries," he laughed. She smiled and put the bags in the cart as the cashier rang up the items. They made it to the doors before Roxie heard her name being called.

"Roxie Jones, is that you?" Freida yelled.

"Hello, Mrs. Poppelton," she replied, turning around slowly.

"What are you doing, White Valley and with Xander Austin of all people?" Frieda gave her a suspicious look and Xander groaned.

"If you must know, he is my fiancé. Goodbye, Mrs. Poppelton," Roxie replied and walked off with Xander following. When they got to their car, Roxie laughed.

"Did you see her face? She can't believe I would get an amazing guy like you!"

"Of course, you got me. I'm your mate forever," Xander remarked with a smirk. She leaned over and kissed him again, happy she could kiss him whenever the feeling struck.

"Are you still worried about your mom?" he asked once they were on their way back to the house.

"No, I've decided I don't care what she thinks. She thought Mitch was the right guy for me," she answered with a smile.

"That's my girl." He squeezed her hand, and they drove home in comfortable silence. She watched Xander out of the corner of her eye as they pulled up to the house.

"What?" he asked once he parked the car.

"Nothing. I just wanted to look at you. I can't help this clingy feeling. During the entire drive, I just wanted to climb in your lap and kiss you," she admitted.

"You keep saying things like that and we won't get dinner made," he threatened, stepping out of the car. She followed, and they each took an armful of grocery bags.

"Maybe I want you for dinner," she flirted and stopped short upon seeing someone on the porch.

"Xander, we have a problem," the man announced, coming out of the shadows. Roxie gasped when she took one look at the man.

"Anderson."

CHAPTER TWENTY-EIGHT

She couldn't believe her eyes; her brother was standing on her porch. He looked older but still the same brother who left fifteen years ago. He had black hair and her blue eyes. She assumed he inherited the black hair from his mom. He stood taller than her and Xander at a staggering six foot five. Thinking back on her conversation with her dad, she knew Anderson was a shifter, but not what kind.

"Roxie?" Anderson walked out into the fading light and stared at her in shock.

"What are you doing here?" she asked, her bags were getting heavy.

"He is my assistant," Xander answered, and without asking, he took the bags from her.

"Did you know?" she wanted to know. If Xander knew where her brother had been all along, she would be mad.

"No, I didn't think your brother would be so close to home," he replied. She knew he told the truth when her eyes connected with his.

"Come inside. We still need to make dinner, and I think a lengthy conversation is in order." Xander motioned them inside and she nodded. Anderson gave a hesitant nod and followed.

Roxie wasn't sure what to say to him. He'd left and never looked back. Roxie knew her mom was the reason he didn't come back. She wanted to know what happened but was scared to hear the answer. She focused on putting away the groceries and setting out everything needed to make dinner.

"What is the big problem?" Xander asked. She knew he was giving her time to collect her thoughts.

"Mitchell Wright threatened to sue us," Anderson stated. She looked up in shock.

"Why?" Xander asked. He opened a beer for each of them and poured a glass of wine for Roxie. She smiled and took a sip as she made the Mexican rice.

"He called me and told me to tell you to back off on the R.J. paintings. He said he has full control over the artist's livelihood. If we showcase the artist, he is suing," Anderson explained, and Roxie gasped. He looked over at her.

"Do you know anything?"

"Mitchell Wright is my ex-husband," she replied, putting the rice in the oven.

"What? Why are you with Xander? Why do you smell like a dragon? Why are you here?" Anderson questioned. She sighed, taking a sip of her wine, walking over to lean against Xander. He wrapped an arm around her waist, offering her comfort.

"You've missed a lot these past fifteen years. I went to art school, then met Mitch through Mom and her rich connections. We married when I was twenty-three. He threw me aside for a younger, much thinner secretary. We've been divorced for about nine months but separated a year before we completed the papers. Xander and I met two weeks ago at a Mate Me event his sister-in-law was hosting. He is my mate, Anderson. Last Friday, we completed the mating process. He asked me to marry him this morning. I smell like a dragon because I am one now," she explained.

"Wait, Roxie is the woman you took a week off of work for?" He looked at Xander. Xander squeezed her hip and nodded.

"Yes. The second I set eyes on her, my dragon roared. I love her very much, and I can answer why Mitch is threatening to sue," he replied.

"Why?"

"Instead of paying me alimony, he has all the paintings I made while we were married," Roxie shared, heading back into the kitchen to cook the chicken, peppers, and onions.

"And let me guess, you are R.J., right?" he asked, giving her a skeptical look.

"Yep. Xander and I called him on Friday trying to get my work back. He hasn't sold a single piece. He kept telling me I was mediocre, and that was why he hadn't sold a single one," she shared and Anderson gaped at her.

"Your work is amazing, Rox. I saw several people make inquiries about your work while I was there. Mitchell gave them the runaround, saying the artist wasn't selling any, that you were purely painting for enjoyment," he replied and she deflated.

"I don't understand why he is so hard-headed about selling my art. I gave him what he wanted, a divorce and he is marrying Barbie," she sighed, flipping the chicken on her grill pan. Xander walked over, wrapping his arms around her waist and kissing her shoulder.

"He is angry. You were the one to ask for a divorce after you discovered his infidelity. You are talented, and I know the work we have will sell immediately," Xander assured her. She melted into his arms.

"Why threaten to sue then?" Anderson asked.

"We are trying to get a court order to make him release all my work. Xander and I spoke to Jordan Howard, and he is working on getting a court order," she said, moving the chicken to a plate to rest. She bent over and checked the Mexican rice in the oven. Deciding it was done, she turned to get the oven mitts.

"I'll get it, baby. You go talk with your brother," Xander offered with a kiss.

She smiled. "Will you heat the tortillas?"

"Of course, go sit with Anderson." He kissed her, giving her bottom a tap. She laughed and walked over to the table.

"You two really love each other, don't you?" Anderson mused, and she blushed.

CHAPTER TWENTY-NINE

"We do. It has only been two weeks, but I feel like a different woman. I've stopped talking to my mom. She doesn't support me in being an artist. She even blames me for my divorce. When she chose my ex-husband over me, I stopped talking to her. I called Dad to tell him about Xander, and he told me about your mom," she said, sitting across from him at the round kitchen table.

"What did he say?" He sipped his beer, and she leaned back in her chair.

"That your mom was his mate, and he married mine to give you a mother. He didn't say why you left, just told me when I quit my job and went to Rome with Xander. He was afraid of a repeat. What happened, Anders?" she asked, using her nickname for him. It made him flinch.

"Your mom happened."

"Meaning?"

"Meredith didn't like that I was a shifter. Turned out, Dad didn't tell her until I was thirteen. I shifted out of the blue, and he knew he couldn't keep it a secret anymore. When I graduated high school, she told me to leave and never come back. She was afraid I'd hurt you or Elizabeth when I was in my shifted form. What she didn't know was I kept you and Elizabeth safe," he shared.

"What do you mean?"

"Dad got into a bit of trouble when I was seventeen. He did the taxes for one of the local bike gangs. When they were

113

audited, they threatened him. They sent some thugs over to take you and Elizabeth. I shifted and fought them off. Dad asked me to keep it a secret from Meredith."

"That is terrible. I'm so sorry she was awful to you. Elizabeth left me a voicemail when I wasn't responding to my mom or Dad. She told me she took her job because it was away from Mom. Where have you been?" she asked, reaching over to touch his hand.

"I got a full ride to college in Washington State. I majored in marketing. When I graduated, Xander picked me up. I've been traveling all over, helping to find artists. Dad knows I live in White Valley but has kept his distance because of Meredith," he explained. Xander brought over dinner for the three of them and refilled drinks.

"Thanks, baby." Roxie kissed his cheek.

"Anything for you, my love," he replied, giving her a kiss in return.

"Dad is coming to my art show in two weeks," she told Anderson.

"Is Meredith coming?" he asked, biting into his fajita. He moaned with how delicious the food was.

"Not that I know of, Dad didn't seem to think she would come to the show." She bit into her meal and smiled. She loved Mexican food, and tonight's meal came out particularly tasty.

"So why did she side with Mitchell over you?"

"He is the son of her best friend in New Jersey. They grew up together in a very rich neighborhood. Turned out, they arrested my grandfather for insider trading and her family lost everything. I think she wanted to feel a part of that world again. You know Dad won't move his practice and so she is stuck here," Roxie offered as a plausible reason.

"So, she was using you?" Anderson asked.

"Yep, but now I have Xander and his family. I would like her to be a part of my life, but she needs to accept all parts of my

114

life. Which leads to my next question, what kind of shifter are you?"

"I'm a tiger."

"That is neat! Are you bigger than a normal tiger?"

"About twice the size of a Siberian tiger."

"Whoa, are you white or orange?"

"White and black striped."

"That sounds pretty."

"Thanks. So does Dad know you are a dragon?"

"I told him I have a mate. Not sure if he put two and two together." She sipped her wine, and Anderson smiled at her.

"What do you look like?" he asked.

"She is a sunset dragon. Her scales are a mix of the colors of a sunset," Xander answered, and Anderson gave him a surprised look.

"I've never heard of that before."

"It is very rare for a dragon to be of multiple colors. Usually, we are varying shades of one color," Xander replied. Roxie gave him a confused look.

"Then why am I colorful?"

"I think it is your artistic nature. You are very in tune with nature because you paint it all the time," he answered.

"True. You seem to understand nature in a way many artists don't. It was the first thing I noticed about your art," Anderson commented.

"Thank you. You are actually the reason I wanted to get into art," she told him.

Anderson raised an eyebrow. "I am?"

"Yes, I looked up to you so much as a child. You saw a piece I did for an art class and told me I should be an artist. I've been trying for years now to build up the confidence to prove Mitch wrong." She finished her meal and sipped the last of her wine.

"I'm flattered that something I said so long ago stuck with you. The dinner was delicious. Thank you for letting me eat with you. I know I was an unexpected visitor." He stood to take his plate to the counter.

"You are welcome anytime, Anders. I've missed you, and I hope you won't disappear from my life again." She followed and started on the dishes.

"I'm sorry I did. I thought your mom would pit you and Elizabeth against me." He sighed. She stopped cleaning the dishes to look him in the eye.

"Dad wouldn't let her. He told her once. She got what she wanted when she ran you off. He would be damned if she spoke ill of you to your sisters."

"He did?"

"Yes. It was about the time Elizabeth went off to college," she replied.

"Thanks, Roxie. I promise I won't disappear from your life. I work for Xander, and we do a lot of work over dinner. Plus if you cook like that every day, I'm coming over a lot," Anderson joked, and she laughed.

"Only if you go home. I've just got my mate, and I don't want you interfering with our alone time," Xander spoke up. Both siblings laughed harder.

"Understood. I'm glad you found a mate Xander and happy it reconnected me to my baby sister. I'll keep you up to date if I hear more from Mitchell Wright. See you later, Rox." Anderson shook Xander's hand and kissed Roxie on the head. She walked him out and leaned into Xander's arms, watching her brother leave.

"How do you feel, my love?" he asked, kissing her temple.

"I'm happy I finally reconnected with Anderson. I'm furious with my mom for throwing him out. I'm disappointed in my dad for letting her," she replied.

"I understand. I'm happy we found Anderson for you. It is funny how life works out. You are my mate, and he is my assistant.

It was fate for you two to connect again. Come, let's finish cleaning up and then I want dessert." Xander nipped at her neck, and she knew exactly what he meant by dessert. Laughing, she let him pull her inside and kiss her senseless.

CHAPTER THIRTY

"The dishes can wait. I want dessert," he murmured into her mouth.

"Sounds like a splendid idea to me," she replied and screamed in delight as he picked her up in bridal style, carrying her to their room.

"I can walk," she argued. He shook his head.

"Nope, I want to keep my hands on you as much as possible." He laid her down on the bed and slowly undressed her. He left biting kisses across her stomach, up to her breasts. He popped one breast out of her lavender bra and licked the tightening nipple. He loved watching her nipples become stiff peaks when he nipped and kissed. Her breasts were his second favorite part of her body, her ass being his favorite.

"Can we expand our repertoire tonight?" he asked, looking up to stare into her eyes.

She lifted her head and asked, "What do you mean?"

"Well, you let me put a plug in you last Friday. Can I go in?" He was worried she'd think he was pushing past her line of acceptable sex acts.

"You want to?" She looked at him in surprise.

"I've wanted to the second I laid eyes on you. I don't want to make you uncomfortable though." He unclipped her bra and tossed it aside. Xander would give her time to think about his

118

question. He didn't want to pressure her into doing something she didn't want to do.

He sucked on one breast while pinching the nipple of the other. Her moan made him feel like a god. He bit down gently and tugged, drawing a louder moan from her. He switched to the other breast and repeated his action. He pressed his cock against her clothed pussy while kissing upwards to capture her mouth in a tangle of tongues and lips.

"I love you," he whispered, reaching down to remove her shorts and underwear. Leaning back to admire his naked mate, she complained.

"You are always wearing too many clothes." Reaching up, she tugged his shirt off and pushed on the waistband of his shorts. He stepped off the bed long enough to toss his shorts and boxers away.

Her hands reached greedily for his cock. He let her push him back onto the bed. Watching her take the tip into her mouth sent his urges racing. He gripped the back of her head as gently as he could and showed her just how he liked to be sucked.

She twisted her hand up and down on the length of his cock until she couldn't fit into her mouth. Her tongue licked up one side and down the other, then twined around his painful erection. She scraped her teeth gently up and down, causing him to shudder. He didn't know how long he would last if she continued to suck on him. Her mouth tightened to suction around him, hard enough that he bucked his hips off the bed. He felt her chuckle against his cock and he groaned. She would be the death of him. He felt like a windup doll, ready to explode. Her tongue dipped into the slit at the top of his cock and he grabbed the sheets to keep from hurting her.

"Don't stop," he moaned, falling back against the pillow, taking deep breaths to calm his racing heart. He wanted to enjoy this for as long as he could hold out. His dragon was pushing for him to take her hard and fast, but he would let her have her fun.

Her hair flowed around her face acting as a curtain, so he couldn't see what she was doing to him. He gently pulled it up out of her face and their eyes connected. She looked amazing, her plump red lips wrapped around his cock. Her eyes were so dark from the desire he could barely see the blue anymore. He lifted his hips, pushing his cock further into her mouth, careful not to gag her. She took the hint and slowed her movements to take him deeper. Each bob of her head, she took him deeper into her mouth until . . .

"God, Roxie!" he called out when she took him deep into her throat, his cock hitting the back of her throat. He almost lost himself. He was so close to his climax. He jerked out of her mouth and flipped them, so she was lying on her back.

"My turn," he said, grinning up at her. He put her knees over his shoulders. He plunged in, sucking hard from her slit to her clit. He knew he was being a little rougher with her, but she could take it. Her cry of passion assured him she enjoyed what he was doing to her. He flicked his tongue into her entrance and had to hold her down or she would have bucked him off.

He took her sensitive nub in his mouth then twirled his tongue around it, enjoying the mews and moans coming from her sexy lips. He loved how she smelled and tasted; he was addicted to her and would never ever stop pleasuring her before sinking home between her legs. Xander held her open, nuzzling his full mouth against her pussy. He took turns sucking gently and hard. He dipped his tongue into her very core, using it to push her closer to the edge. He could feel her pussy tightening around his tongue as her orgasm neared.

Grinning, he slipped two fingers home while sucking and nipping at her clit. He pumped his fingers in and out of her tight, hot, slick pussy. His dick twitched, wanting to be inside of her so badly. He felt the telltale sign of her orgasm just before she squirted all over his tongue. He lapped up all her juices and grinned. His eyes connected with hers. She had a half-lidded look that made him feel dominant and feral; he needed to be inside her now.

"You okay?" he asked when she lay limp on the bed.

"I hope you aren't done," she replied, leaning up on her elbows. He shook his head and kissed her. He wanted her to taste herself on his face.

"Did you give some thought to my question?" He kissed the sensitive spot below her ear, waiting for her response.

"I want you, Xander. I want you to take me how you like it best. I'm willing to try what you want." She looked down shyly, a blush spreading down her neck and across her delicious breasts. Getting up from the bed, he went to a drawer he'd kept her away from. He pulled out a bottle of warming lube and a large battery-operated toy. He wanted her to feel amazing.

"Flip over, ass up," he instructed. She gave him a look of anticipation and rolled over. He came over to kiss each cheek.

"I love your ass. It is perfect." He dropped a trail of warming lube down her crack, using a finger to push some into her puckered hole. She was still tight, even after the plug.

"You do?" her voice came out breathy and he chuckled.

"I do. I want to grab it every time we are together," he admitted, grinning when she moaned as he slipped a finger up to his knuckles. She relaxed, which would help him get inside. He pushed a second finger in, scissoring back and forth to help her stretch. He felt her tensed up when he added a third finger; he knew three would push her pain threshold, but he needed her to get all of him inside. He did not like to brag, but he knew he was thick and long. Sometimes his partner wasn't able to take him all the way. Not Roxie, he knew she could handle anything he did to her. She was made for him.

"Does that feel good, baby?" he asked, leaning down to bite her shoulder.

"More than you know," she moaned. He smirked and flicked on his toy. He pressed it to the entrance of her pussy, chuckling when she jerked away.

"Are you okay?" He wouldn't push her faster than she was ready.

"Yes, just surprised me." He kissed down her spine, teasing her again with the toy. This time she didn't jerk away but leaned into his hand.

"Baby, I'm going to push this in your pussy. When I do, I will enter your ass. Are you ready?"

"Yes," she moaned, pushing her ass further up. He positioned his cock at her tight entrance and pushed until the tip was inside her. He pushed the toy inside her pussy, turning up the speed. Her moan told him she was happy. He continued to push until he settled all the way inside. Her breathing had become shallow, and he paused.

"Don't stop!" she yelled, moving back and forth. He complied with her demand and moved in and out of her ass, letting her get used to him. To his surprise, she took the toy and moved it in tandem to his thrusts.

"Yes, Xander!" Her moans got louder, and he moved faster. She felt amazing. He didn't want it to end just yet.

"Don't cum yet, baby," he ordered. She slowed her movements. He moaned his pleasure, gripping her hips tightly. He knew he was leaving bruises. He pumped in and out until he couldn't wait anymore.

"Cum, baby," he demanded, roaring as his orgasm shook his body. He poured his seed deep into her ass, watching as she brought herself to her orgasm. She screamed out, collapsing forward, pulling him out of her ass.

"You were perfect," he said, kissing her shoulder. He slipped into the bathroom and got a warm washcloth to clean her up. Coming back out, he smiled seeing she hadn't moved. Touching her gently with the cloth, he wiped her down.

"Mmm, that feels nice," she mumbled, and he chuckled.

"Do you want a shower?"

122

"Only if it is only a shower. I don't think I have another orgasm in me," she replied, rolling over to look at him.

"Come on, princess." He scooped her up, walking her into their bathroom. He turned on the shower and settled her on the edge of the tub.

"I didn't hurt you, did I?" he asked once the shower was warm and they were standing under the spray.

"It stung at first, but I really enjoyed it." She kissed him gently and reached for her shampoo. He grabbed it from her hands and turned her around.

"Let me." He put some shampoo on his hands and began massaging her scalp.

"You spoil me," she complained, and he smirked.

"I love spoiling you. You are my love. Now turn around." He pushed her shoulder, and she turned to let the water wash away the shampoo. He reached for the conditioner and repeated washing her hair.

"Your turn," she said, making him let her wash his hair too. He had to crouch to let her do it, but he loved every minute of her ministrations.

Turning off the shower, he handed her a towel and wrapped one around his waist.

"What time do you need to leave in the morning?" she asked, stepping into the closet. He watched as she changed into a silk baby doll nightgown.

"Seven-thirty. Are you trying to seduce me?" he asked, stalking over to her and nipping at her neck.

"No, but it is a perk," she replied, tugging his towel off. He pinned her against the wall and gave her round two of their lovemaking.

Late that night, once Roxie had fallen asleep, Xander lay awake thinking about everything. His assistant was her estranged brother, her ex-husband was threatening to sue, and he still had to meet his in-laws.

Two weeks ago, he would have laughed at anyone who told him he'd meet his mate, be pursuing a court order, and have crazy in-laws. Wrapping his arms around Roxie, he finally let sleep take him.

CHAPTER THIRTY-ONE

Monday passed with no word; Tuesday and Wednesday, the same. By Thursday, Roxie was getting worried. Would Jordan be successful at getting a court order for her art? She paused in her painting and stepped back. She was working on a beach scene from when she was eleven and Anderson still lived with them. Roxie remembered vividly that Fourth of July.

Her family had rented a beach house for a week. Anderson was sitting in the living room working hard on a puzzle. Roxie remembered laughing when he swore at a piece that wouldn't fit properly. She helped him finish the puzzle in under an hour. He was so impressed; he pulled out a second puzzle, and they spent their evenings putting it together. During the day, they hung out on the beach and boardwalk. It was the last family vacation they took before Anderson left.

"I know that beach. What made you paint it?" Anderson's voice pulled her from her thoughts.

"You. It was the last time I felt we were a family. We went back the following summer, but it wasn't the same without you." She gave it a once over and turned to look at her brother. "Wait, why are you here? Where is Xander?" She looked past him and didn't see her mate.

"He got a call from Jordan and asked me to be here with you," Anderson explained. He pulled up a chair and sat next to her.

"Did he get bad news?" She was worried they wouldn't get the court order.

"Don't know. He didn't give any hints. I think he just wanted me here in case he was late. Though he said when you paint, you lose track of time."

"I do. Some nights he comes home and I've ignored my alarm to get dinner on the table. He just makes dinner and comes to get me. I always feel bad, but he doesn't mind at all. Tells me, it is part of loving an artist," she explained, and Anderson laughed.

"I bet. I remember we had Frank Young show at our gallery. He would paint for forty-eight hours straight. Xander had to make him take breaks for lunch and dinner. They fought like cats and dogs, but we had an amazing showing."

"Haha, I've learned to listen to my alarms. Xander even calls me around lunchtime to make sure I eat. I've only missed his call twice in almost three weeks we've been together."

"Impressive. Why did you miss his calls?"

"My phone was on vibrate. I was ignoring my mom before I got a new number," Roxie said. Anderson let out a huge belly laugh.

"I'd ignore your mom too. I was thinking, maybe I'll try to connect with Dad again at your show next week."

"Really? Why?" She looked at him, surprised.

"Well, with you getting married to Xander, having your art show, and I working for Xander, I think it is time to reconnect with Dad and talk things through. I am still mad about everything that happened, and I want Meredith to know she is the reason for my estrangement. I'm sorry I didn't get in touch once you were college bound. I thought about it but was still furious. I didn't want you to feel the brunt of it. Enough about me, show me the artwork for next weekend's show," he ordered and she let him change the subject.

"Sure, they are in the spare room at the moment." She wiped off her hands and led him over to their spare room.

"I've added quite a few more this past week. I've found so much inspiration being here." She opened the door, smiling when Anderson's jaw dropped. She'd finished her Rome series, added to her Grand Canyon set, and painted the woods around her house.

"These are amazing! Rox, you have such talent. I cannot believe Meredith doesn't see it. Your ex-husband was a fool. He would have made a killing if he tried to sell your work." Anderson walked around and took in each piece. He stopped at one. It was of the woods behind her home. "I saw something like this in New York. It reminded me of our house," Anderson said. She looked at him, surprised.

"I never painted one like this while married to Mitch. He wanted me to focus on famous areas."

"No, there are three that remind me of home." He pulled out his phone and showed them. She gasped. They were the paintings she'd made her mother as gifts. Why would they be in the gallery? She hadn't painted them while married to Mitch.

"I made those for Mom for her birthday, while I was in college. Why are they with Mitch?"

"Wait, what? These three are not from your time married?" Anderson asked, calling Xander.

"No, I made them in college. If you look at the lower right corner, I have my initials and the year written," she explained, zooming into the right corner to show the year.

"Anderson?" Xander's voice came from his phone.

"Did you get the court order?" he asked, his voice slightly panicked.

"No, Jordan and Sally are trying to get the paintings," he replied, Roxie deflated.

"I think we have a way. There are some paintings hanging from when Roxie was in college. She said she made them for her mom as a birthday gift. She wrote the date in the lower right corner. I have photo evidence."

"That might just get us an in. He shouldn't have anything, except for the years they were married," Jordan's voice came through the phone.

"If I can see all the paintings he has, I can tell you which ones are from our time married," she said, her body itching to know what other work her mother gave away.

"Let me get back to you after I talk with the judge. Anderson, send me the photos," Jordan replied.

"Will it take long to hear?" she wanted to know.

"No, I'll have something by tomorrow evening. Sally needed a reason to go after your ex. They wrote the divorce agreement to his advantage, but he has art he shouldn't. That should get us rights to have everything back since he violated your agreement," Jordan replied.

"Thank you for everything, Jordan. Xander, when are you coming home?" Roxie asked.

"As soon as I finish up here," Xander replied.

"See you soon then." Anderson hung up, and she did a victory dance.

"I can't believe Mom did something so stupid! I'm mad as hell she gave away the art I wanted her to keep but it gets me all my work back," she told Anderson. They walked down to the kitchen.

"Why would she do that?" he asked, sitting on a barstool.

"I bet Mitch convinced her that all my work needed to be hidden from the world. She also has never been very supportive of my choice of career. I hope she didn't take any I made for Dad," she replied, preparing ingredients to make lasagna.

"What did you paint for Dad? Can I help?" he asked, standing up to come around the island.

"Can you mix the cheeses? I need to boil water for the lasagna noodles," she asked, putting a pot under the faucet.

"So, what did you paint Dad?" He dumped four kinds of cheese into a bowl.

"I made him a painting of his favorite cabin to fish at. You remember the one with an outdoor toilet?" She pulled hamburger meat out to brown for the sauce.

"He loved taking us there. I remember you pushed Elizabeth into the lake once. If I recall, she said mermaids weren't real," he replied, laughing.

"I pushed her in, so she could look for mermaids," she corrected, which only made him laugh harder.

"Did you do any others?"

"One of our houses in the winter time. It was right after a snowstorm, and the snow was up to the front door. I snuck across the street in the early morning to take a picture. I gave it to him for his fiftieth birthday." She walked over to the oven to preheat it.

"Was it this?" He showed her another picture on his phone and she nodded. Her heart hurt to know her parents gave up the work she worked hard on.

"I think his cabin was up too. How many paintings did you make while married to Mitch?"

"Hmm, maybe forty. I had to work during the day and only had a few hours at night to paint. Mitch was not very understanding of my need to paint, one reason we pulled apart from each other. He wanted a housewife, and I wanted a life," she explained with a shrug. She didn't want Anderson to think she still cared about her lying, cheating, sack of shit ex-husband.

"Here, look through my phone and tell me all the work you did before marrying Mitch." He handed her the phone and took over assembling the lasagna. For the next twenty minutes, she pointed out fifteen more pieces of art she made while in college. Each time, Anderson sent the photo to Jordan.

"How many paintings did he have up?" she asked, handing back his phone.

"I'd say about thirty, which means he has some not hung. Another mark in our favor to get a court order to seize all your work. He is not actively showing all your work, which puts him in violation again of your agreement. How dumb is he?" Anderson mused. They were sitting in the living room. She had a glass of wine, and he had beer.

"Probably thought I'd never go after him. He is very arrogant with art."

"I'm home and I have wonderful news!" Xander called, as he walked in through the front door.

CHAPTER THIRTY-TWO

Roxie walked over and gave him a kiss hello. It had become a ritual for them. She would make dinner when he got home. He'd call out he was home, and she'd give him a kiss hello.

"Welcome home. What is the wonderful news?" she asked. He wrapped her up in a hug.

"Jordan called Sally the second we hung up. She said as soon as she gets the proof of your paintings not belonging to Mitch, she will give us the court order. Jordan said it will take forty-eight hours to take effect because we are crossing state lines. This means, on Sunday, we can get your work."

"That is freaking amazing!" Roxie jumped into his arms, smothering him in kisses. Xander laughed and spun them in a circle.

"By Monday, you will have all your work back where it belongs," he promised.

"Congratulations, Rox. This is a big deal. I'm telling you, so many people will buy your work," Anderson said, walking over to join the couple.

"Thanks. You are staying for dinner, right?" she asked. She didn't miss the keys in his hand.

"I figured you newly mated dragons would want to be alone to celebrate," he replied, and she huffed at him.

"No, you are staying and having lasagna. I remember it being a favorite of yours when we were younger. If you don't want to be a third wheel, I'll text Evvy. She and I missed girls's night because of a work event for her." She was already shooting off a text to Evelyn without Anderson answering.

"Might as well do as she says. Your sister can be very stubborn. I also don't want you upsetting her," Xander suggested, a smile on his face.

"Okay, fine," Anderson caved and Roxie whooped for joy.

"Evvy will be here in fifteen minutes. Gives me just enough time to open a bottle of red wine and get the garlic bread done," she announced, waltzing back to the kitchen. She couldn't believe her work was coming back to her. She'd given up hope on ever being successful, and now because of her mother's stupidity, she was getting a chance. Xander and Anderson thought she had talent. Evvy constantly told her that her work should be in a museum. Come Saturday the following week, she would know if her art would be a success.

Leaning against the counter, she stared at her ovens. What would she do if nothing was sold? What was she going to do about her mother's betrayal? You don't give away paintings your daughter worked hard on. Did her father know? She wanted to call her mom and yell, but she didn't want her tipping off Mitch. What a horrid thing to do to your own daughter. *Why?* She wanted to know why. After the art show, she would confront her mother about everything, then cut her out of her life, and enjoy being Xander's mate and the mother to any children they would have along the way.

"You okay? You are glaring at our ovens," Xander remarked. He'd walked back into the kitchen to get more beer.

"Just wondering why my mom did what she did. Am I that much of a disappointment that she didn't want my art?" she wondered. He wrapped her up in a tight hug and kissed her gently.

"No, you are an amazing person. Honestly, I'm upset I didn't meet you before Mitch ever got his hands on you. He ruined your confidence and belittled you to your family. I know you are

132

beautiful inside and out. I just hope you see that too," he replied, and she nuzzled into his chest.

"You know just what to say to make me feel good about myself," she shared. He smiled, kissing her again. "You should feel good about yourself. No one should ever make you feel inferior. Eleanor Roosevelt said it best, no one can make you feel inferior without your consent. You are a powerful, beautiful, talented woman. Show the world the Roxie I know. Prove to your mom and Mitch you are a rockstar. Your brother, Evelyn, and I know it is true," Xander gushed. She teared up and kissed him, pushing her tongue into his mouth. He was the best mate a girl could ask for.

"Ugh, every time I see you two, you are kissing. I better get a niece or nephew as soon as you two tie the knot," Evelyn announced. She walked into the kitchen, and Roxie released Xander.

"I promise you'll get one as soon as Roxie is ready," Xander promised. Evelyn nodded her agreement, taking the glass of wine Roxie offered.

"Hello," Anderson said. He walked into the kitchen with his eyes blazing. Roxie turned her head to watch her brother. She'd never seen him make that expression before.

"Anderson, this is my best friend and former roommate, Evelyn Tate. We met during our freshman year in high school. She works at the art museum in Green Falls. She is a tour guide," Roxie introduced the two and smirked when he took Evelyn's hand in his own.

"Very nice to meet you, Evelyn." His voice dropped almost like a purr, and Roxie had to stop herself from laughing. Her brother was infatuated with her best friend.

"Nice to meet you too," Evelyn replied, pulling her hand out of his grip. Roxie knew the look on her face. She was sizing Anderson up.

133

"Evelyn, this is Anderson, my older half-brother and Xander's chief assistant," Roxie announced and Evelyn's eyes widened.

"The older brother your mom threw out?" she asked, looking at Roxie.

"The very one. I'm happy to meet the woman who supported my little sister," Anderson replied. Evelyn blushed and Roxie had to hide her face in Xander's chest to keep from laughing out loud.

"Evelyn, would you like more wine?" Xander asked, diverting the conversation.

"Yes, please," she replied. Anderson beat her to the kitchen and poured her a fresh glass of wine from the same bottle Roxie had hers from.

"Thank you, Anderson," she said, gently taking the wine from him.

"My pleasure. So, Evelyn, do you enjoy working as a tour guide?" he asked, leading her into the living room.

Roxie grabbed Xander when he was about to follow.

"What?"

"Give them some alone time. If I'm right, Anderson has just met his mate. His eyes flared like yours did when we met. You can help me throw together a quick salad," Roxie explained, taking a sip of her wine.

"Oh! I didn't pick up on that at all," he replied, reaching into the fridge for the salad ingredients.

"How could you miss it? His eyes flared, and Evvy was a blushing mess. It is perfect. I can't wait for them to date." She squealed with glee and began cutting romaine lettuce.

"Don't get your hopes up. Anderson has never dated the ten years he has worked for me. He travels a lot and doesn't stay around long. He is going back out as soon as your show is done," Xander explained. Her smile dropped, and she huffed.

"Well, when you met me, you were willing to go away for a week. Why wouldn't he?" she asked, placing a hand on her hip.

"Rhett fought against Josie being his mate for months," Xander shared and Roxie gasped.

"But they are so happy!"

"Now. In the beginning, there was a lot of fighting. It was mostly because of Rhett refusing to listen to his dragon."

"Of course, he did. I hope Anderson isn't as stupid," she remarked, and smirked when she heard laughter ring from the living room. He shook his head, and when the timer dinged, he took the lasagna out of the oven and went back for the garlic bread.

"Dinner!" Roxie called Evelyn, and Anderson walked in laughing.

"What's so funny?" she asked.

"You at prom," Evelyn replied, and Roxie groaned.

"What happened at prom?" Xander asked as they sat around the table.

"Don't," she warned.

"Roxie thought she was too pale, so she tried a self-tanner. She looked orange, and it coated her hands," Evelyn shared.

"I did it the week before prom. My mom helped me get it off before pictures. She only helped me because she didn't want her pictures of me to look bad," Roxie explained.

"Do you have proof of the orange?" Xander wanted to know.

"No, I threatened not to be her friend anymore if she did. The teasing I endured was bad enough. I didn't need proof of my blunder," she said, serving everyone dinner.

"True," Evelyn replied.

"Besides, Evvy, you weren't much better with your makeup," Roxie shared.

"Oh?" Anderson asked. He looked intrigued.

"She tried to go for a smokey eye look," Roxie began.

135

"By the end of the night, I looked like a raccoon," Evelyn finished, shaking her head over her own folly.

"I did not have prom when I was your age," Xander commented.

"How old are you, if you don't mind me asking?" Evelyn asked.

"A hundred," he replied. Evelyn's eyes widened in shock.

"Whoa, do all shifters live as long?"

"No, dragons are rare and a unique breed altogether," he explained.

"Wow. So, Roxie, are you going to outlive all of us?"

"Probably." She didn't want to think about it, to be honest.

"Anderson, Xander told me you are headed on another trip after my show?" Roxie turned the conversation and let him take over talking about his travels.

Dinner passed quickly, and too soon, Anderson and Evelyn had to leave.

"I'll see you next week for a girls's night, say Velocity Bar?" Evelyn suggested.

"For sure. I'll meet you there at seven," she promised, giving her a tight hug.

"See you tomorrow," Anderson bid them farewell, and with Evelyn, he left.

"Dinner was delicious. Can I get dessert?" Xander asked, and she laughed.

"You don't always have to ask me for love," she teased. To her giggling delight, he grabbed her and ran up to their room to make love to her well into the night. When she was fast asleep, Xander slipped down and cleaned up the kitchen. He didn't want her to have to deal with it in the morning. His hope was tomorrow they could head up to New York and get her artwork. He wanted to explore New York City with her before confronting her ex-husband.

136

CHAPTER THIRTY-THREE

Ring, ring, ring.

Roxie answered her phone absentmindedly, expecting Xander to say he was on his way home.

"Roxanne Leigh Jones!" her mother's shrill voice came through the other end. She sighed; her painting zone shattered by her mother.

"Hello, Mom," she replied, stepping out of her studio. She didn't want whatever her mother would yell at her to contaminate her painting space.

"How dare you change your phone number on me! I just heard from Frieda about you hanging out with Xander Austin. Your father doesn't seem to care about you consorting with his kind, but I won't let you run our good name into the ground." Roxie rolled her eyes and went into the kitchen to pour herself an enormous glass of wine. If she had to listen to her mom, she would need something to take the edge off.

"What do you mean by his kind? Rich? Smart? Another gallery owner?" she asked.

"You know what I mean," her mother hissed. Roxie had an idea but wouldn't help her mother.

"No, I don't, Mom."

"A shifter!"

"Why would that be a dreadful thing? Xander loves me more than Mitch ever did. He encourages my painting, and if you saw, I sent you an invitation to my art show a week from Saturday," she said, seeing it was close to five o'clock. She knew Xander would head home soon.

"I saw it. I will not be coming. Mitch is renowned for his ability to spot talent. I won't come and watch you fail," her mother spat.

"I'm sorry to hear that. If you'll excuse me, I have dinner to make for my fiancé." She hung up, drank her glass of wine, and sighed. Her mother was a terrible person. How could she not support her own daughter?

Ring, ring, ring.

This time she checked the caller ID. It was Xander.

"Hi, baby," she sighed.

"What happened?" he asked. She loved how he could tell her mood even through a phone call.

"My mom found my new phone number. She called to tell me I'm a horrible daughter for being with a shifter."

"You can block her number," he suggested and she sighed.

"I can, but it makes me feel like a terrible daughter. She also told me she will not come to my show. She didn't want to watch me fail."

"That is awful. Well, I have marvelous news."

"What?"

"Pack your bags. We are headed to New York City. On Sunday, we will take your work back," he told her. She screamed in delight, doing a merry dance.

"See you in fifteen minutes," he laughed, and she hung up. She ran to their room and packed.

Xander hung up with Roxie and smiled. It thrilled him that Jordan came through for him. He needed to call his dad, Rhett, and Marcus. Xander wanted all the help he could get when he would confront Mitchell Wright. He'd done his research and knew Mitch used some men from the Italian mafia. Xander dialed Marcus first.

"Hello," Marcus answered.

"Hi, Marcus. I have a job for you and six of your boys," Xander told him.

"When?"

"Sunday. Long story short, my mate has a collection of artwork she needs back from her ex-husband. He uses men from the Italian mafia, and I need extra help to get her work back safely. Do you have enough guys? I'll pay all travel and lodging expenses," he offered.

"I'll see what I can do. I'm in between jobs," Marcus replied.

"Great. Get back to me tonight. I need to know how many men I will have to help," he explained.

"I'll call you by eight," Marcus assured him.

"Good. Talk to you soon."

"Bye."

Xander hung up, quickly dialing his dad.

"Hi, Xander," his dad greeted him.

"Hi, Dad. Wonderful news. Jordan came through with the court order, and we are going up to get Roxie's artwork. I need you and Rhett to come up on Sunday." Xander climbed into his car and drove home.

"Anything for my daughter-in-law. Do you want me to contact Rhett?"

"No, I'll call him. I'm taking Roxie up to New York City tonight. I want to enjoy the city and take her to a Broadway play," he shared.

"That sounds great. Oh, your mom wants you two to come for dinner next week. We want to celebrate your engagement and Roxie's show."

"I'll talk with Roxie and let you know," he said. Looking in his rearview mirror, he noticed a small red car following at a suspicious distance. He turned left, and the car followed.

"Hey, Dad, I'll talk to you later. I think Roxie's mom is tailing me."

"Why?"

"She doesn't approve of our relationship and has no clue where Roxie moved. They have a complicated relationship. I'm going to lose her and then call Rhett," he answered.

"Good luck," his dad replied and hung up. Xander quickly made several random turns until he could no longer see Meredith Jones. He called Rhett and explained the situation. Rhett agreed to meet him in New York City on Sunday. They would meet up at their Austin Luxury Hotel at 8 AM. Pulling into the driveway, he saw Roxie sitting on the porch with a book in her hands.

"Hi, sweetheart," he called, walking up to give her a kiss.

"Hi, baby, how was your day?" she asked, kissing him back.

"Good, until your mother tried to tail me home," he joked, and she gasped.

"She did not?" Roxie groaned, closing her book and hiding her face in her hands.

"I think so. Does she drive a little red Mazda?"

"Yes, she made my dad buy her one when she turned fifty-five."

"Then it was her. Don't worry, I lost her. Come, I want to pack and get us on the plane to New York. I have big plans for tomorrow." He kissed her on the cheek and pulled her to her feet.

"I'm so sorry about my mom. I have no clue why she would want to know where we live. She hates me." Roxie sighed. She let Xander pull her to their room. Roxie sat on the bed and watched him pack. "Are you sure you want to marry me?" she asked, her eyes on the floor, as she picked lint off their comforter.

"Of course, I do. Why would you ask me that?" He walked over and knelt at her feet, taking her hand in his.

"My mom is insane, and we are fighting my ex-husband. Most men would walk away after my mother stalked them," she said, her voice soft and tears coming to her eyes.

"I love you, Roxie. You are my mate. We will be together forever. We will deal with your ex, and once we come back from

New York City and have your show, we can deal with your mom," he promised.

"I don't deserve you," she whispered. Instead of answering her, he kissed her. Pushing her back onto the bed, he slipped his hands up her shirt, caressing her breasts through her bra. Slipping his tongue in, he kissed her until her body softened. "I love you. You are all I want," he assured her. She smiled with tears pricking the edge of her eyes and kissed him. Her arms wrapped around his neck, and she pulled him close against her chest.

"I love you too," she told him, giving him another kiss.

"Good. I really want to take you here and now, but I need to pack." He gave her a sad look, and she laughed.

"You can have me on the plane. I promise." She nuzzled his neck, nipping gently.

"Mmm, just like our first date." He smirked. She smiled and gave him a push towards their walk-in closet. "I hope you know I am holding you to that promise," he warned and she giggled.

CHAPTER THIRTY-FOUR

He did just that. When she got off the plane late that evening, Roxie's legs were wobbly. Xander laughed when she gripped his arm.

"It's your fault," she hissed, which only made him laugh harder. Once he had the keys to their hotel room, he scooped her up in his arms and carried her to the elevator.

"Xander put me down!" She felt extremely embarrassed by him carrying her.

"Why? Your legs are weak and I get to show the world you are mine," he replied.

"No one else wants me. People stare at you, not me," she remarked. To her surprise, he growled.

"Men stare at you. Every time we go out to eat, someone is lusting after you. Can't you sense their arousal?"

"No, because all I can smell is yours," she retorted, and he shut up. She could tell he was proud to have her undivided attention when they were out.

"That is the best compliment I have ever gotten. Let's shower when we get in the room. I want to show my appreciation." She giggled and nibbled on his ear to stoke the flames of his desire.

Striding into the room, Xander made his way to the bathroom, never letting go of Roxie. He turned the shower on and slowly set her down on her feet.

"Strip for me," he begged, sitting on the edge of the jacuzzi. She blushed but nodded. She was wearing a simple t-shirt and shorts. Gripping the edge of her shirt in shaky hands, she pulled it over her head, showing off her bright red lacy bra. She smirked when his eyes widened. She'd gone shopping for new underwear one day while Xander was working. She'd chosen this set because it reminded her of his dragon. Earlier that week, they'd gone out for a flight. Her dragon wanted to let Xander take them on a mountainside, but she held back.

Her shorts were next. She saw his breath hitch as she revealed her excuse for underwear; it was a small patch of red lace covering her most intimate spot.

"Roxie, I'm trying very hard not to pin you to that wall and take you," Xander groaned. His eyes were almost reptilian when he looked at her.

"Why hold back?" she wanted to know. Reaching back, she unclipped her bra and dropped it to the floor. Hooking her fingers into the waistband of her underwear, she watched him stalking over to her.

"Allow me." He reached down and tugged, ripping her thong right off her legs.

"That is so hot," she moaned. She felt branded by his hands on her hips.

"You are the sexiest woman, Roxie," he growled into her ear.

"Mmm, you are wearing too much," she pointed out. He was still wearing his shirt and khaki shorts.

"Help me," he demanded. She smirked and pulled his shirt over his head. He was an Adonis, with his six-pack abs and broad shoulders. His tan skin looked sun-kissed, even though she knew he spent most of his day inside. She placed kisses across his chest, her hands quickly undoing his belt and zipper. She shoved his shorts and boxers to the floor, freeing his cock.

Greedily stroking him, she stepped forward to capture his mouth in a kiss.

"God, Roxie," he moaned, his fingers found the entrance to her pussy, and he stroked. She was dripping down her legs and onto his fingers. "You are so wet, baby."

"That is what you do to me," she moaned as his fingers plunged deep. Her nails dug into his arms to hold her upright.

"I can't wait anymore!" He lifted her up, pinning her against the wall. She wrapped her legs around his waist, her pussy poised just above his cock.

"Xander!" He plunged into her in one fell swoop. She screamed; he covered her mouth with his own. Their tongues danced as he thrusted in and out of her. She bounced up and down, the telltale signs of her orgasm coming. Her body tightened, and a tingling sensation built in her womb.

Setting her down, he turned her to face the wall. Reaching forward, he massaged her breasts, slipping back inside of her. She gasped at the fresh sensation. Bending down further, he hit a spot she hadn't known was sensitive.

"Yes, baby, more," she begged. His hands gripped her hips so hard his nails bit into her skin. He was losing control of his dragon, and she knew it. Moaning loudly, she let her orgasm overtake her, her knees going weak. Xander roared behind her, spilling his seed deep within her. He braced his arms against the wall, breathing heavily.

"God, Roxie, you are amazing," he huffed, placing kisses across her shoulders.

"That was amazing. I'm not sure I can stand for a shower though," she admitted. He chuckled and picked her up, stepping into the warm spray of water. She nuzzled his neck.

"You are forever carrying me."

"I enjoy holding you. You calm my dragon and smell amazing."

145

"What do I smell like?" She looked up at him when he set her down on the bench in the shower.

"Like a field of tulips, the ones in Holland," he answered, handing her a loofah and body wash. She scrubbed down quickly and thought about what he said.

"Can we go see the tulip fields in Holland?"

"Sure. When do you want to go?"

"When are they blooming?" she asked, standing on shaky legs to rub down his body.

"Not sure. We can look it up once we are done here," he replied, closing his eyes. He practically purred as she washed his body. "Keep that up and I'll take you again," he threatened.

She gave a deep-throated laugh and shook her head. She knew she couldn't go another round. They'd made love the entire flight from DC to New York. Her body was sore and ready for snuggling in bed with a movie playing and maybe dinner.

"I can't go again. I'm sore. Can we snuggle in bed and watch a movie?" she asked, looking up at him. He ducked his head under the water to wash his hair and face. She admired the three-day beard he had going. She liked him with just the scruff of a beard, not a full one.

"Sure. What movie do you have in mind?" He turned off the water and they got out, wrapping towels around their bodies.

"A superhero movie. I like The Avengers with Scarlett Johansson," she answered, and he nodded his agreement.

"I love anything Marvel, so let's order a movie and room service," he suggested. She kissed his cheek and walked out into the room, stopping short upon seeing the bellhop. She was still wrapped in a towel, her tattoos on full display.

"I'm so sorry. I was sent up here with a gift for Mr. Austin," the bellhop stammered. Roxie nodded and walked over to her suitcase. She grabbed a nightgown and a pair of underwear.

"Xander, there is a bellhop for you," Roxie called. He stepped out of the bathroom in his towel. She escaped into the bathroom to dress. Coming back out dressed, she saw Xander holding an envelope and a bottle of wine.

"Who is it from?" she asked.

"I haven't opened it yet," he replied, sitting on the edge of the bed. She sat next to him and leaned into his body. He opened the card, and she gasped when she saw Mitch's handwriting.

"How does he know we are here?" She stood to pace. Her ex-husband had ties to the Italian mafia, and she worried about Xander's safety.

"Probably the same way I know what kind of business he runs out of his warehouse," he replied, standing and wrapping his arms around her.

"Remember me talking about my friend Marcus Zephyr?" he asked.

"Yes, he runs a protection agency of some sort."

"Yes, he is coming up tomorrow with six other men to help me. I know what kind of man your ex is, and I am prepared. Marcus and his men are all shifters. Plus my dad and Rhett are coming on Sunday. We will have plenty of protection. He is just trying to scare us into leaving. We will not leave until we have all your artwork," he promised.

"You swear?" she demanded, wrapping her arms around his waist and looking up into his hazel eyes.

"I swear. Come on, let's get to our movie and dinner." He pulled her into their bed, dropping his towel before climbing in.

CHAPTER THIRTY-FIVE

They watched the movie and enjoyed their first night in New York City. Xander recalled what the note said. Roxie caught one look at the handwriting and panicked. He was happy that she didn't read the letter.

> *Xander Austin,*
>
> *I know you are in New York City, and I want you to know I have eyes everywhere. Should you or Roxie come within a hundred feet of my gallery, I will burn her paintings. Enjoy the bottle of champagne I sent, consider it my congratulations on you two being engaged. Her mother has been a font of information pertaining to your relationship.*
>
> *Mitchell Wright*

Xander fumed. *How dare he threaten his mate!* Thankfully Marcus was coming up tomorrow, and they could make a plan. He didn't want to tip Mitchell off that they were coming for her work. He wouldn't let him burn a single canvas. He shot off a text. He wanted his dad and Rhett in town as soon as possible.

While all the men were scouting the area, he would take Roxie around for a day in the city. He knew she'd lived close when married to Mitchell, but he had a sneaking suspicion she rarely came into the city. She probably came for art shows and nothing else. He was excited to see the city with her. He didn't come here often because of Mitchell. They had never gotten along when at art exhibitions. Mitchell saw him as competition and he would stake his reputation on him being pissed he stole Roxie. Seeing responses from both his dad and Rhett, he fell asleep worrying about his mate.

He awoke the next morning to an empty bed. He sat up quickly, scanning the room for his love. When he spotted the balcony doors open, he got up, tossed on his boxers, and went outside. She was sitting at a miniature easel with a small canvas in front of her. He watched her paint the city with the sunrise behind it. Her strokes were sure, and he could see the piece coming along. Leaning against the door, he stayed silent as she worked. He loved watching her. She would scrunch up her button nose when she contemplated what color to use next.

"I know you are there," she remarked, not looking away from her work.

"Of course, you do," he chuckled. She'd only had her dragon for a week but had learned to hone her senses quickly. He bent and kissed her cheek.

"How long have you been up?" he asked, sitting next to her.

"Since four. Mitch is a dangerous man, and I read the letter. How the hell are we going to get my work now?" She set her brush down and angrily wiped away a tear. He pulled her into his lap, not caring that she got paint on his bare chest.

"I have a plan. Trust me and everything will work out. I have everyone coming up to meet us in an hour. We will enjoy our day like normal and the guys will put our plan into action," he explained.

"I don't know if I can pull off acting normal," she murmured.

"That is where I come in. We have a full day planned out, starting at the Delicious Spa for a couple's massage. We have lunch at Gramercy Tavern, window shopping around Times Square, dinner at Bemelmans Bar, and the Broadway play Hamilton to finish out our day."

"That is a full day. I'm not sure I'll be able to keep up," she laughed, and he nipped at her neck. "No marks. I don't have makeup with me to cover them," she warned, and it made him want to leave one even more.

"I'll make it below the collar," he promised and went to work sucking on her shoulder.

"Baby," she moaned, tipping her head to the side. He renewed his suction until a blooming red mark appeared right by her red rose tattoo.

"I want you," he whispered in her ear. She nodded and stood up, slipping her panties off. She left her nightgown on and reached for his hard cock. Slipping it free from his boxers, she lowered herself down on him. He moaned and watched the sunrise as she rode him. Gripping her hips, he guided her up and down until she had the perfect rhythm.

He kissed her, slipping his tongue into her mouth. He matched her strokes with his tongue. His moans got louder as she increased her speed. His orgasm came unexpectedly, and she followed soon after.

He held her in his lap, not wanting to remove himself from inside her. With the amount of sex they had had the past twenty-four hours, he was convinced she would get pregnant. The idea of having children warmed his heart. He was so ready to be a father. Was Roxie ready to become a mom?

"That was so liberating," she whispered, and he had to ask.

"What was?"

"Having sex out in the open with you. I mean, I know no one could see us this high, but the fact we are outside is exhilarating," she answered with a bright smile.

"My little exhibitionist," he joked and stood, keeping himself still inside of her.

"Don't get any ideas. We were practically in private," she warned, giving him a gentle kiss.

"I know, love. Want another shower? We both have paint all over now," he suggested. She nodded and they took a long, intimate shower.

CHAPTER THIRTY-SIX

"So, what happened to you to want us all here a day early?" Rhett asked him. James had arrived five minutes ago. Roxie and Xander had just finished eating breakfast.

"I'll explain all when Marcus and his guys get here," Xander replied. He and Roxie were sitting on the couch, wrapped in each other's arms.

"How many did you ask for?" James wanted to know; Roxie observed the three men. They looked so much alike. They were good looking, tall, and built.

"Six. I figured with ten shifters we should have enough muscle to get her work safely," Xander explained.

Knock knock.

Roxie stood and answered the door. Standing there were some of the biggest men she'd ever seen.

"Hello, I'm Marcus Zephyr. Xander is expecting us," the man with bright red hair and green eyes said. He had to be close to six foot six.

"Yes, come in." She stepped out of the way and watched as five more men came in behind him. They weren't as tall but equally intimidating.

"Marcus!" Xander called, getting up to exchange handshakes.

"Good to see you," Marcus replied, his face remaining impassive.

"Now that everyone is here, I'll do introductions," Xander started. He beckoned for Roxie to come over to him. She stepped next to him, and he wrapped an arm around her waist.

"Roxie, this is Marcus Zephyr. He is a bear shifter. With him, he brought Grayson." He pointed to a blond with shoulder-length hair pulled into a low ponytail.

"He is a lion shifter. Troy and Peter are brothers, both wolves. Kevin is the black-haired one. He is a black bear. Last is Orion, and he is also a bear, but a grizzly bear like Marcus." Roxie took in each of them. Orion was almost as tall as Marcus. Troy and Peter were the shortest but both over six feet tall. Orion had light brown hair with chocolate eyes.

"Nice to meet you," she said, feeling shy around such tall, intimidating, handsome men.

"Let's all sit. We have a lot to discuss," Xander suggested. Everyone quickly found places to sit, except Marcus. He propped himself against the wall closest to the balcony. Roxie could see him checking for safety and smiled. These men were trained to help protect. She would be fine.

"So we all know Jordan Howard got us a court order to take back all the artwork created by Roxie. The artworks are being shown at The Golden Painting here in New York City. I believe Mitchell is not aware of the court order. He sent me a note yesterday threatening to destroy them if we step within a hundred feet of her art. He has a working relationship with the Italian mafia, and they use his warehouse for illegal activities."

"I believe some of her work is at the warehouse and some at the gallery. The two are thankfully in the same area of Manhattan. Jordan will meet us here tomorrow morning with the court order to help us put it in effect," Xander explained. Roxie was clenching his hand the entire time. She worried they wouldn't be successful in saving her art.

"What's the plan?" Marcus asked from his spot on the wall.

153

"Roxie, Jordan, Dad, Rhett and I will go to the gallery with the order. Marcus, you and your men will go to the warehouse with a copy of the order. You are to use any means necessary to get her art. They are marked with R.J."

"Wait. I thought we weren't allowed near the gallery?" Roxie asked, looking up at her love.

"If my hunch is correct, he won't hurt the gallery. His family has spent too much money perfecting it. He will burn down the warehouse and claim the insurance money without blinking. We distract him at the gallery, while Marcus and his men save your art from the warehouse. They are all ex-military and know how to handle dangerous situations," he told her. She looked over all the men and realized they had a hardened edge to their look.

"Oh, what are they going to do today?"

"Marcus and his men will scope out the warehouse and locate your work. This way, tomorrow, they can get them quickly. Dad and Rhett will do the same at The Golden Painting. We will go around New York City, keeping Mitchell and his goons busy. He won't think anything of my dad visiting because he visits when he opens a new hotel looking for art."

"You've thought this through," James remarked. He looked proud of his son.

"I know how Mitchell works. He thinks with the power of the mafia behind him, he is untouchable," Xander answered.

"I want us all to meet back here at midnight. We can discuss any issues, and once Jordan arrives tomorrow morning around eight, we implement our plan." He looked at each man, and they nodded their agreement.

"See you at midnight. Enjoy your day. Roxie, please don't worry. Everyone will come out unscathed, and you'll have your work back," James assured her. He walked over and kissed her cheek.

"Thank you, James. Rhett, how is Josie?" she asked. She didn't know how he felt being away from her, now that she was pregnant.

"Good. Her morning sickness has been pretty bad lately," he replied with a wry smile.

"I'm sorry. I hear ginger helps with that. My friend Missy had such terrible morning sickness when she was pregnant with her daughter. She ate candied ginger and sucked on ginger pops. They seemed to help," she offered. Rhett nodded and quickly texted Josie.

"Thank you, everyone, for helping me," Roxie said, looking at each man to let them know she meant it.

"Anything for family," James replied, tapping Rhett on the arm. They left.

"I'll keep you up to date on my progress," Marcus told Xander and motioned for his men to follow. Once the room was empty, Roxie sighed.

"Just think that by tomorrow afternoon, you will no longer have to deal with Mitchell Wright," Xander remarked. He kissed her on the top of her head.

"I hope so," she replied, shaking her head.

"Come on, love, we have a full day to enjoy. I want you to not worry about anything today. We need to leave in a minute for our massage. Part of it is them teaching us how to give each other massages, and I can't wait to get my hands on your naked body." He nipped at her neck, and she squeaked.

"You are too much," she giggled and let him kiss her until they needed to head over to the spa.

CHAPTER THIRTY-SEVEN

Stepping into the private massage room, Roxie glimpsed Xander standing in just a bathrobe. She'd been told to disrobe, leaving only her underwear on, no bra. In the first half, they would teach them how to massage each other and the second half would be their actual professional massage. She worried they'd ask her to strip off her robe and show off her naked body to everyone.

"Don't be nervous, sweetheart. They won't see anything," Xander promised, walking over to her and kissing her gently. Roxie melted into the kiss, gripping the edges of his robe as she pulled him in for a hot and steamy kiss. She would never get used to this man loving her. She wanted to touch him as much as possible. If they continued on the pace for their lovemaking, she would be pregnant in no time.

"Ready to get started?" a youthful woman with black hair asked. A gentleman with blond hair followed her. He had muscles for days. His polo shirt did nothing to hide his buff body.

"I am Rita, and this is Marco. We will be your masseuses for the day," Rita said. Stepping toward Xander, she motioned for him to sit on the table.

"Sir, lay down and I will instruct your fiancé on how to properly give a back massage." He laid down and turned his head to see Roxie. She lifted an eyebrow and smirked. He slipped under the sheet, removing his robe as carefully as he could. Roxie could glimpse his black boxers, but nothing else.

"Excellent. Miss, if you will come over here?" Rita motioned for her to come over to the table with lotions and oils. "Most couples use lotions to spice up their sex life. A massage can be a very sensual experience if you let it. Oils make the skin slick and easy for skin to skin contact. Which would you like?" Rita asked. Roxie looked at Xander.

"Lotion, please. Oils have a tendency not to sink into our skin the best," Xander said. Rita nodded and put the lotion into a warmer. A minute later, she pulled it out and handed it to Roxie.

"Put a small amount on your hands. We will start at the base of his back and work up. Most people keep the most tension in their shoulders. The problem is if you jump right to the shoulders the muscles have nowhere to go. You need to relax the muscles working up," Rita explained. Roxie did as she was told and put a small amount of lotion into her hand. She noticed Marco stood off to the side, arms crossed, making for a very imposing view.

"Don't pay Marco any mind. He is not an adept teacher. He is watching me, so one day, he can run his own couple's massage," Rita said. She gave Roxie a push toward Xander.

"Okay, now I want you to place your hands like a butterfly on the center of his spine." Rita showed her what she meant. Roxie did as she was told and laughed when Xander jumped from her touch.

"Surprise you?" she asked.

"No, your fingers are icy," he replied, which only made her laugh harder.

"Next time, I'll try to warm them up for you," she promised. For the next fifteen minutes, she followed Rita's instructions on how to properly massage Xander's back.

"Switch," Rita demanded, and Roxie paused. How was she supposed to get under the sheet and get her robe off with no one seeing anything?

"Would you and Marco turn around? My fiancé is a very private person," Xander explained, understanding her predicament. Rita and Marco both turned around. She quickly stripped off her robe and slipped under the sheet. The entire time Xander stood blocking her from view, in case Marco got any ideas.

"You can look now," she replied, placing her head in the hole for her face on the massage table.

"Excellent. Xander, do you want to use lotion or oil on her?" Rita asked Roxie to lay still, wondering what he would pick. They'd played with some lubricant before in their bedroom, but nothing like massage oils. She bet they would make it even easier for her to accommodate some toys Xander liked to use. She found in the past three weeks being with Xander that she really enjoyed anal play. She'd heard horror stories from some of her friends in college, but with Xander, she never worried about being hurt.

"Lotion, please. I think her skin could use the extra lubrication," he replied, and Roxie could hear the double meaning behind his words. She felt a shiver run down her spine and did her best not to wiggle. This position was one she lay in when he would get the toys they'd be playing with for the night.

"Excellent choice, sir." Rita's voice came out in a slight squeak, and Roxie felt her cheeks flush. Seemed Rita understood his double meaning, and now Roxie was extremely embarrassed.

"Now place some on your palms and put your hands in the same butterfly position as I showed your fiancé." Roxie felt Xander's gigantic hands sit at the base of her spine and push up. She bit her lip to keep the moan from escaping her mouth. He worked up her middle, then down each side before getting to her shoulders. She knew she was very stiff from painting, and it would hurt like a bitch when Xander pressed down on her body.

"She is a painter, and her shoulders hold a lot of tension. Is there a way I can help it release without causing undue pain?" Xander asked. She felt through their connection his concern for her.

"Start at her neck and work outwards. If the pain gets to be too much, shift to using just your palm. There is to be some pain, but it shouldn't be so painful that she jerks out of your hands." Rita put her hands on Roxie's shoulders and showed him how to press down, just enough to push out the tension. Xander's hands replaced Rita's, and Roxie moaned when he pushed down.

"You like that, baby?" he whispered, placing a gentle kiss on her shoulder.

"Very much. If you do this every night for me, I will have as many children as you want," she promised. That drew another chuckle from him.

"Don't make promises we both know you won't keep," he nipped at her shoulder and she jumped.

CHAPTER THIRTY-EIGHT

"Don't worry, baby. Rita and Marco have stepped out of the room and I locked the door. This is the next part of the package, just the two of us spending some time massaging each other and maybe making that baby you just promised me."

"Xander! We can't have sex in here. Everyone will hear," she objected, sitting up, keeping the sheet wrapped around her chest.

"Not if you are quiet. Up for the challenge? I may have brought a little friend with me to play." He walked over to her bag and pulled out a silver butt plug with the initial X on the base.

"You are serious?" she asked. He nodded and walked over to her and kissed her gently.

"I won't push you, but now I am so turned on from touching you." He guided her hand down to stroke his cock through his boxers. She closed her eyes. There was no way she could say no to him. She nodded her head, and he kissed her, pushing her back down onto her stomach.

"Ass up and hands down," he ordered. She shivered and did as he said. The sheet fell from her body, and she shivered when the cool air hit her skin. He reached up and removed her underwear, kissing her ass gently.

"You ready?" he asked, trailing kisses down her back and stopping at the base of her spine. She nodded, her body humming with anticipation as he used the oil to lubricate her hole. His finger slipped in and she moaned. The oil heated the muscles, helping them relax.

"Deep breaths, baby, and don't clench. This one is a little bigger than last night's toy," he told her, and she nodded. Her blood hummed in anticipation as the toy circled her ass.

"Stop teasing, Xander," she moaned, wiggling her hips.

"Hold still, baby girl," he commanded and gave her ass a light slap. She jerked forward and moaned softly. "Oh, you like that, do you?" he asked, smacking her other cheek just enough to leave a slight sting.

"Xander," she moaned, almost losing her ability to stay still. He chuckled and finally gave her what she wanted. He pushed the tip in slowly. She gasped at the size. He was right; it was bigger than the one they had most recently played with. With a few pushes and pulls, the plug sat snugly inside of her. She felt pleasantly stretched and moaned with pleasure. Xander climbed up behind her and slipped his head between her legs.

"I am going to try my hardest to make you sing," he growled and attacked her pussy. Spreading her lips, his tongue dove in and she jerked forward. Jolts of desire raced through her body, settling in her womb. She pushed down with her hips, taking his tongue further into her pussy. He smacked her hip, and she pulled back. Using his teeth, he clamped onto her clit and she had to bite down on her arm to keep from screaming.

"Cheat," she gasped out when he let go.

"I told you. You will sing for me, baby." He leaned up and dove back into sucking on her pussy. Roxie had to take deep breaths to keep her orgasm from consuming her too fast. She wanted to enjoy the sensation of his mouth on her for as long as she could. One of his hands slipped out and tugged on the plug in her ass. He pushed it deeper, and at the same time, two fingers entered her pussy. She bit her arm again to keep the scream from ripping out of her throat. She felt amazing and loved him playing with her. His teeth bit down on her clit again. This time she couldn't hold back her orgasm, and she squirted all over his face, a scream leaving her lips.

"Xander," she moaned. She knew that he knew what she needed. Slipping out from underneath her, he plunged his cock deep into her pussy. She jerked forward from the force of his entrance and groaned. She felt so full with him and the plug in her ass. Her body moved on its own; she needed her second release. Xander's hands gripped her hips, his nails digging in just slightly painful.

"Roxie," he growled. Leaning forward, he caged her with his arms and nipped at her neck. His rhythm never faltered as he kissed across her back and down to her ass. His hands found the plug, and he pulled it almost all the way out, then plunged it back in with his thrust.

"Oh god!" she moaned and gripped the massage table.

"You are so fucking sexy," Xander grunted, pumping in and out, hitting her pleasure spot every time. Roxie reached down, pressing on her clit as she sent herself into another blinding orgasm. Xander shouted out and squirted his cum deep inside of her body. She collapsed onto the table, her breathing ragged.

"I can't believe we just did that," she rolled over to face him.

"That was the hottest thing. Roll over, so I can take the plug out, baby. We still need to get our professional massages." He motioned for her to roll over. Roxie did. He gently removed it, placed it in a Ziploc bag, and tucked it away in her purse. She watched him slip his boxers back on and climb under the sheet. She fished around for her underwear, and once she was settled again, Xander rang the bell.

162

CHAPTER THIRTY-NINE

Her massage was anticlimactic after her massage with Xander. Marco did a suitable job working out the knots in her shoulders, and she felt very good at the end.

"Make sure you drink plenty of water or your muscles will seize up," Marco told her. She nodded and thanked him for the massage.

"We need to head to lunch, sweetheart," Xander murmured against her ear, his arms wrapping around her waist. She pushed her bottom into his crotch, and he groaned.

"Baby, you keep that up and I might just have to take you in the restaurant bathroom," he threatened, and she giggled.

"You can have me again tonight, my love," she promised and kissed the edge of his lips.

"Damn right." He smacked her butt and led her out onto the sidewalk.

"It is a five-minute walk to Gramercy Tavern from here," he explained. Taking her hand, they set out to get lunch.

They enjoyed a quiet lunch, but Roxie couldn't shake the feeling they were being watched. Several times, she caught the eye of a server. He had muscles for days, and his white shirt strained against his chest.

"Xander," she whispered after seeing the same server for the third time.

"Yes?" He looked up from his phone. He had been texting back and forth with the other guys.

"See the server who looks like a wrestler?" She nodded in his direction, sipping on her water.

"What about him?" he asked, looking up discreetly.

"He keeps staring at me," she replied. The man gave her an uncomfortable feeling.

"Maybe he finds you attractive?" he suggested, looking around the restaurant.

"He makes me feel uncomfortable. He keeps staring at me. When I look up, he is always watching our table," she explained. She hoped he could feel her discomfort.

"Give me a minute." He stood and made his way to the bathroom. She sat back, pushing away her lunch plate. She no longer felt hungry enough to finish her salad.

"Excuse me, but are you Roxie Jones?" The large server asked, coming up to the table.

"Why?" she asked, crossing her arms over her chest.

"I have a note from your husband, Mitchell," he told her, holding out an envelope.

"I don't have a husband," she argued back.

"I beg to differ." He set the envelope on the table and walked off. Xander appeared instantly.

"I'm sorry. You were right," he apologized and sat down. "What did he want?"

"He gave me an envelope and said it was from my husband, Mitchell. When I told him I didn't have a husband, he disagreed," she explained, lifting the envelope.

"Open it up. Let's see what your delusional ex wants." She lifted it up and carefully broke the seal. Pulling out a piece of paper, her old engagement ring fell out.

"Oh my god," she gasped and jerked away from the offending ring.

"What is that" Xander leaned forward, looking at the small ring.

"My old engagement ring," she answered. Xander scowled and motioned for her to read the letter.

My Dearest Roxie,

I want to apologize for my behavior when we got divorced. I miss you and your artwork in our house. I miss your cooking and how wonderful you were at parties. My parents have expressed their distress over our divorce. I am no longer engaged to Barbie and want you to come home. I promise we will try to show your work. I should have never told you that you were not good enough. I have had a lot of interest in the art I have up in the gallery. Come home to me, Roxie.

Love,
Your husband, Mitchell

She almost threw up reading the letter.

"He is insane. Why would I go back to him when I have you?" she asked, shaking her head over his craziness.

"I did not expect that," he replied, rubbing a hand down his face.

"Should we be worried?" She gave him a concerned look.

"No, I'll contact Marcus. He can send one of his men to do some recon." He waved the server down to get their check. She tapped her fingers on the table, while Xander shot off a text.

"He is sending Peter to meet us in the center of Times Square," he told her.

"How are we going to handle this?" she wanted to know, calling in Peter told her nothing.

"We will discuss everything away from prying ears," he answered, nodding his head toward the watching server. She nodded her understanding and fiddled with her phone. The server brought them their check. He paid in cash, so they could leave quickly. Stepping onto the street, she took a deep breath.

"Why does he want me back? He always made me feel like a failure in everything I did," she commented. They hurried down the street.

"Probably realized what he lost. Plenty of people want your work. He has seen that when so many people asked about them. You are also an amazing cook, and as much as I hate to agree with him, you are great with people." He kissed her gently, and she sighed. "Look, there is Peter. I'll have him look into Mitch. You still have his office address and his home address?"

"He didn't move. I did," she replied and quickly jotted down both addresses.

"Excellent. For the rest of the day, I won't let you out of my sight. No one will get close to you again," he promised. She pulled him down for a fiery kiss. She wanted him to know how amazing he made her feel.

"I love you, Xander Austin. I cannot wait for the day we get married."

"I love you, Roxie Jones. Once we get back home, we should start planning our wedding," he suggested. She smiled widely and gave him one more kiss.

"You two are sickly sweet. What did you need me for?" Peter asked, coming around the corner.

"Read this." Xander handed him the letter, and his eyes widened in surprise.

"Wow, so what do you need me to do?" he asked, handing the letter back.

"Check on Mitchell. Here are his home and his office addresses. Please observe what he is doing," Xander informed him, Peter nodded and left just as quietly as he came.

"Now we enjoy our day." Xander took her hand, and they went shopping. They stopped at the New York branch of her favorite designer to find her a dress for her show the following week. Dinner was delightful, and the Broadway play surpassed her expectations. All day, Roxie knew they were being followed but did her best not to let it bother her.

CHAPTER FORTY

By twelve-thirty at night, all men were seated in the hotel room.

"We should share what happened today first," Xander started. He gripped Roxie's hand as they sat side by side.

"At lunch today, a server kept watching me. When Xander stepped away from the table, the server gave me a note from Mitchell. He knows I am here in New York with Xander. He told me in the letter that he made a mistake and wanted me back. Xander contacted Marcus, and he sent Peter to come talk with us," Roxie explained.

"I went to his office, and he was there. I slipped into the hallway and listened to his conversation. He is planning on moving all R.J. paintings tomorrow night to an undisclosed location. This leads me to believe he does not know about the court order yet. I followed him home, and meeting him at the door was a very pregnant blonde. She wrapped her arms around him, and her large ring shone on her left hand." Peter took over, sharing his news.

"I knew the letter was a fake. There is no way that after everything Mitchell had put me through the past two years, he would have changed his mind. I bet it was his ploy at trying to get me to leave my artwork with him," Roxie growled, slamming her fist on the couch next to her.

"Easy killer. Tomorrow, you will get your revenge on him. You will take back your life, so Mitch will never manipulate you again." Xander kissed her gently, and she melted into his side. His muscular arm wrapped around her shoulders, making her head rest on his shoulder. She felt protected and cherished, something she hadn't felt in a very long time.

"We scoped out the gallery today. Roxie, I have to say, your work are very impressive. We asked the young lady working on the floor about buying a piece. She told us they were on loan from the artist and the pieces were sentimental and not for sale. I took a picture of each one," James explained, handing the phone for her to go through.

She flipped through the pictures and gasped when she found the one she had made for her parents's anniversary. It was of her family home in the fall, just as the leaves changed color. She loved this painting and had worked for days on it. She continued to flip. Every painting she made for Christmas, birthdays, and anniversaries were on display. Not a single one was of the work that she would sell.

"I didn't paint any of these to sell. They are all gifts to my parents for holidays and birthdays. I am sure my mom gave them to Mitch when he told her I was mediocre at painting." Her throat was tight with emotion, and she needed a minute to herself. "If you'll excuse me." She got up and rushed to the bedroom. Locking the door, she slid to the floor with her back against the door. Wrapping her arms around her knees, she put her head down to cry silently. It hurt to see all her gifts given away like that. She'd put her heart and soul into those paintings. Her mother tossed them away as if they meant nothing.

"Baby?" Xander's voice came through the door. She didn't feel like being around anyone.

"Leave me be, Xander. I need to process this alone," she replied, not lifting her head from her knees.

"I will finish talking with the guys and then we are talking," he told her, and she knew she wouldn't get away with wallowing in her own self-pity.

169

"Okay," she whispered and crawled into their bed. Pulling a pillow into her arms, she rested.

CHAPTER FORTY-ONE

Xander sighed and walked back to the living room. He didn't enjoy leaving his mate to her thoughts for too long.

"We need to make this quick," he demanded. His entire demeanor changed, and he brought them back to the task at hand.

"We could get inside the warehouse. For someone working with the mafia, it was easy to get inside," Marcus said, pulling out a roughly drawn sketch of the place. "Troy and Grayson located Roxie's paintings. They are being kept in a pile at the back of the warehouse." His blunt finger pointed to a marked spot on the map.

"They are not being kept in the same condition as all the others. There is a sign on them that reads, 'salvage don't touch,' " Troy explained. He pulled out his phone to show Xander.

Good thing Roxie went to lie down. He didn't want her to see what Mitchell had done to her art.

"Did any of it look damaged?" he asked, handing phone back. He wanted to kill Mitchell with his bare hands. The man never deserved such a jewel like Roxie.

"No, it almost looked as if they had just been stacked there recently. From what Peter said, it sounds like he had them placed there to send them off," Grayson answered, his voice deep and low as if he didn't use it often.

"The plan tomorrow is for Jordan to come with Dad, Rhett, Roxie, and I to the main gallery. Marcus, you will take Troy, Peter, Grayson, Orion. Kevin will go to the warehouse and gather

her paintings. Before you do that, I want you to stop and get bubble wrap. We will wrap them properly when we all gather back at the hotel." Xander paced around the room while sharing his plan.

"Shouldn't one of my men come with you? I know you, Rhett, and James are dragons, but Roxie is human and Jordan has sworn off fighting," Marcus suggested.

"Wrong. Roxie is a dragon too," Xander corrected, and all the men stared at him in awe.

"You damn dragons never like a small shifter," Kevin joked. Everyone gave a slight chuckle, and the tension in the room settled a little.

"She may be a dragon, but can she handle facing her ex? Her reaction upon seeing those paintings doesn't give me much hope," Rhett commented. He was lounged across an armchair with his feet hanging off one side. He wore basketball shorts and a t-shirt, very different from his usual three-piece suits.

"I'll let you in on a secret. You know how our parents have always supported our work?" Xander asked, training his blazing eyes on his younger brother. He felt tired and irritated, and all he wanted to do was comfort his hurting mate. His dragon huffed. They needed to shift and fly above the city. When this finished, he would take Roxie for a flight.

"Yeah?" Rhett gave him a cautious look. They'd been brothers for ninety-five years; they knew when the other was close to blowing their top.

"She doesn't have that. Her mother has taken Mitchell's side when they divorced. She blamed Roxie for the marriage failing, even though he cheated on her with his secretary. They threw her half brother out of her home for being a shifter. Her sister moved two states away to get away from her mother. Don't get me started on her weak father. He let all of these happen to his children. He is weak and lets her mother control every aspect of their lives. Roxie changed her phone number to avoid her mother. Then she finds out all the art she gave as gifts was given away."

"How would you feel? Would you be able to hold it together if Josie suddenly left you for someone younger? Would you be able to handle it if Mom and Dad suddenly told you they wanted you to sell all your clubs, that you were giving our family name a bad image? Could you keep your dragon from raging?" He was seething with anger by the time he finished his rant. He was furious with Roxie's family for being a poor excuse and with her mother for caring more about her image than about her daughter's success.

All the men sat in silence, afraid to be the one who pushed him over the edge. He could feel the claws threatening to extend from his fingers. His breath was smoking, and his eyes were taking on a reptilian shape.

"Xander Richard Austin, if you blow up and shift in here, your mother will have a fit," his father roared.

Roxie came sprinting out of their room. He set his eyes on her, and his dragon paused. She rushed over and wrapped her arms around his waist.

"Xander? Please come back to me. Calm down." Her whispered plea was the nail in the coffin. His dragon calmed down and purred. His mate was just the cure to his temper. He buried his face in her hair and breathed in. Her scent washed over him. He relaxed his shoulders and looked down at his mate. Her eyes were red-rimmed from crying over those who were supposed to love her. He would do anything to keep her from feeling that pain ever again.

"Are you okay?" she asked softly. He nodded and looked up at the men in the room.

"We all know the plan. Let's call it a night and meet up here at eight-thirty. Marcus, you and your men will go to the warehouse when you see fit. Retrieve her paintings and come back here to package them carefully for the trip back home. The rest of us will confront Mitchell and get the paintings from the gallery." Xander looked around at all the men and they nodded. They stood up one by one as they left the room. Rhett and James left last.

173

"I am sorry for pushing." Rhett clapped his hand on Xander's shoulder and gave Roxie a kiss on the cheek.

"This will all be over tomorrow. Get some sleep tonight," James told them both, giving Xander a pat on the shoulder and a hug for Roxie.

"Thank you for all your help," Roxie said, hugging James tightly. Xander watched with pride. His mate was an amazing woman who deserved a loving family.

"Good night." James bid them both goodbye, and the door shut. Roxie sighed against Xander's side as the day hit her.

"Want to go for a flight?" he asked. He knew he needed a chance to shift, and if he did, then Roxie's dragon would push for one too.

"Absolutely. Let's go," she said, stripping out of her clothes and walking to the balcony. He laughed and followed, licking his lips over her delectable naked body. He couldn't help but reach out and smack her ass. She laughed and arched an eyebrow.

"How are you going to shift if you are still dressed?"

"I'm coming, my love. Patience is a virtue." Xander laughed and slowly stripped off his shirt, watching her eyes dilate with desire. He pulled his belt off achingly slow. She slipped her tongue out and licked her lips. He felt his cock stir. She was hard to resist. His pants came next, unzipping. He hooked his fingers into the waistband, his eyes connecting with hers.

"Like what you see?" he asked, cocking an eyebrow, and she nodded. He chuckled and dropped his pants, leaving his boxer briefs.

"Those too," she remarked, pointing to his underwear, his cock straining at the fabric.

"As you wish." He nodded and slowly drew them down his legs. When he stood up straight, he almost lost the resolve to go for a flight. He could smell her arousal and wanted to sink his cock hip-deep into her calling pussy.

"Let's go!" she whined and pranced from foot to foot. He made a full-bodied laugh and nodded.

"Watch me," he instructed and took a diving leap from the edge, shifting into his scarlet dragon as he fell. Turning on his back, he watched his mate do the same. Her sunset dragon burst out and flew to join him.

"I will never get used to seeing you. You are beautiful, Roxie." Xander mind linked her. Her dragon turned its head to look at him, and she nodded her head.

"I love seeing you. You look like a fire at the very center. Now take me around New York City and then make love to me when we get home," Roxie replied.

"As my queen commands." He shot straight up with her and did exactly what she asked of her. He showed her New York City.

CHAPTER FORTY-TWO

Roxie dove over the edge of the balcony and screamed her delight, which turned into a roar as she shifted into her dragon. She felt powerful; no one could touch her when she shifted into her dragon. She and Xander had shifted twice since they mated. Each time, she got better at controlling her dragon.

"*Let's go!*" her dragon cried, excited to be out in an unknown city.

"*Just don't let us be seen. What would people say when they see an eight-foot-long dragon flying in the sky?*" she warned her dragon, rolled her eyes, and shot higher. This time, Xander was right behind her.

"*I will never get used to seeing you. You are beautiful, Roxie.*" Xander's voice came through her mind. She turned to look at him and sighed.

"*I love seeing you. You look like a fire at the very center. Now take me around New York City and then make love to me when we get home,*" she told him with a jerk of her head.

"*As my queen commands.*" He shot past her and took her to Central Park. They spiraled around and Xander called to her.

"*This place is beautiful at dawn. If we come back, I'll take you,*" Xander said. She looked at it from the view of a painter and mentally smiled.

"*I have a question,*" she called to him. His dragon's head turned to look at her. They were high above the clouds, hidden from any nighttime eyes.

176

"Shoot, my love."

"Do you breathe fire? I saw you smoking when your temper was fraying." Her dragon circled around him, nudging his head with her own. His dragon replied kindly and wrapped one claw around her own.

"Yes, I breathe fire. All the dragons in my family do."

"Can I?" she asked. She hadn't thought to try.

"Since you are mated to me, most likely. If the mate isn't a dragon, he or she will take on the same qualities as their mate. Usually, they are the same color too, so you are unique."

"Why didn't I take your color?" Were they not truly mated if she didn't look like him?

"I think subconsciously you wanted to remain your own dragon. You still have fiery colors, except you have taken on a myriad of colors. Give breathing fire a shot. We are high up, so it will damage nothing." His dragon shifted back, using his wings to keep him hovering in the air.

"All right, dragon. What do we get?" she asked her dragon. Her dragon smirked.

"Watch this!" Roxie let her take over and mentally gasped when a ball of fire came shooting out. Xander shot to the left and dodged the ball.

"Sorry!" Roxie called to him.

"No harm was done. That is a unique power too. I just breathe streams of fire. You shoot balls of it. If you ever were in danger, you could do some serious damage," he told her. She let those thoughts settle in her heart, and she spun in a circle.

"Interesting. What dragons are Antonio's family?" She remembered the wonderful family she met a few weeks ago. Marta was coming to her show. She promised to buy any paintings she loved for Anthony's restaurant.

"Water dragons. Come, we should head home and get some sleep. I also want to wrap you up in my arms and that is hard to do when we are dragons. Follow me and do exactly what I do to shift back. This is harder than

177

shifting into our dragons because of the angle we'll have to land. I'll give you the all-clear, then you land." His voice brokered no argument.

"*Okay, Xander.*" She nodded her head to reiterate her agreement and followed behind him. She thought about how she would react tomorrow, seeing her artwork displayed for people to look at. Roxie had a lengthy conversation coming with her mom and dad about their connection to Mitchell. She'd decided if they insisted on keeping ties with his family, she would cut ties with them. She couldn't have Mitch continue to be in her life, even with a distant connection between her mom and his mom.

"*Watch carefully,*" Xander called. She turned her attention to his dragon. He hooked on with a front claw and shifted. He was a naked man hanging off the balcony. Xander pulled himself up and over and waved her in. She hooked both front claws to the balcony. It gave a precarious groan. Quickly envisioning herself as a human, she shifted back, hanging onto the edge. Using her newfound strength, she pulled herself up and over.

"That was exhilarating!" she yelled, running over to hug him close. He wrapped her into a tight hug and kissed the top of her head.

"I love you. Let's get another shower and head to bed. I have some loving to shower on you once we are out." He kissed her and walked them into the enormous bathroom. Her legs were jelly.

"Can we get in the tub?" she asked. He smirked and nodded.

"I'll massage your back, maybe even repeat what we did earlier," he whispered, nipping at her neck. She jumped at the pain and looked into the mirror to see a very visible hickey.

"Marking your territory?" She lifted an eyebrow, and he laughed.

"Maybe. I just want Mitchell to know you will never be his ever again. I know what Peter said this evening, but I don't trust him to want both of you," he growled into her mouth, pressing his

178

lips firmly to hers. She smiled into the kiss and let him slip his tongue in to mate with hers. Wrapping her arms tight around his waist, she tried to convey all her love into the kiss.

"I need you," he moaned. She knew he did. His cock was pressing into her soft belly.

"Get me in the bath," she commanded. He chuckled and stepped away to get the water going. Once it was warm enough, he put the jasmine-scented bubble bath in the water.

"Get in," he ordered. She smiled, loving the commanding side of him. She stepped into the water and sank down to her shoulders. Closing her eyes, she felt her muscles slowly relaxing. Xander slipped in across from her and pressed the jets on. He rubbed the arch of her foot. She moaned as he pressed up to the ball of her foot and then down to the heel. He switched to her other foot, then moved to the top, rubbing each of her toes. She couldn't keep her pleasure anymore.

"Oh, God, Xander!"

"I take that you like it?" he chuckled. His hands moved up to her calves, and he gave them the same attention he did her feet. He worked up to the top of her thighs. She wanted him to touch her so badly, her body on fire for him to sink into her wet pussy.

To her disappointment, he skipped her core and grabbed her hands. She watched in fascination as he rotated her wrist and pulled on each of her fingers.

"You are spoiling me. I could get used to this," she sighed.

"Get used to it. I will do this for you whenever you need it. I love you, and you deserve to be spoiled." He bent down and kissed her hand. "Turn around," he instructed, putting his hands on her shoulders.

She turned around and pressed her back against his chiseled chest. She would never get used to how amazing his body was. He should be on the cover of a fashion magazine. Instead, he was all hers for the taking.

He put his hands on her lower back and worked upwards, just like how the masseuse taught them. She leaned forward, her head lolling against her chest. The pleasure building in her body was becoming unbearable, and she needed relief.

"Xander," she moaned, and he placed a kiss in the center of her shoulders.

"Do you need more?" His husky voice washed over her. She knew he was just as affected as she was. The proof was poking her in the back.

"I need to be riding your cock." She turned around and straddled his waist. Even in the water, she was slick enough for him to enter her. Her eyes connected with his, and she gasped. He had his dragon's eyes. She felt her pussy flush and couldn't contain her need anymore.

She placed her hands on his shoulders, maintaining eye contact as she slid down on his rock hard cock. She pushed down an inch, then pulled up, inching down further. Roxie took her time torturing him and herself.

"You are so fucking tight, Roxie. Please stop tormenting me," he growled, his hands gripping her hips tightly. There would be no escaping him tonight. She loved him skating on the cusp of losing control of his dragon. She shot down, impaling herself so hard on his cock, it spurred on her orgasm. Roxie had no idea she could orgasm just by being fully seated on him.

"Baby, you've got to move," his voice came out as churned gravel. She bounced up and down, letting him guide her hips. Capturing his lips on hers, she pushed her tongue deep. Her belly slowly tightened with the signs of another mind-bending orgasm. Her nails dug into his shoulders, and she sped up.

"Fucking sexy. I love watching your tits bounce." He bent his head. Using one hand, he gripped her breast and sucked her nipple into his mouth. Her head dropped back, and she gasped. He wasn't being gentle. He switched to her other breast, and she moaned when he bit down.

"I love it when you are rough with me." She clenched her pussy tightly on his dick, and he sucked hard on her tits. "I'm close," she moaned.

The other hand he had on her hip reached between her wet folds and stroked her clit. The shock sped her along. He touched her again, and she shattered. Jerking in his arms, her pussy clenched his cock so hard it hurt. Her nails dug deep enough to draw blood. She couldn't get out a scream because her breath got caught in her throat. He took over, slamming into her until he too went rigid. He spent his hot seed deep into her. She collapsed onto his chest, her breathing erratic.

"I love you," he whispered into her hair.

"I love you too." She lifted her head for a gentle kiss. She was limp like a noodle and didn't think she'd be able to move soon.

"We should get out," he remarked, wrapping his arms around her and standing. She didn't know how he had the strength to move, but at the moment, she was grateful. Quickly, he wrapped them both in towels, drying her off. He carried her to their bed and lay down, pulling her back against his chest.

"Sleep. We need to be up soon." He kissed her head, and they fell asleep. She dreamed of confronting Mitchell and winning.

CHAPTER FORTY-THREE

Roxie awoke wrapped in Xander's arms. She felt warm and content, her head resting on his chest. Stretching out her legs, she opened her eyes, and it took her a minute to place her surroundings. She wasn't in her king-sized bed at home. Their walls were a warm peach, but this room had a stark white. Their comforter was a blanket made for her by her grandmother; this one was a thick white down comforter. The sheets were soft but not her jersey sheets at home. The only similarity was Xander wrapped around her body, keeping her warm against the air conditioning blasting in the room.

She sat up and groaned as a sharp pain stabbed behind her eyes. Why, of all days, did she have to wake with a headache today? Debating on whether she wanted to get up and dig around her bag for a painkiller, she felt Xander stir. His warm hand settled on the back of her neck and rubbed. Slowly the pain dissipated, and she could lay back down on his broad, sculpted chest. She would have to get Xander to pose for her one day. Roxie didn't normally do portraits, but with him, she wanted to capture his beauty. Maybe she could get him to let her draw his dragon in flight over the woods in White Valley.

"You okay, baby?" he mumbled. She smiled. She could tell he wasn't fully awake.

"Now I am. I think the stress of today is already hitting my body. What time did Jordan say he would be there?" she murmured into his shoulder, her eyes closed, and sleep slowly gaining on her again.

"Eight-thirty. We have another hour until we need to be awake," Xander answered. She nuzzled her face into his neck and surrendered to sleep once again.

Xander woke her with a gentle shake. Rubbing her eyes, she sat up and saw the clock read eight. She took in her handsome mate wearing a pair of black pajama bottoms that slung low on his narrow hips. He wasn't wearing a shirt, just the way she liked her man in the morning. Admiring his body, she once again marveled at how this handsome man who could have anyone in the world wanted her. She was a big girl, one society actively shamed for being overweight. She knew she was big; it took her a long time and many scars from her teen years to come to terms with her body. She ate healthily, went for walks regularly, and did her best to take care of herself.

When she married Mitchell, he had put her on a strict diet, one that made her lose twenty pounds but made her so light-headed that she fainted at one of his art shows. The doctor berated her for eating too little and told her to make sure she ate proper portions. He directed her to a nutritionist. She had been wonderful and helped Roxie gain a new outlook on her life. Mitchell was still unhappy with her progress, and when he became angry at her, he would call her a "fat cow" and moo at her.

At the height of their divorce proceedings, he had argued that she owed him money for her going to the nutritionist. Her lawyer and the judge shut him down when she brought out the medical charts from her passing out. It was the only time the judge had sided with her on anything. Mitchell kept the house, cars, her artwork, and art supplies. She'd come home to Evelyn crying about losing everything. Evelyn helped her find a cheap, used car and move out of Mitchell's mansion and in with her.

"Baby?" Xander called her. She looked up and realized he had been talking to her while she went down the memory lane.

"Yes?"

"I said breakfast is here. Come eat and then you can get dressed," he repeated with a gentle smile. When she got lost in her head, he would be patiently waiting for her to come back to him. He never seemed to mind. If anything, he found it endearing. She nodded and grabbed his shirt to wear. He insisted she sleeps naked as he did. At first, she objected. Enough body parts stuck together when she got hot. She didn't need to peel her legs apart every morning. His shirt hugged her curves but was long enough to reach mid-thigh.

"Mmm, I love you in my shirt. It makes me want to take it off and make love to you again." His deep voice strained as his eyes dilated. She blushed and pulled him down for a gentle kiss.

"I'd say yes in a heartbeat if I weren't starving and if everyone wouldn't be here in thirty minutes," she replied.

"Damn, the second everything is over today, I am making love to you until neither of us can stand anymore," he promised and she felt a bolt shoot through her body and settle in her core. Her body could never reject him and almost always was ready for him the instant he looked at her.

"Then let's get this done quickly," she demanded, and they walked out to have breakfast before everyone showed up. She sat down to see a pile of pancakes, a bowl of strawberries, and plenty of coffee.

"You always know just what I need. I could never ask for a better mate," she flirted and kissed his cheek. He smirked and sat in the chair across from her, his feet intertwined with hers.

"I always know what you need. I never want you to feel anything less than loved for the rest of our lives. Being dragons, we will be together for hundreds of years. I hope you are prepared to be spoiled," he warned. She beamed at him and took a bite of her pancakes. The pancake was fluffy with just the right amount of butter to syrup ratio. She devoured her plate and the entire bowl of strawberries before she felt full. It was something she was slowly getting used to. In the past, she would eat half of the pancakes and most of the strawberries and felt full. Being a dragon, she could eat more but still maintain her curvy figure.

"That was delicious. Thank you." She looked up to see his eyes far away. She could tell he was thinking about what they had to do that day.

"Penny for your thoughts?" she asked, touching his hand to gain his attention.

"You know Mitchell best. I just know him from conventions, and he struck me as the competitive type. Will he cause a scene today at the gallery?"

She considered his question. *Would Mitchell explode?*

"Possibly. He never enjoyed losing at game night. I would purposely lose to avoid his anger. He was pretty volatile. Any insignificant thing could set him off. The only time I ever saw him control his temper was in front of his clients. He has plenty of celebrities and billionaires who ask for his help in finding the right art piece. He could go back and forth with one all day and never lose it. The second he got home, he would throw something, and it would break. He threw a picture of my family once. After that, I hid all of my breakable things. I didn't want him to take his temper out on my precious memories. I think it depends on who is around. If we go and the gallery is empty, I think we will see the angry Mitchell. If there are any clients around, he will do his best to be cooperative," she explained, watching his eyes burn with anger when she mentioned Mitchell's behavior toward her.

"He never hurt me. If he had touched me, I would have left him long before I did," she promised, patting his hand. He turned it over and laced their fingers together.

"If he had put a finger on you, I would kill him today, not just humiliate him. Are you done?" he asked, changing the subject with a nod to her plate.

185

"Yes, I will run through the shower quickly and get ready for today. Let me know when everyone gets here." She got up, kissed him quickly on the lips, and made her way to the bathroom.

"Want company?" he called. She turned to see him still sitting at the table, his hands clenched tightly in front of him.

"Not today, love. I will make it quick, and our showers are anything but quick." Roxie punctuated her words with a wink and a blown kiss before shutting the door. She loved Xander, but today she needed a little space to get in the right mindset for her showdown with Mitchell. She wanted to be the one to demand her work back. Roxie wanted to shove the court order in his face and learn how he got his hands on the work she made for gifts. Today, she would stand up to her ex-husband and get him out of her life once and for all.

CHAPTER FORTY-FOUR

Roxie sat at the small kitchen table with a cup of coffee while listening to Jordan explaining their plan.

"I have several local shifter police officers meeting us at the gallery. I spoke with Sally and she got me in touch with the chief of police here in New York City. He could spare three officers to help us enforce the court order. Sally purposely left the order vague, meaning we have the right to every single piece of artwork that has Roxie's signature," Jordan explained.

"Do you know about all the artwork kept in the warehouse down the street from the gallery?" she asked. Marcus and his crew were in the room listening to everything carefully.

"Yes, I have a copy of the order for them and Officer Brown is a bear shifter. He will accompany them to make sure they give your works back without damages. I will come with Officers Killen and Montrose. Both are wolf shifters," Jordan said.

Roxie looked at the three men. Officer Brown had rich chestnut hair with almost black eyes. His skin was a deep tan, and his muscles bulged under his uniform. Officer Killen had white hair and bright blue eyes. He was much thinner than Officer Brown but still towered over her. Officer Montrose had black eyes, black hair, chocolate skin, and was, in her opinion, the most attractive of the three. He had an amiable smile and didn't overwhelm her by glaring at her. She felt she was an inconvenience for the other two officers.

187

"Thank you for helping me get my artwork back. You do not understand how wonderful it feels to almost be through with my ex-husband and his poisonous ways," she thanked each man and gave them a soft smile. Xander was standing behind her with his hand on her shoulder, lending her some of his support. She knew he could tell that she was nervous around these officers.

"We should thank you," Officer Montrose said, his voice a rich baritone.

"Why?" She gave him a confused look and looked up at Xander to see if he had any idea why they would thank her. He shrugged and nodded toward Officer Montrose.

"We've been trying to pin your ex-husband with charges for almost a year now. We know he is dealing in black market artwork. This gives us an opportunity to snoop officially. Officer Brown will do the official investigation. We will question Mitchell Wright subtly while getting you your work," he explained, patting her hand and nodding at Xander.

"What has Mitchell done exactly?" She wanted to know. She had been married to the man. If he was doing illegal things while they were married, she wouldn't want to be connected to it in any way possible.

"Mitchell has Jenner Kingsly as a client. Kingsly is known for his mob connections. He is the mastermind behind some high stake robberies of museums and banks. He is never caught because it is the henchmen we capture and can never connect him to them in any capacity to arrest him. Your ex-husband has sold him several pieces of art in the past three years. We have a hunch he is letting Kingsly use his warehouse for drug deals and weapons storage."

"Oh my god, I cannot believe Mitchell would be so stupid! His family has worked so hard to build their name, and he is going to let it all go to waste." She shook her head, and her phone buzzed with an unknown number.

"Answer it," Officer Montrose encouraged her.

"Hello?" she whispered into the phone.

"Roxie, why are you in New York?" Her mother's shrill voice came on the other end. She hung up and tossed her phone away. Xander caught it midair and saved it from crashing onto the floor.

"Who was it?" Officer Montrose asked.

"My mother. She loves Mitchell more than she could ever love me. She gave him all the artwork I painted for her and my father to put up in the gallery. He couldn't legally sell them because they were all gifts. My art available for sale is in the warehouse," she explained. She watched as Xander rubbed a hand down his face and shook his head.

"I bet Mitchell called her to tell her I was causing problems for him," she hypothesized.

"She is close to your ex-husband?" Officer Killen questioned and Roxie nodded.

"Our mothers were best friends in high school and college. My mom is always looking for a way to stay connected to the high society of New York. My father is content to live as an accountant in Virginia." She was furious at Mitchell and her mother. "When do we get my work back, I need to have a chat with my mother about her behavior," she growled and several of the surrounding men took a step back. Her dragon echoed her feelings and was making herself known.

"Now, Marcus and his men will go to the warehouse directly from here. He will let us know when they have your works safely. While they do that, we will confront Mitchell and make him return all work with your signature from the gallery. I had Rhett swing by the gallery before he came over, and it looked like Mitchell slept in the small office. I think he expected us to steal them in the night and be able to arrest us," Xander shared. Roxie laughed at the idea of Mitchell sleeping in his small office. There was no way he would have enjoyed that; he was spoiled rotten and refused to sleep on anything less than a high count Egyptian cotton.

189

"Now that I would have liked to see. Mitchell's idea of roughing it was sleeping at a four-star hotel." She giggled and the others chuckled. None of them besides Xander's family knew Mitchell at all, but she would bet with the picture she painted for them, they got the idea that he was a spoiled rotten man-boy. Someone who would never grow up and expect his partner to be his mother.

"Okay, let's get going!" She stood up and marched to the door.

"Whoa, we need to let Marcus and his men get in place. I want them inside the warehouse before we get anywhere near Mitchell." Xander stopped her with a firm hand on her wrist. She almost yanked her hand out of his grasp but did not want to make a scene in front of the others.

"*Let go,*" she mind linked Xander. He dropped her hand like it was on fire, and she glared up at him.

"*Calm down, love. You look ready to blow your top. I don't want you to do something you are going to regret when your dragon isn't fighting you for control.*" Xander's voice filled her head. Her dragon huffed but relaxed so Roxie could function as a wholly human again.

"*I want Mitchell to feel how I felt when I found out he was cheating on me. I want to break him!*" she replied, her eyes narrowing at him.

"*You will just let the others get into position. We don't know what he is up to. He could have some of his mafia buddies waiting for Marcus and his men. I want to know if they can get a hand on your work before we tip off Mitchell,*" Xander urged. She knew he made sense; she was just tired of waiting. He bent his head and kissed her. She melted into his arms and wrapped her arms around his neck. His tongue dove in, distracting her from the others in the room. She fought for dominance in the kiss and enjoyed losing to his small growl. His hands cupped her face, holding her captive as he explored every inch of her mouth. His agile tongue tangled with hers, pulling small mews out of her mouth.

"Enough, Xander!" Jordan called. Roxie blinked and looked around. She had completely forgotten the men were still in the room. Looking up at Xander, he gave her a smug look. She knew he had planned the kiss. Looking around, Marcus and his men were gone, as well as Officer Brown.

"I will get you back," she warned, and Rhett laughed.

"You've turned into a feisty one, Roxie," James commented and she beamed with pride. Ever since meeting Xander, she felt she was taking control of her life more each day. She liked her newfound confidence and couldn't wait to see how it helped her against Mitchell and her mother.

"Time to go," Xander called out ten minutes later, after looking at a message on his phone. She bounced up, and using some of her nervous energy, she kissed him quickly, putting all her emotions into the small kiss.

"I love you," Xander told her. She stared up into his hypnotizing eyes.

"I love you too."

CHAPTER FORTY-FIVE

Xander climbed into the cab with Rhett, Roxie, his dad, and Jordan. The two officers were going in their own vehicles. "You okay?" he asked her. He could feel her shaking in his arms. He wasn't sure if it was nervousness or anger. When she growled earlier, it had worried him. She'd only been a dragon for a week, and here he was asking her to keep her temper under control while confronting her ex-husband. He was beyond angry with her mother. Xander guessed Mitchell called her to tell her Roxie was bothering him, and he wanted her to put an end to it. When he had researched her mother, he found out some interesting things about her family.

She had lied about her father being arrested for insider trading. Her family disowned her when she failed a semester in college. Meredith Jones had lied about her fall from grace to her family, and Xander knew her parents rather well. They always bought their art from him. He wondered if they even knew about Roxie and her sister Elizabeth. He would ask Roxie if she wanted to meet them. He didn't know how much he could dig into her past and not be overstepping.

Her phone buzzed again. He looked down to see it was the same number that called her that morning. She clicked reject the call and huffed, staring out the window, watching New York City pass her by. He watched her. She still hadn't answered his question.

"Roxie," he probed and her head whipped around to look at him.

"What?"

"Are you okay? You never answered when I asked earlier," he repeated. She stared at him in confusion.

"I'm sorry. I've been stuck in my head for too long. We should be at the gallery soon. I recognize the shops around. Mitchell loved that he was in the middle of-the-art district and a very important person in New York society." She leaned her head on his shoulder, and he kissed her temple.

"No worries. I get lost in thoughts too. How long do you think your mom will keep calling you?" He wanted to get her thoughts on something different.

"Not sure. I know after we take everything from Mitchell, she will have a field day. I don't get why he is so important to her. She has other friends besides his mom. Why can't she talk to one of them?" she questioned.

He paused and replied, "I did some digging into your mom after she called you. I suspected how she found your number."

"She probably grabbed it from my dad," she suggested.

"I don't think so. I got the feeling that the two of them weren't actually on speaking terms and he may sleep at a hotel," he answered. He knew it to be true because he did a background check on her father.

"Why would he be at a hotel? Every time I see them, they are always together with a united front against anything I've ever wanted to do in my life," she shared. Her eyebrows scrunched together as she thought through his suggestion.

"Parents hide many things from their children. Xander and Rhett don't know about every disagreement his mother and I have had. We are mates, but that doesn't mean we see eye to eye on everything. It is okay to disagree. Just don't go to bed mad. That is how resentment builds, and you wake up just as angry. There have been nights Koraline and I didn't go to bed because we were

193

working out a huge argument," his dad interjected. He looked at him in surprise.

"You and Mom fight?"

"Usually with building a new hotel, we both have sound ideas, and with almost two hundred years together, things get heated. It makes the sex that much more enjoyable though." He laughed. Xander paled and Rhett covered his ears.

"Gross, Dad! I may be a hundred, but I still never want to know you and Mom are doing it," Xander objected.

"How come you only have Xander and Rhett?" Roxie asked.

"Once a dragon reaches two hundred, they cannot breed anymore. We managed Xander and Rhett right before Koraline turned two hundred. You, being only twenty-seven, can have as many babies as you like. Koraline and I have always wanted lots of grandchildren. We were worried about Xander reaching a hundred with no mate in sight."

"Dad," he warned, and his dad stopped talking as Roxie laughed. He was glad to see her laughing again. All too soon, the laughter died from her lips and the taxi pulled to a stop. Xander paid the driver, and they all stepped out onto the steps. The Golden Painting had gilded columns holding up a large balcony, a banner hung inviting people in to see the mysterious R.J. artist. The name was written in gaudy golden script over the door and Mitchell's face placed on the door with his name underneath stating he was the current manager.

"This place is even worse than I remember. He didn't have his face plastered on the door before." Roxie curled up her lips in disgust and took Xander's hand.

"Just goes to show how big a head he is getting." Rhett scoffed and Roxie nodded her agreement. Xander watched his mate. She was amazing. Standing here, he could feel the nerves in her body dissipate completely.

"Where are Jordan and the officers?" his dad asked Xander, looking around and humming. Xander cautiously looked around. He didn't want to look worried. Out of the corner of his eye, he saw Jordan and the two officers walking. The officers changed into plain clothes. Jordan would do the talking, and if needed, they would reveal who they were.

"There they are." Xander motioned with his head. Roxie, Rhett, and his dad turned to see them walking. Jordan looked confident. He struck an imposing figure at almost 6'4. He had broad shoulders and was dressed to impress in a dark gray three-piece suit. Xander had only ever seen him once out of a suit, and it was at a barbecue his parents had hosted a few years back. He wondered if Josie had her sights set on him next to find a mate. He knew they were good friends before Rhett met her.

"We are ready. I want only Roxie and Xander with me when I first speak to Mitchell. If need be, I will ask Officer Montrose to come. I want Rhett and James to walk around the gallery and remove the R.J. paintings. Officer Killen will go with you. Do you have a way to store them?" Jordan asked Rhett and James, smiling.

"We will pack them in the waiting van across the street. We parked it there this morning to make sure we have an easy place to load the paintings." Rhett pointed the black unmarked van. Xander approved their plan last night after Roxie had slipped into their room to calm herself down.

"Perfect. Let's get this over with," he said, pulling Roxie behind him. He pushed open the door to the gallery. No one paid them any attention until the three of them were at Mitchell's office door.

"I'm sorry. The manager is not taking appointments today," a short woman with light blonde hair and black brows announced. Xander felt Roxie stiffen.

"Barbie," Roxie whispered. He knew at once this was the woman who had taken Mitchell from his mate. He couldn't say he

195

was mad because he met Roxie, but it upset him she was around. He took in the small woman and couldn't see how Mitchell would have ever let Roxie go. Barbie was the quintessential beautiful woman. Yes, she was beautiful and had long legs and perky breasts. She was wearing a tight-fitting dress of blood-red. Her nails and lips matched perfectly. Her hair, he could tell, had been dyed a light blonde. He would never put a woman down for her looks, but he just preferred his woman on the curvier side, not afraid to let him pound away while making love.

"Hello, Roxie, why are you here?" Barbie asked. She crossed her arms and tapped one manicured finger on her arm.

"I am here to speak to Mitch," she replied and opened the office door, storming in with the men hot on her heels.

CHAPTER FORTY-SIX

Roxie was fuming. Mitchell refused to let her work for him because it was mixing business and pleasure, but here was Barbie, still working as his secretary. She wanted to slap the rich right out of Mitchell but knew it would not make her feel better. The only thing to make her feel better was taking back what was rightfully hers. She slammed the door open and watched Mitchell jump to his feet and glared at her.

"I told you if you come within a hundred feet of the gallery, I am going to have you arrested!" he yelled. She laughed and put her hands on her hips. It was time for her to find her inner dragon and stand up to him. She let him get away with far too much when they were married and during the divorce proceedings.

"You won't call the police, because if you do, they will want to know why you are keeping my artwork," she replied, enjoying the shade of red his face was turning.

"I have every right to those paintings. That was our agreement in the divorce," he shot back, his hands curled into fists at his side. She couldn't believe she had ever fallen in love with this man. He was not much taller than her at 5'7, and his hair was oily from the amount of product he put in it to make it stay slicked back. She could tell he had put on a significant amount of weight since she last saw him. She almost felt sorry he had to see her with her new fiancé, but not enough to cave in to his wants.

"Our agreement was for you to sell my art, not keep it locked away in a warehouse and show off the work I gave my family as gifts. You have no right to any of the artwork out there and how you got them is beyond me." She kept her voice calm. She knew it irritated him the most to be the one losing his cool.

"Your mother was kind enough to give me all the pieces after I explained you would never make it as an artist. I told her they were wasting space on her walls, and if she wanted to ever show her face in New York society again with her parents, she would need to get rid of them. She was more than happy to send me everything you made, even from the time you were in college. You've improved since college. I've had plenty of offers on your art. Unfortunately, since they are not the ones you made while we were married, I can't sell them. Poor pitiful Roxie, your family will never accept you. Just come back home and everything will be back to normal. I will even put your other art up and sell them if only you become my wife again." Mitchell came around the desk this time, his hands outstretched. She laughed and pushed him away from her.

"I will never come back to you. You were a horrible husband to me. You cheated on me with Barbie, and I bet she wasn't the only one. You put me down about my artwork and never once complimented me after we got married. You were two different people, the Mitchell who courted me and the Mitchell who married me and discarded me for the next best thing.

"I have Xander. He is my mate, and I know how mates are supposed to be there for each other. They build each other up, not put each other down to make yourself feel better. Xander and I are partners in everything. He will help me sell my artwork, and you won't see a penny of the money. We gave you a chance to work through things in the most civil way, but now I have a court order demanding you to return any artwork with my signature on it. That means all those hanging in the gallery plus the ones you have in your warehouse." She motioned for Jordan to step forward. He did and handed Mitchell the court order.

"It is all there. All artwork created by Roxie Jones are to be returned to her. If you prove noncompliant, it will force me to get the police involved. Judge Sally Truitt signed the court order, and it goes into effect today," Jordan explained. Roxie watched Mitchell's face turn purple.

"She can have everything hanging in the gallery. Unfortunately, I ruined all her work in the warehouse in a fire." Mitchell smirked, pressing a button on his phone, and Roxie gasped. What did he mean by fire?

"Impossible. We checked out the warehouse yesterday," Xander interjected, pulling Roxie toward him.

"The button I just pressed detonates explosives all around the warehouse. I told you, I would burn all your work before I let you have them back." Mitchell cackled with glee and Roxie cringed. This was not the man she knew. What happened to him?

"Why would you do that? What did I do to you?" she demanded, wrenching out of Xander's grasp and stepping toward her deranged ex-husband.

"You left me! You humiliated me! Now I am stuck marrying that plastic barbie because you told everyone I cheated on you. Not one of my clients trusts me anymore. They feel because I cheated on someone as amazing as you, I will swindle them out of their money," he sneered and she flinched back as his hand came down on the desk hard.

"You were the one who cheated. Why would I keep quiet about it?" She wanted to know who in their right mind would cover for the man who betrayed her.

"You are the granddaughter of one of the most powerful couples in New York society. You were my ticket to making a fortune. This place is going bankrupt, thanks to your mate," he spat and she turned to look at Xander. She didn't understand why her grandparents were part of the issue.

199

"Roxie, I've been in this business for a long time. Mitchell was mismanaging his funds, and those last few artists he showcased, they did not sell many pieces. I have picked talented artists and sold all their work on opening night. Some of Mitchell's clients have come to me to find art for their homes and businesses. He blames me for taking them, and I suspect when he found out we are together from your mother, he saw me as taking away his woman too. He knows you are a goldmine for selling art, now that your work in the gallery are getting attention. The problem is, with only getting five percent of each painting, he won't be able to make back the money he is in debt to the Italian mafia. He needs you back and all the money from your sales in order not to die at their hands. I did some digging after the threat and the letter asking you to come back as his wife again. Turns out, he is several million dollars in debt and the mafia doesn't take lightly to debtors who can't pay. The insurance from your warehouse fire might get you close," Xander commented. He had pulled Roxie into his arms, shielding her from Mitchell's vile gaze.

"That explains a lot, but not why people won't trust him anymore. Many high power men cheat on their wives. A lot of the men I met while married to Mitchell had mistresses on the side." She glared at Mitchell when he stepped toward her again. This time she felt her dragon pulse and her eyes change. Mitchell recoiled and hissed.

"What the hell?"

"Oh, did I forget to mention? Xander and I mated. We cannot be pulled apart ever, and I may have taken on some of his characteristics." She laughed and let her dragon shift one of her hands into a claw. Mitchell cowered back.

"Take all your damn art back and get out of my office! I don't want to be married to a thing like you!"

"I wasn't ever going to come back," she quipped and turned to look at Jordan and Xander.

"I want my artwork back now. Then we get out of here and let Officers Killen and Montrose have a crack at Mitchell. I am sure they have quite a few questions about his connection to the mafia." She sent one last glare at Mitchell, who was huddled into the back corner of his office.

"Sounds like a plan. You go get started. I need a word with Mitchell." Xander sent her on her way. She wanted to stay and know what they would talk about, but she'd wait until tonight. Roxie knew Xander would never keep secrets from her. She kissed him, making sure Mitchell saw the change in Xander's eyes as his dragon surfaced in a fit of desire.

"Just don't kill him," she remarked and walked out of the office, feeling a million times lighter than when she had stepped inside.

CHAPTER FORTY-SEVEN

Xander watched his mate walk out of the office with Jordan following behind. He turned back to the cowering piece of shit his mate once called a husband.

"Here is what you will do, Mitchell. You will never contact Roxie again. You will never talk to anyone in her family again, and that includes trying to manipulate her mother. We both know I can blow the whistle on your warehouse fire. If any of the men I have at the warehouse get so much as a scratch on them, you will burn in hell. Roxie showed you a little of what she is capable of. Remember, I have been a dragon for a hundred years; Roxie has been one for about a week. I am much more deadly and can show up. You will never see me coming. Now tell me why you really need Roxie back, aside from the money her artwork will bring in," he demanded, forcing Mitchell to sit in a chair. He took the desk chair and waited. His fingers steeped in front of his face.

"I, uh, um . . ." Mitchell stuttered and Xander smirked. He wasn't so big and bad when an alpha was around him.

"While you are still young, Mitchell," Xander roared. He enjoyed watching Mitchell cower and stumble over his words.

"Her grandparents want to meet her. They came to see the artwork and recognized her name. They are estranged from her mother, but they want Roxie and her sister, Elizabeth, to be a part of their lives. They want to show off their successful granddaughters to everyone." Mitch ducked his head when Xander growled.

"Why now?" he demanded.

"I don't know. I just know Jacob Lunsford approached me the other day and said if I got Roxie back, he would erase all my debt with the mafia," Mitchell explained and Xander sighed. He knew Jacob Lunsford; he was a powerful senator and was ruthless in his business deals. His parents had to go through him to get their hotels in New York City approved.

"Thank you. Now I believe Officer Montrose has some questions about your illegal activities." He stood with a sinister smile on his face and strode out of the office.

"Officer, he is all yours," he told Officer Montrose with a nod of his head. He walked over to where Roxie was, ordering around several gallery employees.

"I want you to get me bubble wrap, tape, and a wooden crate to put all these in," Roxie told a thin boy. He looked no older than eighteen. His eyes were wide at the way Roxie was snapping at everyone.

"Don't just touch it with your bare hands! That will ruin the paint," she chastised a young woman.

"Roxie, calm down, sweetheart. No one is going to purposely damage your work." He wrapped her up in a tight hug, pushing her face into his chest, trying to pass some of his calm on to her.

"I just want out of here. Too many terrible memories of sucking up to clients as they walked around the artwork. I am also furious my mother was so stupid for giving away all the work I put my heart into. How could my dad let her give them all away?" she whispered into his chest. He felt her tremble and knew she was close to tears again.

"I think you need to talk to your parents about that. You won't ever get closure until you talk with them," he suggested, pulling back enough to look down into her beautiful shining blue eyes.

"I'll talk to Dad first. I am so angry with my mom, I think I might accidentally lose control of my dragon like I did with Mitchell." She nuzzled her nose into his chest, taking a deep breath.

"We can set up a dinner for him to come over. I know you want me to meet him," Xander replied, and she beamed at him. He loved making her happy. It made him feel good.

"Come, let's get all your work put away and then call Marcus. I don't like how quiet he has been since this morning. I sent him a message when Mitchell claimed to have blown the warehouse. He hasn't answered." Worry passed through her eyes. She nodded and turned out of his arms and began directing four employees on how she wanted the paintings packed up.

It took three hours for her to be satisfied with the way they had packed them; she made one kid redo his work three times before she was happy. He should have her come down to his gallery and teach his workers how to handle art. She knew just how to wrap her canvases to keep them in pristine condition. He heard from Marcus finally, saying they would meet everyone at the hotel and explain what happened. He promised all of Roxie's art had been rescued before the fire took hold of the building, and it had hurt no one.

"There, now we just need to get these into the van and we can go." Roxie came over to him, wiping the sweat from her brow. He watched the four employees step back. He didn't blame them. Roxie had come into her own and took no nonsense.

"Rhett and Dad can put them in the van. Let the poor employees go back to work," Xander said, laughing when she gave him a confused look. She turned around in time for the employees to run off in the opposite direction.

"What did I do?" she wanted to know.

"You might have scared them with how particular you were with your protective measures. That one boy you made redo his

204

work three times looked close to tears." He laughed. She blushed, and he bent to kiss her soundly on the lips.

"You are so sexy when you blush," he murmured into her lips and she smiled.

"Seems to me, you make me blush an awful lot." Her lips reconnected with his, and he gave into a passionate kiss with her. Her tongue pushed in to tangle with his own. She had such an agile tongue. Fighting for dominance over the kiss, he pushed her against a wall and slid a thigh between her legs. He had her pinned with her hands above her head, his mouth ravishing hers. His cock pulsed hard against the unyielding fabric of his dark wash jeans. He needed to be inside of her soon, or he would be in a lot of pain.

"Oh for Pete's sake!" Rhett roared, the two pulled apart reluctantly. Roxie buried her face into his chest. Her breathing was labored. He could tell their kiss affected her just as much as it had him.

"I hope everyone leaves quickly today. We have one more night in the hotel before we go home on Monday. I plan to use every second of that time trying to get you pregnant," he whispered into her ear. He felt her body shudder and couldn't resist kissing her once more.

"Don't start again. I want to get out of here," Rhett complained. Xander and Roxie turned to see him covering his eyes. They laughed, and slinging an arm over her shoulders, he walked her out of the gallery for the very last time. Her body relaxed when they stepped out of the doors.

"I will never have to see this place again," she commented. He nodded his agreement and hustled her to the van.

"Dad and I will drive the van over to the hotel. There is a taxi waiting for you two and Jordan. We will meet everyone back at the hotel, get the other artwork packed up the way Roxie wants, and drive it home," Rhett informed them. He pointed out the taxi. Xander took her hand, and they climbed into the taxi, waiting for

Jordan. He followed them a minute later with a smug look on his face.

"What's so funny?" Xander asked him once the taxi pulled away from the curb.

"You two. You are so perfect for each other. Xander, you have a fierce mate there. I hope you never piss her off. Did you see the look of panic on Mitchell's face when her hand shifted to a claw? I didn't know you had it in you, Roxie."

"I lost control of my temper," she admitted, and Jordan laughed again.

"Remind me never to piss you off. If you don't mind, I will head home after checking in with Marcus. I could only get someone to watch Daisy for me for one night."

"Who is Daisy?" Roxie asked and Xander tensed. Daisy was a sensitive subject for Jordan, although he had brought her up in front of Roxie.

"My niece. I have custody of her after her mother died last year. Her father was a drug addict and hasn't been heard from in three years," he explained. Xander could feel the pain radiating off him. His brother had been a deadbeat, and Jordan hated being related to him.

"How old is Daisy?"

"Three."

"So, she never met her dad?"

"He was arrested and never knew about her. Her mother died from cancer last year. No one else could take her financially. My parents are too old to take on a toddler. I didn't want her going into the foster care system, so I took her."

"That is impressive. You and Daisy should come over for dinner. I love little kids, and it would give you a break," Roxie offered. Xander smiled down at her, one of the many reasons he loved his mate. She was always thinking about others.

"That would be great. I don't get to go out to restaurants often. Daisy is not good at sitting long enough to manage a meal," he replied.

"Then coming to our house would be perfect. She can eat and then run around while you eat." Roxie beamed. Jordan gave her a relieved smile and nodded his agreement.

"You are amazing," Xander whispered into her ear and then kissed her temple.

"I am only doing what a decent person would do. I can feel the exhaustion coming off of him in waves," she murmured back. Xander could feel it too. When she suggested bringing Daisy over, he felt Jordan's relief.

"We are back," Roxie announced as the taxi pulled in front of the hotel. She was the first one out and gasped when she saw Marcus and his men covered in soot. Xander stopped behind her and frowned. He saw everyone was still in one piece but with a few scrapes and brusies that were already healing, thanks to shifters quick healing.

"What happened?" Roxie demanded, hands on her hips.

"Can we all get inside before we explain. I have soot in places that shouldn't have soot," Marcus complained, a deep frown on his face.

"You all can shower and then we will discuss what happened. I can have clothes brought to the room. We have two showers, so you can go two at a time," Xander suggested. He was happy he did when he saw the relief on their faces. He knew how uncomfortable it was to be covered in soot. Xander was a fire-breathing dragon. Grabbing Roxie's hand, he followed everyone up to the penthouse suite.

CHAPTER FORTY-EIGHT

Roxie settled onto the couch; her body suddenly exhausted from her showdown with Mitchell. Looking at the clock, she realized it was past lunch and her stomach growled. Xander looked over at her from the door of the suite.

"Hungry?"

"Very. Can we order room service? I bet everyone is hungry," she replied, looking around at the group of men.

"Sounds good. Everyone look at the room service menu and let me know what you want. I'll write the order and have a bellhop pick it up," Xander ordered. Roxie got up and passed out copies of the menu before walking over to her mate.

"What do you want to eat?" she asked him, wrapping an arm around his waist and resting her head against his shoulder.

"Anything is fine with me. Do you want to share something?" he asked, kissing her temple. She couldn't get enough of touching him. She wanted to always be close enough, so she could get a kiss anytime she wanted. Looking up at him, he knew what she needed and gave her a gentle kiss on the lips.

"Want to share an everything pizza minus the mushrooms?" she asked once he had released her lips.

"Sounds good, but let's get extra-large. Dealing with your ex made me hungry," he replied.

"Perfect. I'll get the orders from everyone, and you call the bellhop." She walked away and took everyone's orders. While writing Marcus's order, she noticed he was cradling one of his hands. Upon closer inspection, she noticed a nasty burn.

"What happened?" she demanded, taking his hand in her own.

He jerked out of her touch and gruffly replied, "Nothing that won't heal in a couple of days."

"That doesn't look like nothing. You need to take care of it or it will scar," she countered, trying to grab his hand again. This time Marcus stood up and walked away from her and into the bathroom.

She huffed and put her hands on her hips, looking at Greyson as she asked, "Is he always so stubborn?"

"He doesn't enjoy being fussed over. When we served together, he rarely let the medics care for any of his wounds. We shifters heal quickly, but if not properly cared for, we would have scars. Marcus doesn't seem to care, and I've learned a long time ago not to push him. He is a grumpy bear who needs a mate," Greyson replied with a shrug. She shook her head over crazy shifters and finished taking everyone's lunch order.

"You did a very brave thing today, standing up to your ex-husband," James told her as she passed by him.

"I did?" she asked. She had done what needed to be done. She wanted her artwork back and needed Mitchell out of her life forever.

"Yes, we could hear you yelling at Mitchell. I am proud of you for standing up to him and not letting him manipulate you. I am sorry about your mother giving away all the work you made for her and your dad. Koraline and I love the painting you made us. Koraline has it displayed in the main hallway, so whenever people come over, it is the first thing they see," James explained. She blushed a deep red. Roxie didn't know her gift would have been so well received. When she gave paintings to her family, they always gave a polite nod and faked their enthusiasm. She had truly found a family to accept her as her own.

"Thank you, James. That means a lot coming from you. I am excited to be joining your family," she replied, blinking back the tears that had sprung to her eyes. She loved Xander and his family. She loved how they accepted her since day one. Now she would get them as her chosen family. She still needed to have a talk with her mother about her behavior and to make an ultimatum; either she learn to accept Xander and any children who would come along or they would cut her off her life.

"Here are the orders, Xander," she said, handing him a full notebook page of orders. He gaped at the amount and laughed.

"We are feeding an army. The bellhop should be here any minute." As he finished speaking, there was a knock on the door.

"Speak of the devil," he chuckled and opened the door. Standing there was a youthful man with a mop of black hair on his head and bright green eyes. Roxie had never seen him before. Usually, Linx was their bellhop.

"Where is Linx?" she asked.

The bellhop grinned and replied, "He has been unexpectedly detained. Do you need anything?" His voice raised hackles on her neck, and she looked up at Xander. He was frowning as well and looked over his shoulder at his dad. Roxie knew this was the one hotel James frequented the most and would recognize the bellhop.

"You are not a bellhop here," James stated, and without a thought, Roxie grabbed the boy by the ear and yanked him into the room.

"Why are you here?" Xander demanded. His voice boomed throughout the room, making the teen cringe.

"I am here to take your lunch order," the teen replied, trying unsuccessfully to make Roxie let go of his ear.

"Try again," she hissed, her grip tightening. The boy whimpered and pulled at her arm to no avail.

"They sent me to get your lunch order and then poison yours. The boss did not take kindly to you blowing up his

210

warehouse," he finally confessed. Roxie released his ear and motioned for Xander to take over detaining the boy.

"Who sent you?" he demanded, walking the boy over to a chair in the middle of all the men. The teen looked around and shivered. Whoever sent him did not understand how many dangerous men were in the suite.

"I can't say," the teen replied, giving a defiant jut of his chin. Roxie sighed and leaned on one arm of the chair.

"Look, we can do this the easy way where you tell us everything, or I will let these nice men have a crack at you. Six of them are former military, two are navy seals, the others are dragons and a high power lawyer. You have a minute to decide your fate. I really hope you chose the peaceful way. You are still so young and have a life ahead of you. I bet you have a girlfriend, and she'd be pretty upset if you disappeared," Roxie coaxed, her hand touching the teen gently on his shoulder. He deflated and nodded his agreement.

"Excellent. Who sent you?" she asked, keeping her voice soft and calm.

"Jenner Kingsly. He is pissed that all his artwork just went up in flames this morning."

"We are not responsible for the fire. Mitchell Wright blew the warehouse," Roxie replied. The teen looked up in fear.

"What?"

"Mitchell Wright blew it up when I went to see him this morning. I'll give you a bit of background. That slimy sleazeball used to be my ex-husband, and I was taking back what was mine. You can tell Jenner Kingsly that Roxie Austin had nothing to do with the warehouse being blown and he should talk to the sniveling snake Mitchell." She gave him a patient smile, looking down at her nails, acting as if she were bored with the conversation.

"Yes, ma'am. I'll report back right away," the teen promised, getting to his feet and running his hands through his hair nervously.

"Wonderful. Have a delightful day and please release Linx from wherever you stashed him. I am hungry and would like my lunch brought up quickly," she replied, and the teen nodded again, running for the door.

Roxie slid into the seat he vacated and closed her eyes. She was now sporting a decent headache.

"That was amazing, and remind me never to make you angry," Peter broke the tension with his joke. The others laughed, and she gave them a tight smile.

"Marcus, while we wait for Linx to come up, why don't you tell us why Jenner Kingsly thought we blew up the warehouse," Roxie suggested. Marcus looked from her to Xander, and she saw Xander nod from the corner of her eye. She bet Marcus wasn't used to taking orders from a woman.

Xander could not believe what he had just witnessed. Roxie was amazing. She snagged the boy before he even thought about grabbing him, and her grip on his ear was impressive. Her ability to question him and get him to share what he knew was fascinating. She used a touch of sternness with a mix of gentleness to make him spill.

CHAPTER FORTY-NINE

"Well, we arrived at the warehouse just after nine o'clock. I sent Orion and Kevin in to check out the security. Turned out there were several security cameras but no actual guards. I had Greyson hack the alarm and Peter, Troy, and I went inside to retrieve the paintings. Someone had moved them from their original position in the back of the warehouse to the front marked for shipping. The nice thing is they were packaged like the rest of the artwork and easy to roll out of the building. We had just removed the second to the last crate when he heard an explosion. Greyson and Orion were still inside getting the fourth and final crate. I rushed back in to find several beams flaming and one pinning Orion down. With the help of the others, we were able to get the beam off of him. Thankfully, he only had minor cuts and no broken bones. We tried to save some other art, but the flames caught onto the oil paints and spread rapidly. It was all we could do to save Roxie's work. Troy called the fire department, and we stayed to help the firefighters fight the flames. We are a little more fire retardant than humans. It is possible when the explosion went off, Jenner Kingsly sent some men to find out what happened. When they spotted us, I am sure they called Wright and wanted to know what happened."

"Where was the explosion set?" Xander asked. Looking at his mate, he noticed she had gone silent. He knew she had the same question he did. Why were her artwork suddenly packed up and marked for shipping?

213

"In the back of the warehouse where the paintings originally were being kept. They were sitting at the front with the symbol of a raven on each box. You can look. They are in our van," Marcus answered. Xander nodded. He would look at the symbol when they left for home.

"Why were they packed up? If Mitchell wanted them destroyed, why have them protected?" Roxie mused aloud.

"That is an excellent question, one I have no answer to," Marcus explained, and Xander watched her deflate.

"Was there a name on the boxes?" she asked, trying to figure out what they would do with her work.

"No, just the raven. Know anyone with that symbol?"

"Well, it isn't the symbol for the gallery. They stamp a gold seal on the front with their last name in the middle. You don't suppose Jenner Kingsly has a raven for his symbol, do you?" she suggested, and everyone stopped to stare at her.

"I don't know, but I can look into it when I get home," Marcus replied with a thoughtful look.

"If Mitchell was selling my paintings behind my back, I would sue him for everything. His family would never sell artwork again!" she raved. Xander put his hand on her shoulders and pushed down. He hoped the pressure would stabilize her and her dragon.

"We don't have proof, Roxie, only how the paintings were stored," James argued. He, too, could see the anger rising off of his almost daughter-in-law. Roxie was steaming, literally. Her eyes had changed to slit pupils, her skin had taken on a reptilian texture, and her color had changed to her dragon's color.

"Calm down, sweetheart. The first thing we need to do is get food for you. You'll be less angry after you eat. The second thing we do is go home and set up for your show next Saturday. You might have to touch up some paintings Mitchell has had, then we will hold a successful art show and you can shove your success in his face. There is no need to get violent with the man. Just

214

humiliate him and take all his clients that way." Xander hoped his plan would sink in and his sweet, peaceful Roxie would come back to him. He'd forgotten how emotional young dragons were. He hadn't been one in quite some time. Looking at his dad, he nodded his approval of the way Xander was handling his mate.

"Is that what I have to look forward to when Josie becomes a dragon?" Rhett asked. Xander glared at him. He didn't need Rhett to set her off.

"She isn't nearly as bad as either of you. Her personality doesn't allow for her to get too dangerous. Your Josie, she will be a handful," his dad supplied, laughing at his youngest.

"Is that why I am so angry?" Roxie asked, looking up at the three dragon shifters.

"Partly. You wouldn't be reacting so strongly if your dragon was more mature. Remember, you and her have only been a pair for a week. It will take time for you two to find a balance between beast and woman," Xander's dad replied. Roxie looked up at him with fear in her eyes.

"How long will I be like this? I don't particularly enjoy being a volcano that's about to erupt all the time."

"I'd say about a month. You are an adult, so it should take you less time than a teen to get a hold of your dragon. Take her out flying every night next week and you'll be able to connect with her more. She won't push to come out when you are angry if she feels rested. Restless dragons push for control and spark anger like yours toward that teenager earlier," Xander told her. It exhausted him, her constant mood changes. No one ever mentioned helping their mate come to terms with her dragon. Marta came from an ancient line of dragon shifters, so Antonio never mentioned the change in her when they mated. He'd never thought to ask his dad about changing his mom. They had always been the most amazing mated pair.

Knock knock.

Rhett opened the door, and several carts were laden down with delicious smelling food pushed into the room. The kitchen staff announced each dish and walked it over to the person who ordered it. There were no words exchanged as everyone fell on the food, too hungry to be polite. Xander and Roxie demolished their pizza in record time. When he looked around, he saw everyone else had finished their meals too.

"If we leave now, we can be home in about five hours. Do you want to spend another night here in New York or do you want to go home?" Xander put the question to Roxie.

"I want to go home. I never want to come back here. I want to be in our bed, in our home, near my paints," she replied. He laughed at her comment about her paints. They had brought some with them, so if she got the urge, she could paint.

"Done. Everyone, we are going home today," Xander announced. All the men shared relieved smiles and cleaned up their dishes. Roxie slipped into their bedroom, and Xander said his goodbyes. Marcus and his crew would take one van home; Rhett and his dad, the other. He and Roxie would take a new car home, one he had bought for her as a surprise. Her car was almost a decade old and needed to be bigger, especially if they would expand their family.

CHAPTER FIFTY

Wednesday evening at 7:30, Roxie was sitting at a two-person round table, telling Evelyn everything she'd been through over the weekend.

"Xander is still trying to figure out who the raven symbol belongs to and what Mitch would do with my paintings. I've had to do touch-ups on almost all of my work. They were not stored properly, and some color faded. I really hope it doesn't diminish the value of my art," she explained.

"You're telling me Mitchell blew up his own warehouse to keep you from getting to your artwork, but in reality, they had packed them and were ready for shipment?" Evelyn sipped her cocktail, her chocolate eyes wide with surprise.

"Exactly. Oh, and Jenner Kingsly, the mafia boss? He sent someone to kill Xander and me because he thought we were the ones who blew up the warehouse," Roxie added. She leaned back in her chair and looked around the chic restaurant Evelyn had suggested. The place had an airy feel to it. The tables were dark wood under white table cloths. They adorned the walls with mass-produced art of flower fields, and they dressed the waitresses in light blue dresses. The waiters were dressed in black slacks and light blue button-up shirts.

"That is insane. You've moved out for a week and are already in trouble without me," Evelyn joked. Roxie laughed.

"What have you and Anderson been up to?" she asked, knowing Evelyn and Anderson had gone out on a date, thanks to snooping through Evelyn's social media pages.

"He took me to the park and we had a picnic, then we went to a bar for a few drinks," Evelyn shared as their server came over to take their orders.

"What can I get you, ladies, to eat?" the adolescent boy said.

Roxie smiled up at him and replied, "I'll have the barbecue chicken salad."

"The steak salad for me," Evelyn answered. He nodded and walked away.

"So, tell me, have you and Anderson had sex yet?" Roxie blurted out. She wanted the details on her best friend's life. Evelyn deserved to be happy, and she knew Anderson was the one to make her happy.

"Roxie!" Evelyn pretended to be shocked. Roxie shook her head.

"Oh no, you don't get to be shy now. As soon as I had gotten back from Rome, you bombarded me with questions. I want to know about you and my brother. I think it means you two are mates."

"Fine. Yes, we've had sex, and it was the best I've ever had, mind-blowing even. I felt a deeper connection to him, and I've never wanted to pick up and follow a man on his adventures. Anderson is leaving for Washington state next week. He hasn't asked me to go with him yet, but I am hoping he does," Evelyn gushed. Roxie could see the love Evelyn had for Anderson. She felt the same way about Xander; it hadn't taken over twenty-four hours for her to know Xander would be hers forever. She loved him with a fierceness that honestly scared her a little.

"I am sure he will. If you are his true mate, he won't be able to be away from you for long. Xander said mates go into a depression without each other. He said the week after Rome, he

218

couldn't sleep well. He got maybe two or three hours of sleep a night and instantly wanted to see me when he woke up."

"That is sweet. I wouldn't want Anderson not to get sleep, but it makes me feel good to know he needs me. My job at the museum is getting boring. The exhibits haven't changed in six months, and I am tired of my current tour. I need something new and exciting," Evelyn replied. Her friend had a far off look on her face as she thought about Anderson.

"Would you be interested in doing what Anderson does? Travel and look out for new artists? He leaves for one week a month. His last trip was a unique one because they were desperately looking for unknown talent," Roxie explained. Evelyn tipped her head to the side and thought about it.

"To be honest, I'd like to be the manager of Dragon Lore. Xander put an advertisement out for a manager as soon as you two came back from Rome. I've been toying with the idea of sending in my resume, but I don't want to get the job just because you and I are best friends."

"You would be perfect for the job! I promise not to say anything to Xander," Roxie promised, holding up her hand to show how serious she was about not influencing Xander's choice.

"Thanks, that means a lot. When are you going to talk to your mom?" Evelyn changed the subject to the one Roxie did not want to talk about.

"I don't know. I think I might wait until after the show, so I can tell my mom how successful I am. I will have the art she gave away up for sale. We will save the ones I made for my dad until he and I have time to talk. He is coming for dinner on Friday, so he can meet Xander. I am pretty nervous about the two of them meeting," she confided in her friend.

"Why? Wasn't your dad with a shifter before your mom?" Roxie drained her glass and signaled the server to bring her another.

"Yes, but this is his daughter having chosen a forever mate. I also changed into a dragon. According to Xander, only dragons transform their mates. That is because they can live hundreds of years. Most shifters live a normal life span like humans," Roxie explained and Evelyn nodded her understanding.

"I can see how that would be hard to tell your dad. 'Hey, Dad. I am mated to Xander, and oh, I am now a dragon and can live for a very long time,' " Evelyn replied, pitching her voice to sound like Roxie. Roxie laughed at her friend.

"Something like that. Thanks for making me smile, Evvy." She patted her hand and finished her own drink.

"Your dinners. Ma'am, would you like a drink?" the server asked, placing their salads in front of them.

"No, could you bring me a glass of water, please?"

"Yes, be right back with your water." He walked off and Evelyn gave her a raised eyebrow.

"I might be pregnant and don't want to risk anything," she whispered. Evelyn squealed with delight.

"It isn't for sure. I've just felt different these past few days," Roxie explained.

"When are you due for your next period?"

"Next week."

"Too early to take a test too. If you are pregnant, that will be so exciting. You and Xander have been together for almost a full month, so it is possible you are pregnant." Evelyn sipped on her fresh drink while Roxie picked up the water the server brought over.

"Have you been to any other Mate Me events?" Roxie asked and listened as Evelyn dove into a tale about meeting a coyote shifter who ended up getting banned from the events and the club for going after a bartender last week.

CHAPTER FIFTY-ONE

Roxie ran around the house all of Friday, cleaning from top to bottom. She wanted her dad to have a wonderful impression of Xander. All her life, she never cared what her parents thought of the boyfriends she had, but Xander was her mate, her genuine love. She wanted her dad to get along with him and approve of her choice. She spent the entire afternoon mopping, dusting, vacuuming their rugs, and making sure all the bathrooms were in pristine condition. She had been too worked up to even think about painting. It was something that shocked Xander when he suggested she take a break while he took care of the yard.

"Roxie, baby, everything will be fine. I know your dad, and we will get along great," Xander tried to reassure while she was fretting over the chicken pot pie in the oven. She had made a salad earlier and put it in the refrigerator to be ready along with the chicken pot pie. For dessert, she bought all the things for brownie sundaes, her father's favorite dessert. It's one dessert her mother frowned upon, always saying it contained way too many calories.

"I just want everything to be perfect," she replied, turning the oven light on once again to make sure the crust wasn't getting too brown.

"It will be because we both love you and know how much tonight means to you. I don't want to ruin your mood, but have you spoken to your mom?" He slipped his arms around her waist and kissed her neck. She relaxed into his arms. He always knew when to touch her to give her a sense of calmness. Thankfully, she and her dragon were getting better at working as one because she and Xander had been shifting daily.

Bringing up her mom always made her tense; she was so worried about the reasons behind her mother giving away her work. Did she really believe Mitchell? Did she hate Roxie for being an artist so much she was willing to get rid of anything that reminded her of Roxie's current passion? She wanted answers—no, she needed answers but was afraid of what they would be.

"No, I was thinking of waiting until after the showcase tomorrow. I want to prove to her I will be successful as an artist. Then she can't throw Mitchell's words back at me," she answered. Xander hummed his agreement and latched onto the back of her neck, sucking and nipping. He was trying to pull a moan from her lips. She did her best to resist; she loved when they tempted each other to the point they were both a mass of writhing desires. He moved up to the nape and bit with a little more force. She gasped and turned around in his arms. She grabbed his face between her hands and planted her mouth on his, forcing her tongue in to mate with his.

He pushed her onto the counter and she grunted. Not a second later, she had been lifted to sit on the counter and Xander was between her legs. Wrapping her legs around his body, she pressed her heat against his erection, gaining a moan from his lips. Smirking, she pushed again, and this time he growled against her mouth. She captured his bottom lip between her teeth and tugged just enough for him to grunt and shove his hips into hers. She moaned and released his lip, her arms wrapped around his neck. She pulled him as close as she could.

"Do you think we have time for a quickie?" he asked, his voice strained from holding back his desire for her. She could feel the amount of effort he was using to restrain from taking her right there on the counter.

"As long as we only remove the bottom half of our clothes," she offered. No sooner had the words come out of her mouth, her panties came down her legs and the skirt of her dress hiked up past her hips. Xander had his pants and boxers off within seconds of her being freed. She reached down and stroked his cock; she would never get used to how big he was. He always filled her to the brim, and she loved knowing he desired to be inside of her daily. Lifting her off the counter he slid home into her pussy. She held on with her legs and arms, moaning as he fully embedded in her. She felt like liquid lava, burning hot and ready to explode.

"Xander," she whined, and he finally moved in and out of her at a slow pace. She groaned and threw her head back, moving her own hips, trying to get him to go faster.

"All in good time, my love," he promised. She wanted fast and hot, and he was giving her slow and steady.

"There is a time for patience later. I need it now!" she demanded, tugging on his hair. Their eyes met, and she sucked in a breath as his eyes changed to his familiar dragon. She felt her own dragon push forward, and they needed no more words. The two molded into one as they moved in tandem. She kissed him, pushing them both closer to the edge of their climax. She wanted him to come with her today. Usually, he gave her multiple orgasms before he sought his own. Today she needed him to pump his seed inside her as her pussy contracted around his cock.

"Faster," she hissed, and he sped up. He pushed her against a wall and pumped in and out of her. She held on and moaned as her orgasm rushed through her body, making her go stiff and then limp while tiny ripples continued to pulsate each time he entered her. His orgasm was just as powerful. His neck strained and he huffed a little smoke, shouting out his release. She felt branded inside out, his hot seed coating the walls of her pussy.

"That was fucking amazing," he huffed. She nodded, unable to find her own voice. Slowly releasing her grip on his hips, she slid to the floor, holding onto his arms for support.

"We might need a shower," Xander commented. She took a sniff and agreed. They smelled like sex, and she now needed to clean off the kitchen counters again. He swooped in and carried her all the way to their bedroom. She loved their bathroom. It had a standing shower big enough for several people to fit inside. It had two shower heads, one like a waterfall and the other at an angle. The tub fit them both perfectly, with jets to massage away the tension in her back from painting all day. There were his and her sinks; both had their own products lined up neatly around each sink. She had quite a few more products, thanks to her skincare routine. The floor was polished gray tiles; the walls, a warm cream. All fixtures were a shining chrome with black accents. She loved the sleek look of the bathroom and would never tire of being in it with her mate.

They showered quickly, knowing her dad would arrive shortly. Roxie reapplied her makeup and watched as Xander changed into a button-down black shirt, dark wash jeans, and a pair of Oxford shoes. She changed her dress. Flipping through the hangers in her walk-in closet, she settled on a slightly fitted dress of navy blue with white flowers splashed across. It had a sash that she could tie under her chest, giving her a defined shape.

"You look beautiful," Xander whispered, coming up behind her and slipping a necklace around her neck. She looked in the mirror and saw a beautiful ruby heart surrounded by tiny diamonds.

"Why get me a present?" She wanted to know, looking up to meet his eyes in the mirror.

"Because you deserve to be treated like the queen you are," he answered with a small shrug. She turned around and gave him a kiss to convey all her feelings at the moment—love, desire for him again, and thankfulness to have someone so wonderful in her life.

"You are the best mate I could have ever asked for. I love you." She kissed him once more, and he smiled down at her.

"You are my one and only Roxie. I love you more than life itself." He returned her kiss and then they heard the doorbell ring.

"I'll get it. You grab your shoes and touch up your lipstick," he told her. She turned to see it had smudged from kissing him. She quickly fixed it and found a pair of pale pink ballet flats. Walking down the steps, she stopped up short when she saw her dad standing there giving Xander an enormous bear hug. She'd never seen him do that until she noticed Anderson standing behind him.

CHAPTER FIFTY-TWO

"Thank you for giving me back my son," she heard her dad say, and she had to keep the tears at bay. She hadn't known Anderson was coming over or she would have warned him their father would come to dinner.

"Hi, Dad, Anderson." Her dad turned to her and beamed. He wrapped her in a tight hug.

"I miss seeing you every day. I know quitting your job was the right thing to do, but I miss you. How have you been?"

"I am wonderful. Come sit down and we can catch up on what has happened this past month." She took his arm and led him into their living room. Xander went into the kitchen to grab drinks while Anderson stood shocked in the doorway.

"You too, Anderson," she beckoned, and he followed.

"What brought you here tonight?" she asked Anderson once everyone had a drink and was comfortable. She took her favorite armchair. Anderson sat in the other, and her father sat in one corner of the couch.

"Just a final check-in with Xander about your show tomorrow. I didn't know you had company coming over or I would have just called," Anderson replied.

"No worries. Now you and Dad can spend some time together in a neutral space. I just ask, no fighting in the house." She was very serious. She didn't know how much anger Anderson still felt against their dad for letting her mom toss him out.

"I promise," Anderson murmured and her dad nodded.

"So, tell me about your upcoming show. I cannot wait to see it tomorrow," her dad asked, steering the conversation to be about her. She smiled and looked up at Xander, who was perched on the arm of her chair.

"Well, we had an adventure last weekend in New York. You remember how Mitchell weaseled his way into keeping all the art I painted while we were married?" Roxie started. Her dad nodded and she continued, "Well, Xander helped me get a court order for all my work to be released to me. Turned out, Mitchell had more than just the art I created to sell. He had all the work I made for you and Mom from before we were even a couple. He told me he manipulated Mom into giving them to him because I would never amount to anything as an artist. He said he was saving her the embarrassment of having useless art upon her walls."

"I had wondered where all the art from my study went when I went over to the house last time," her dad said, which gave away more than she thought he meant to.

"So we got all my art, but Mitchell was so mad he tried to blow up his warehouse and destroy all my work."

Her dad reared back as if he was struck when she told him. "That rat bastard! I hope he gets what's coming to him," her dad growled, and she nodded.

"He won't be able to get the insurance money. The fire marshal claimed the fire had been set. Turned out, Mitchell has also been working with the mafia, so I fear he won't see a very happy ending," she remarked. Xander had placed his hand on her shoulder throughout the retelling. She reached up and put her hand on his. Her father's eyes followed her movement, and he relaxed.

"So, Xander, tell me about yourself and how you and Roxie met. I know you are a shifter, but not what type." Her father turned his gaze to Xander, and she felt him stiffen beside her. It was her turn to comfort him. She leaned into his side and he relaxed.

227

"I am a dragon, sir. I am a hundred years old, and I own an art gallery. Your daughter and I met at a shifter event called Mate Me. My sister-in-law, Josie Austin, created the event in order to help shifters meet their mates. I met Roxie at the very first event, and I have been head over heels in love with her since then. It took some convincing, a trip to Rome to be precise, before she entertained the possibility of becoming my mate. Anderson found her work in Mitchell's art gallery and didn't know she had created it. He called me with a brand new talent he knew I had to see. Turned out to be Roxie. My temporary assistant also recommended Roxie from when they were in art school together. I knew if she kept popping up in my life, then she was the one fate had meant for me." Xander looked down at her, and her heart swelled with pride and joy for her love.

"If you are a hundred, how do you and Roxie plan on making it work? She is human and won't live as long as dragon shifters do," her dad asked. She took a deep breath. Here was the moment she had dreaded since inviting him over for dinner.

"When Xander and I mated, we made a blood pact. When our blood mingled, it gave me the power to become a dragon shifter myself," she explained, her foot bouncing from nerves over his reaction.

"Huh, so now I have two shifters as my children?" he asked. She looked at him bewildered. She thought he would be angry.

"Uh, yes," she replied.

"I assume you needed to change into dragon form in order to survive as mates?" he questioned. She nodded and looked up at Xander. He had a smile on his face. She knew right then he knew it would not upset her father.

"So you are okay with this?" she asked, wanting to hear it for herself that her dad wasn't angry.

"Yes, you do what you do for love. Anderson's mother and I were mated. She, being a tiger, bit my neck to mark me as her mate. It devastated me when she died after giving birth. If I hadn't had Anderson to care for, I would have wasted away to nothing." Roxie's dad looked at her with tears shining in his eyes. She got up and hugged him gently around the shoulders.

"I love you, Dad."

"I love you too, sweetheart, and I am so sorry about your mom. After talking with you the other week, I decided it was time for me to be happy again. She doesn't make me happy, so I've moved out into an apartment here in town," he told her. She pulled back and gaped at him.

"What?" she asked.

"Your mom and I are getting a divorce. I realized when she kept taking Mitchell's word over yours that she wanted desperately to get back into New York society. I know she told you her family went bankrupt because of a scandal. The truth is, she failed out of law school and her parents disinherited her. She was the laughingstock of New York. You and Elizabeth were her tickets to getting back there. She had a brief taste when you married Mitchell, but now I fear it has taken over the way she looks at everything. When we came over to tell you to stop painting, it nearly killed me to see your face when your mom told you about Mitchell. Then you quit and I knew I didn't want to lose you like I did Anderson. I've made so many mistakes in my life, and I don't want to continue to live a life of regret. I will never hate my time with your mom because it got me you and Elizabeth, but she has turned into a different person. Elizabeth took a job two states away to get away from her, you flew off to Rome and came back with a mate, and Anderson disappeared from my life for fifteen years. It is time to make amends, and I am here to start tonight. I am so sorry I didn't stand up for you and I hope you will forgive me." He was looking at her and Anderson when he said his last sentence. Roxie immediately nodded and hugged him tightly. She could see the hesitation on Anderson's face.

"I don't expect an answer tonight, son. Just know I want to reconnect. Can you do that for me?" he asked and Anderson nodded.

"Good. Now come to the kitchen and we can have dinner. I made chicken pot pie and salad, and we have brownie sundaes for dessert." Roxie stood up and led everyone into the kitchen to sit around the small four-person table. Xander refilled everyone's drinks while she brought over the pot pie and went back for the salad.

"This smells delicious, sweetheart," her dad praised her, and she blushed.

"Her lasagna is out of this world," Anderson commented, and she turned even redder.

"Roxie is an excellent cook. I am spoiled having her," Xander complimented, and she took a long sip of her water. She'd never been praised so much in her life. She proceeded to cut everyone a piece and dish out the salad. She settled and watched as Xander and her dad launched into a conversation about baseball. Her father loved sports of all kinds, but baseball and hockey were his two favorites. She knew enough to follow along. Even Anderson added his two cents here and there. Watching the three most important men in her life get along made her heart feel light. *This is what a family should feel like.* Yes, fights were natural, but no one should be out to hurt the other purposefully. Sipping her water, she watched and listened, content to be in their presence.

With the dishes cleared away and leftovers in take away containers, she pulled out gooey brownies and vanilla ice cream. She also pulled out her favorite mint chocolate chip with whipped cream, cherries, fudge sauce, and caramel sauce. She didn't want anyone to feel they didn't have enough options for their sundaes.

"Who wants which ice cream?" Xander asked, wielding the ice cream scoop.

"Dad first." She motioned for him to step up. He laughed.

"Vanilla, please."

"Anderson, you next," she ordered once her dad had his scoops of ice cream.

"Vanilla," Anderson replied.

"I know you want mint chocolate chips," Xander supplied when it was her turn. She laughed and kissed his cheek.

"You know me so well. What do you want on yours?" she asked, walking over with his bowl to put toppings on.

"I'll do it. Go sit with your dad and Anderson outside. This is the last pleasant night we will see in September. I feel an early cold spell coming on, unusual for October around here, but it is coming." He kissed her and, with a gentle smack of her butt, pushed her out to the patio.

He had outdone himself for his backyard; He had an outdoor kitchen, a huge stone patio with a large fire pit, umbrella, and chairs. Further out was a gigantic swimming pool. The cool thing about the pool was it looked like a lagoon. You wouldn't think of a swimming pool when you looked at it from far away.

He'd told her when she asked, "I want it to look amazing all year round. I'm only able to use the pool for part of the year when the pool is covered. The backyard still looks amazing."

"You have a wonderful home here, Rox. Your mate is one of a kind. I want you to know I am thrilled you found him. I worried after what had happened with Mitchell you would be off men entirely. I am so proud of you for taking a chance on being an artist. You've grown into quite the woman this past month." Her father patted her hand when she sat down next to him on a deck chair.

"Thanks, Dad. He is one of a kind. He even helped me find Anderson, even if it was by accident. When we were on our way to Rome, we talked about our families and he offered to help me find Anderson. Funny how life reconnects people when they least expect it," she replied and smiled when Xander kissed the top of her head. She watched him take the chair next to her and dig into his sundae.

231

"Xander, as her father, I must tell you if you hurt her in any way, I will find another dragon shifter and have you killed," her dad said in all seriousness. She gasped, but Xander nodded.

"That would be your right, although you wouldn't have to look too far. Both my parents love Roxie more than me and have given me the same threat." Her dad laughed, and she couldn't help chuckling herself. Koraline and James were amazing, and she loved being their daughter-in-law.

"Excellent, and call me Calvin." Her dad held out his hand and Xander shook it, an unspoken connection being made.

"Anderson, tell me about your date with Evvy." Roxie turned her attention to her quiet brother, and he blanched.

"She is a wonderful woman. We've been on a few dates," he replied, keeping his voice neutral. Roxie knew he was trying to hide how he really felt and didn't want to scare him off.

"She is an amazing best friend. Be nice to her," she begged, and he nodded. Soon the conversation drifted to her art showcase tomorrow. Time flew by until it was close to midnight by the time her dad and Anderson went home.

"I think tonight went perfect," she told Xander while being wrapped in his arms after a round of lovemaking.

"It did. Your dad is a funny man, and I really enjoyed talking with him. Maybe we can do a family dinner again and invite my side too," he suggested, and she quickly nodded her agreement.

"I think our families will get along perfectly. I love you Xander, and thank you for believing in me and never letting me go." She kissed him softly. His eyes glowed gently in the moonlight streaming through their window.

"I love you too, and thank you for giving me a chance after Rhett royally screwed everything up that first night." He kissed her back, and she laughed, remembering how angry she had been for thinking she was just another hookup.

"I always believe in second chances, and tomorrow is mine. I am so excited about the showcase. I don't know if I will ever be

232

able to get to sleep," she replied and Xander rolled on top of her, pushing his semi-hard cock against her thigh.

"I can think of a way to tire you out," he offered, and she giggled.

"I was hoping you would." She wrapped her legs around his waist and let him make love to her until the early hours of the morning. They eventually fell asleep through the exhaustion.

CHAPTER FIFTY-THREE

Dressed in a gown of deep rose-pink, Roxie shifted from foot to foot. She was nervous about her art show. It would start in ten minutes, and her brain was freaking out. She was walking back and forth inside Xander's office, banned from helping set up.

"You will break something. Go sit in the office," Evelyn ordered, pushing her toward Xander's office. She'd moved several paintings around, only to put them back where they originally had been hung.

"Baby," Xander's hesitant voice floated through the doorway.

"I'm in here," she replied. Her hair had been swept up and out of her face into an intricate updo Evelyn had created. She had kept her makeup natural, and she wore the necklace Xander gave her the night before. Her half sleeve tattoo was on full display, and she worried what her dad would say. He didn't see it last night because her dress had quarter length sleeves.

"You look amazing," Xander pronounced, opening the door and taking in her appearance. She had to take a minute and collect her breath. Xander was dressed in a formal tuxedo. His hair had the top gelled and his sides shaved. She salivated looking at him.

"I know that look, and there is no time for a quickie," he warned, which made her pout. It just meant their lovemaking later would be even better with the anticipation building.

"Fine, how does it look out there?" she asked, bringing her thumbnail up to worry away. Xander snagged her hand and kissed her knuckles.

"It looks perfect. Why are you in here anyway?" he asked, taking in his office.

"Evelyn banished me here and said I would break something." She huffed, pushing out her bottom lip.

"Were you moving paintings around again?" He gave her a serious look, and she ducked her head.

"Maybe," she mumbled, and he pulled her in for a tight hug.

"I love you. Everything will be perfect. You and I will greet people as they come in. Once most of our guests are here, you and I can walk around and you tell them about your work. I have a surprise for you too," he told her and she looked up.

"What surprise?"

"You'll see when it is time," he promised, and she frowned. His surprises were always wonderful. It's just irritating that she always had to wait.

"Can I get a hint?" she asked, walking her fingers up the buttons of his shirt and slipping one open at his neck. Pushing her hands away, he redid the button and fixed his bow tie.

"No, come on, we are needed at the front." He took her hand and walked her to the door. She could see a crowd of people already waiting, her dad at the forefront. He was dressed in a tux just like Xander. She'd never noticed how handsome her dad was until she saw all the women eyeing him. Her dad had the same light hair and eyes as she did. He was tall and broad-shouldered. Their eyes connected and his went wide. She knew why, her tattoos. He smiled and gave her a thumbs-up, which she hoped it meant he approved.

"See? Your dad doesn't hate your body art. It is just another extension of you," Xander murmured into her ear and she smiled. He always knew what she was thinking, and she bet he had witnessed their exchange.

"I hope so," she whispered back and hooked her arm with his as they readied to greet their guests.

"How many people are coming tonight?" she asked, eyeing the ever-growing crowd.

"I had Lauren send out an invitation to everyone on my client list, and there are about five hundred people on that list. I didn't want a single person to miss out on seeing your art. I told you, tonight we will sell everything you painted," he replied with a smirk on his lips and a twinkle in his hazel eyes.

"You are insane. Not everyone will be able to buy a painting," she remarked, and his smirk became bigger.

"That is the key. You keep people clambering for your work. You won't ever have to worry about selling one again. Not everyone will see a piece they like. They will wait to see what else you produce, which gives you a following," he explained, and she shook her head. He really was amazing. He had everything planned out, and she knew tonight would be a success.

"Time to open the doors," Evelyn announced. Xander had given her an opportunity to show her skills by putting her in charge of handling the event with his assistant manager. Roxie watched as Evelyn clad in a gold ballgown, her dark hair curled gently around her face, and her makeup daring. She then opened the doors. People walked in, and it distracted Roxie from her worry as she greeted and was introduced to many of the guests coming through the door.

About a half-hour into the event, she heard children's voices.

"Aunt Roxie!" Four little bodies clad in suits and dresses came flying through the doors to hug her tightly. She looked up to see Antonio and Marta dashing after their kids, trying to pull them off her. She laughed and knelt to return their hugs. Her heart swelled when she heard them call her Aunt Roxie.

"What a wonderful surprise!" she gushed, touching each child on the head.

"When Mama said she was coming to see your paintings, we all begged to come too. Daddy called Uncle Xander, and he said you would be happy to see us. Well, are you?" Austin, the oldest child, asked her.

"Oh, very happy to see you. I've missed you so much, and you've all grown." She pulled them in for another hug, and they all laughed.

"Did you really paint these, Aunt Roxie?" Isabella asked, her eyes wide as she took in Roxie's favorite piece—the Trevi Fountain.

"Yes, I did. My trip to Rome is all over here. Come and I will show you." She took Isabella and Mary's hands, Joseph and Austin following along, eyes wide with curiosity.

CHAPTER FIFTY-FOUR

Xander watched Roxie walk away with Antonio and Marta's four children.

"No hello for us?" Antonio joked and Xander laughed. It had worried him that Roxie wouldn't want the children around her art.

"Can you blame her? Those four are delightful distractions. Thank you for making the trip all the way from Italy. It means the world to have your support. Did your painting arrive in good shape?" Xander asked. Roxie had painted their comfortable house in Rome as a present.

"Yes, it is beautiful, and we immediately put it up. Mary couldn't stop staring at it in awe. I think she will be creative like Roxie," Marta shared. Xander watched as Roxie slung Mary up on her hip without caring about her dress, so Mary could get a better look at one of her paintings.

"Can we expect a wedding soon?" Marta asked, nodding at Roxie's left hand.

"Yes, we want to get through the showcase before we plan the wedding. I think she has her heart set on a November wedding. Would that be too much for you to come back out here again around then?" he asked. He knew traveling with four kids was a lot of work.

"We wouldn't miss it for the world," Antonio assured him, clapping him on the shoulder.

"Come help me pick the painting I should have in my restaurant." Antonio tucked Marta's hand in the crook of his elbow, and the three walked over to join Roxie and the children.

"This one is of the colosseum. I snuck out of our hotel room to get a picture of this before Uncle Xander was awake," Roxie was telling the children. Antonio raised an eyebrow at Xander; it was rare that someone snuck in and out on him.

"Papa, I want this one." Isabella pointed to the painting they had been listening to Roxie share about.

"This is a beautiful piece. Why don't we walk around and look at all of them before we make a choice. Roxie, this is exquisite. If they all look like this, we will have a hard time choosing," Marta complimented, patting her arm.

"Thank you so much." Roxie squeezed her hand, and Xander took a moment to admire his mate. She was a natural around people; some artists had a hard time connecting with others because they were so immersed in their art. Not his mate. She walked that line without falling.

"Roxie," Evelyn came up and whispered in her ear. Xander watched her stiffen. He followed her line of sight and saw her mother walking through the door. She was on the arm of an older gentleman, probably around the same age as her.

"Get rid of her," Roxie demanded in a harsh whisper and walked away to speak to another client admiring her painting of the Rocky Mountains. Evelyn nodded and walked over to where Meredith Jones was waiting to be greeted. Xander followed but kept his distance. He wanted to see how Evelyn handled an unwelcome guest.

"Meredith, I will have to ask you to please leave," Evelyn said, blocking her from coming further into the gallery.

"Why? They invited me?" She waved her invitation in Evelyn's face. Unphased, Evelyn flipped open the guest list.

"I am sorry. Your RSVP said you would not be attending, and we are at max capacity for this event. If you like to come back

239

and look at the paintings, they will hang them for the next month," Evelyn replied, her voice calm.

"No, I was invited and I intend on watching my daughter fail," she hissed. The gentleman on her arm gave an alarmed look.

"Were you not going to come tonight?" the man asked. Xander recognized his voice immediately. He was Jenner Kingsly.

"I am sorry. We are at max capacity and can get in trouble should the fire marshal show up." Evelyn tried once again to usher them back out the door. Xander walked over and stopped behind her.

"Any trouble, Evelyn?" he asked, eyeing up Jenner Kingsly.

"I was just explaining to Meredith and her guest. She declined to come, and we are at max capacity for the building," Evelyn replied.

"I am sorry, ma'am. As my manager stated, we cannot allow you to enter. If you like to come again, we will be open for people to admire her work tomorrow. I cannot guarantee any of them will still be available for purchase, though. We've already sold about half in the past hour." He gave her a tight smile, and her eyes widened when she realized who he was.

"Damn you, Xander Austin. You couldn't have left Roxie well enough alone. You've ruined everything!" Meredith turned and stalked out, Jenner Kingsly staring after her in shock.

"I apologize for my date's rude behavior. I came tonight to offer my apologies to the artist about the abominable events of last weekend. One of my associates stepped over his authority and led me to believe she caused the fire. I am here to offer to buy a painting. The ones you took from the warehouse were supposed to go to my private collection. After hearing they were obtained illegally, I was glad you took them back. Her mother said she wouldn't be able to sell any. I see she was wrong. I will be in touch about purchasing one of her paintings. I saw plenty when they were on display in New York." Jenner bowed and walked back out into the night. Xander and Evelyn exchanged a confused look.

"We tell Roxie nothing. Just tell her, her mother left and took her guest with her," Xander ordered and Evelyn agreed without question. "You are doing an excellent job. If the night goes off with no major problems, the manager's job is yours," he told her.

"It's not because your mate is my best friend, is it?" Evelyn demanded, hands on her hips.

"No, you are more than qualified to be in charge, and tonight you are proving it by keeping your cool with her mother," he replied, looking around for his mate. He spotted her talking with an elderly couple about one of her Grand Canyon paintings.

"Thank you. That means a lot," Evelyn thanked him and walked off to make sure everything was working smoothly. Xander looked around and took in the number of people. He hadn't had a successful showcase like this in quite some time. Roxie came into his life at the perfect time, when he was struggling to find an artist who spoke to his soul. Who knew she would also turn out to be his mate? Xander couldn't wait to see where life took them. He only knew she would always be by his side, loving him as much as he loved her.

CHAPTER FIFTY-FIVE

The showcase was more successful than Roxie could have imagined. Every single one of her paintings was sold and several were bid over until one buyer backed out. She was commissioned to paint several specific pieces, including one for Jenner Kingsly. She knew Xander didn't think she recognized the mafia king, but she'd met him at several of Mitchell's events. She hadn't known who he was, but after hearing his name and seeing him with her mother, Roxie knew who her mother was seeing now that she and her father were getting a divorce.

Now it was almost a week later. She parked outside of her childhood home. She'd called her mom and asked if they could meet and have a talk. Her mother had been reluctant, but Roxie pushed for her to agree.

"I already know you and Dad are getting a divorce. Dad told me last week before my showcase," she'd told her mom. Reluctantly, her mother agreed, and here she was, too scared to walk up to the door. Xander was at work. She wanted to do this on her own. She needed to face her mother and get closure.

She and Xander had dove right into wedding planning the day after her show. They decided to get married on the first weekend of December. His father would act as the officiant; Evelyn would be her maid of honor; Josie, Marta, and Elizabeth would be her bridesmaids. Xander asked Antonio to be his best man. Anderson, Rhett, and Marcus were to be the groomsmen.

Just get out of the car Roxie. There is nothing she can tell you that you haven't already heard, she told herself. Taking a deep breath, she turned off her car and climbed out. Xander had been right. A cold front moved in and the leaves had all changed in just a week's time. She walked up the familiar cobblestone walk and onto the creaking front porch. She knocked gently on the door, not feeling she could just walk in anymore. This was no longer her home; it hadn't been since she was twenty-three. The shutters were a pale blue color with chintz curtains in the windows. The siding was a dingy white; the house looked in need of repair. She wondered just how long her parents had been separated—maybe not in different homes but in separate rooms in their own home.

"Roxie." Her mother gave her a stiff nod, and she tried to smile.

"Mother," she replied. Her mom backed out of the doorway and, with an impatient movement, motioned for her to come inside. Roxie walked in and immediately didn't recognize the place. Meredith had replaced all the furniture with luxury items. Gone was the worn plaid sofa and in its place sat an antique settee. Her mother replaced the two comfortable armchairs with fragile-looking wooden chairs.

"You've really changed up the place," she commented, not sure where she should sit. She was afraid she'd break something or, worse, ruin it with the paint still on her hands. She'd tried her best to clean as much off but didn't want to take a full shower just to come out and speak with her mom for what she bet was twenty minutes tops.

"When your father moved out, I changed it to better suit my preferences. Have a seat on the settee and I will bring us tea." Her mother walked out of the room. Roxie had the chance to observe her. She was wearing her traditional fifties housewife style dress. Today it was covered in cherries. Her hair had been expertly curled and set to complement her heart-shaped face. Roxie sat gingerly on the edge of the settee, afraid to get comfortable.

Her mother walked back in with a tea tray, a very delicate-looking china teapot, and two cups. She was more of a coffee kind of girl, but she wasn't about to upset her mother when she wanted answers.

"Here." Her mother thrust a cup and saucer at her. Roxie carefully took them from her manicured hands and sipped. The tea was a little sweet but gave her suddenly dry throat the moisture it needed.

"I came to talk to you about what I had seen displayed at The Wright's Art Gallery," she announced. She wanted to get this over with and back home to her love.

"What did you see?" her mother asked, sipping her own tea and leaning back in her chair. Roxie watched, awed by how graceful her mother was.

"All my artwork from when I was in college. The agreement with Mitchell was to put up the art I made while we were married to sell for my alimony. Instead, I saw every single piece I had made for you and Dad. Obviously, Mitchell didn't have permission to sell them and put all my art available to sell in a warehouse. Why did he have it?" she asked, setting her teacup down. She was getting angry and didn't want to break the glass cup by accident. Taking a deep breath, she thought about Xander and how in just an hour he would be home from work. She had a crockpot with cheesy bacon potato soup and would stop for crusty bread at the local bakery.

"Mitchell told me you would never amount to anything as an artist and were better suited to be a homemaker. I didn't want your ugly work cluttering my walls, so I gave him all the art. I had no attachment to it. You were a disappointment as a daughter," she spat, and Roxie had to force herself not to shift.

"I was a disappointment?" she asked through gritted teeth.

"You couldn't survive a marriage. You couldn't overlook Mitchell cheating. That is what New York society is, cheating behind closed doors," her mother told her. She made it seem like it was normal for spouses to never be faithful.

"That is not how I see marriage. It is for life and you are faithful to your partner. Were you cheating on Dad before you separated?" she asked. Suddenly she felt like her parents's entire relationship had been a farce.

"Not until you and Elizabeth moved out. Your father could never make me happy. He didn't want to be a part of that world, I did. So while I came to visit you and Mitchell, I met a new man to make me happy." Her mother gave her a smug look, and she knew she was talking about Jenner Kingsly.

"I see. Well, thank you for my answers. I will let you know, Xander and I are mates. He gave me the privilege of becoming a dragon like him, and we won't ever be contacting you again. Enjoy your life with New York society. Xander and I will make a life for ourselves in White Valley. Oh, and I sold every single painting last night, which means I made over a million dollars selling the art you said would never be good enough, the art that Mitchell thought was useless. Just know we want nothing to do with you. You will not meet any children we will have. You will be nothing to me." She stood up, placed her teacup on the table, and walked out.

She felt free her mother was behind her. She had a wedding to plan with the love of her life and her art career had taken off with a flash. Roxie Leigh Jones almost Austin was taking life by storm.

EPILOGUE

Xander stood at the front of the massive church he and Roxie were holding their wedding. Today, he would marry his mate. It had been almost four months since he met the love of his life. They had gone on a wild adventure to Rome, using travel to convince her she was his mate, then fought Mitchell for her art, dealt with Anderson and their father's estrangement, and stood up to her mother. They'd been through a lot.

Wedding planning had been a breeze compared to everything else. Today he was on pins and needles waiting for Roxie to enter. He hadn't seen her since their rehearsal dinner the night before. He ached to touch her again. Last night, he didn't sleep, his dragon not understanding the tradition of spending the night apart. Xander wholeheartedly agreed with his dragon, but his mother had declared that Roxie would stay at her house. All the women were spending the night there and were getting ready for the wedding.

"Nervous?" Anderson asked as they dressed him in a dark gray suit with a navy-blue button-up shirt and ivory-colored tie. Roxie had picked out the clothing choices for men and women.

"No, just ready to have Roxie mine in the eyes of the law and mated to me," he replied. Anderson laughed and clapped him on the shoulder.

"The wedding should start in a few minutes, then she is all yours. As her older brother, I want you to know I will kill you if she cries." Xander laughed this time.

"Understood. Everyone who loves her has given me the same speech. She is such an amazing woman. Everyone who meets her instantly loves her," he shared. Anderson nodded and Rhett leaned over.

"Very true. Josie has declared Roxie her sister along with Evelyn. Ellie at the club loves both of them nowe. They've become regulars at the Mate Me events."

"How is Ellie?" Xander asked. Him and Rhett had rescued her from a rogue coyote shifter.

"Still refusing to work any Mate Me events. I need to talk to Marcus after the wedding," Rhett replied.

"No business at the reception," Xander warned. Rhett nodded his understanding and straightened up. The music began. Xander couldn't help holding his breath. First came his mother, then the bridesmaids—Josie, Evelyn, and Elizabeth. They were wearing floor-length gowns of navy blue with ivory sashes. Finally, as the music changed to the bridal march, Roxie appeared at the end on the arm of her father.

She took his breath away. Her gown was the epitome of a princess ball gown. The bodice had ruching with crystals adorning the sweetheart bustline. The bottom half was covered in sheer lace, stopping part way down. There were crystals spread across the material. The gown matched the ivory in the bridesmaid dresses. He couldn't keep his eyes off of her.

Watching her walk down the aisle to him, Xander felt himself become emotional. The love of his life was walking down to him, ready to pledge her life to his forever.

Roxie couldn't believe the day had finally come. She was to officially become Roxie Austin. The night before, she wasn't able to sleep a wink. Koraline had insisted that all women in the bridal party were to stay at her house. If she had it her way, she would have spent the night with Xander making love. Instead, she had spent the night sharing a bed with Evvy and not sleeping. She'd been on edge all day, her dragon complaining about being away from their mate for too long.

"You look amazing," her dad whispered. Looking up at him, she smiled. Her parents's divorce had just become official. Her sister, Elizabeth, had moved back home and had taken a job as a pediatrician for the local hospital and maternity ward.

"Thanks, Dad. I'm super happy today. I'm finally getting the man of my dreams, my art are sold out, and I've been getting requests left and right." Looking down the aisle toward Xander, she felt tears prick her eyes. She was very emotional these days. Everything made her cry. She and Xander would announce at the reception they were expecting twins come May of next year.

They made it down to Xander. Roxie could see his eyes were misty with emotion. Her father handed her off to him and the ceremony began.

"I love you," Xander whispered in her ear. She smiled up at him.

"I love you to the moon and back. I love being loved by a dragon," she whispered back. They'd chosen to go with their own vows, and she couldn't wait to share her words of love with him. Xander's father began the ceremony thanking everyone for coming, before turning to the two of them.

"The bride and groom have written their own vows. Roxie, you will go first," James announced.

"Xander, I love you very much. The day I met you, I wasn't looking for love. I went to the event because Evvy wanted to go. I am so glad she didn't take no for an answer. You helped me find myself again. You made me whole again. In our first month together, we went through more than any couple should. Thank you for loving me and embracing the artist you knew I was meant to be. I cannot wait to see where this journey takes us. I love you," she said, staring up into his captivating hazel eyes.

"Roxie, the second my dragon and I saw you, we knew you were our mate. What we hadn't expected was for you to not believe us. A trip to Rome and I knew there would be no other for me. I love you and am proud to be your mate. You are amazing and my forever. I cannot wait to see where this wild ride takes us next. Thank you for saying yes," Xander shared. Roxie dug out her tissue and dabbed at her tearful eyes.

"Now repeat after me." James walked them through the rest of the ceremony until he announced, "You may kiss the bride!"

Xander grabbed her and dipped her back, thoroughly ravishing her mouth. His tongue pushed in, tangling with her own. She wrapped her arms around his neck and held on for the ride. The crowd broke out in cheers and whistled as they kissed. Setting her back up on her feet, Xander scooped her up and carried her out of the church.

"Xander!" she shrieked. He didn't put her down until they slipped into the waiting limo.

"I love you, Roxie Austin. Thank you for becoming mine and carrying our children. It has been so hard keeping your pregnancy a secret." He kissed her again, his hand slipping down the bodice of her gown. He found one of her sensitive nipples and tweaked it. She moaned with pleasure. He pulled the bodice down and captured a nipple in his mouth. Arching her back, she pushed more of her breast into his mouth.

"Tonight, I will not let you sleep. We have a flight to Bora Bora in the morning. You can sleep then." His lips captured her own. They stayed locked in a passionate embrace the entire ride to the ballroom where their reception would be held.

"Mr. and Mrs. Austin, we have arrived," their driver announced. Roxie sighed, sitting up and fixing her wedding dress.

"Ready?" Xander asked.

"For anything," she replied, and let him pull her out of the limo to enjoy their reception.

Do you like fantasy stories?
Here are samples of other stories
you might enjoy!

DRAGON OF LEGEND

DESTINY

ANGELIKA MEYER

CHAPTER I
Beginnings

A shape hurtled through the air, casting a shadow on the lands below. Creatures of all shapes and sizes scurried for cover, none wanting to catch the eye of the majestic beast that passed overhead.

In a meadow, far away from the approaching danger, birds chirped as they flew over a small grassland. Eyeing the ground below for fat worms, they dove every so often to catch any unlucky ones.

As they gobbled down their early breakfast, a single butterfly flew through the field. It settled down on a yellow flower for a moment, as though to rest its weary wings before it took off once more, flying past a sleek doe, which stepped out from among the foliage.

The doe looked around cautiously before she gracefully walked over to the bubbling stream that made its way through the meadow. Her nose twitched as she followed the smell of water. While her ears rotated, her eyes darted around the clearing, searching for any signs of danger.

Finding none, she relaxed. Upon reaching the stream, she took one last look around before lowering her head. As she drank, the cool water trickled down her throat, and the doe's tail twitched in satisfaction.

The butterfly continued on its way. The gentle breeze making it wobble slightly off course, yet it bravely flew on. Passing by a rusty sword, which had certainly seen better days, the butterfly descended and landed on a hand. Here, it folded its wings, as though deciding to rest.

The hand belonged to a girl. Her eyes closed as she lay there in the middle of the grassy field. Her long black hair spread around her and a smile touched her lips as she soaked in the warm sunshine. Were it not for her rising chest, any passerby would have thought her dead.

A large shadow passed overhead, momentarily blocking the sun. The doe's head snapped up as she tensed in visible fear. The birds's singing ceased; forgetting the worms, they flew for the shelter of the trees. As her whole body trembled, the doe turned and followed the birds's lead as she bounded for the cover of the forest behind her, away from the danger she sensed was coming.

The only remaining creatures were the girl and the butterfly, neither of whom seemed to have realized the approaching danger.

Suddenly, a majestic male dragon landed but a few feet away from the girl. His feet sank into the ground, crushing the grass and soil beneath his weight. His scales, an eerie silver which verged on becoming white, glittered as the sun's rays bounced off them. He gracefully arched his neck and folded his wings as his eyes came to rest on the figure lying on the grass.

Parting his lips, he revealed rows of razor-sharp teeth. His tail swished as he advanced and the ground trembled with every step he took as he approached the girl who still hadn't moved an inch. The butterfly on her hand quivered slightly, as though ready to flee, yet it stayed bravely with the girl it had decided to use as its perch.

The dragon was upon them. As he came to a stop, his yellow eyes gleamed as they stared down at his prey. His mouth opened to make use of his arsenal of teeth before he lowered his head.

"*Akira . . .*" H   is voice echoed almost hauntingly in the girl's mind.

He was inches away from her face when Akira's nose suddenly wrinkled in obvious disgust.

"Scales!"

The dragon froze.

"What did you eat?" Akira lifted a hand to pinch her nose. "That smells like a rotting carcass!"

The dragon withdrew his head; its lips falling to cover his teeth. Disappointment filled his eyes at the obvious lack of surprise. His tail dropped and he sat on his haunches with a heavy thud.

Akira's eyes flew open to reveal a pair of clear blue orbs. As her other hand twitched, the butterfly took off. It fluttered into the sky, seemingly without a care in the lands as it left behind the girl and the dragon.

"I'm sure it doesn't smell 'that' bad," the dragon's voice spoke in Akira's head.

"Redemption, trust me. One whiff of that and every female dragon in the lands would make a beeline for the mountains." Akira sat up as she thought this.

The dragon, now known as Redemption, responded with a snort of obvious disbelief.

With a mischievous grin, Akira got to her feet.

"Sure, don't listen. You can't say I didn't warn you." She brushed herself off. Looking up, her gaze wandered to the white dragon's back. Her eyes narrowed before they darted to Redemption's face, then back to his back.

"Ree, where's your saddle?"

Her dragon tipped his head back to stare at the sky.

"You know, I think I may be getting hungry."

Akira crossed her arms on her chest.

"How about a juicy deer?" The dragon got off his haunches and stretched. *"I think I smell one nearby."* He turned, his tail flattening the grass on either side as it swished.

Akira wasn't about to let him go.

"Redemption!" she spoke out loud.

Her dragon slowly turned his head.

"The saddle."

Redemption blinked innocently.

"Err . . . I lost it?"

"How does one lose a saddle?"

More blinking.

"Oh, it's quite possible."

"It was strapped to your back!"

The white dragon raised his head, as though to try and look somewhat more dignified.

"It came loose."

"Both straps?"

"I told you it wasn't worth your mother's pearls."

"And you didn't notice it slip?"

"I was a bit preoccupied."

"With what?"

Redemption paused for a moment, as though considering his answer.

"With flying."

With an exasperated sigh, Akira let her hands drop to her side. She glared at her dragon.

"I should have known better than to entrust it to you. Destiny would surely have looked after it."

Redemption cocked his head. *"Oh, cheer up. It was itchy and uncomfortable in every way. I say we're better off without it. Who needs a saddle anyway?"*

"And how do you suppose I stay on your back?"

The white dragon's tail swung in thought.

"Ah . . . I see." His tail stopped swinging. *"Well, it looks like we have a slight problem."*

Without a word, Akira picked up the sword that lay in the grass. She pointed it at Redemption.

"This is your fault."

The dragon's head lowered in shame.

Ignoring him, Akira raised the sword so that she could better examine the blade. Her fingers traced its dulling edge.

"Perhaps if I traded this in, we could get another . . ."

A snort from her dragon made her eyes snap to him.

"Sorry." His head lowered even further.

With another sigh, Akira returned her attention to the blade.

"Who am I kidding? I don't think anyone would pay even a draco for it." She tilted her head back and stared at the sky. *"What we need is a miracle."*

Another large shadow passed overhead.

"She's here." Akira thought, her eyes lifting to the sky. Redemption did the same. They were in time to witness a female dragon circling above once before she made a graceful descent.

Her blue scales, which had once been the bluest of blue, were now fading with age, yet they made the dragon look all the more noble.

No sooner did she land than she dropped a brown bundle she had been carrying in her mouth.

"You found it!" Akira rushed over to the object which now lay in the grass. She dropped to her knees next to it, and placed the sword down before her hands carefully examined the leather bundle. Its edges were frayed and was tattered to such an extent that the cords that hung from it looked like they would snap at any moment.

Akira felt it all over before she let out a sigh of relief. *"It's alright."*

Redemption reluctantly   made his way over. His head stretched as though to see if the object really was the same detestable item he had so conveniently lost earlier.

Akira's eyes lifted to briefly meet those of the blue dragon. *"Where was it?"*

The dragon hesitated. Her eyes darted to meet Redemption's.

"In a tree."

"A what?" Akira turned to glare at her white dragon. He refused to meet her eyes.

"Ridiculous," Akira muttered out loud. She picked up the saddle and got to her feet.

"Ree."

The white dragon hesitated for a moment before he slumped over with his head down. He shot a glare at the saddle on the way, baring his teeth slightly at the loathsome thing.

Akira ignored her dragon's reaction. When he reached her, she threw the saddle on his back, and readjusted it before she started working on the straps. Redemption squirmed, yet he didn't think a word.

The blue dragon watched; her wise eyes filled with amusement. Standing next to the white dragon, it became apparent that she was smaller in build—as most female dragons were, and unlike Redemption, her scales were smoother and thus, more delicate looking.

"There." Akira stood back to admire her handy work. *"I'm sure it won't fall this time."*

The white dragon arched his back. He turned his head and sniffed the saddle on his back before he recoiled in disgust.

Ignoring him, Akira turned to the blue dragon.

"Thank you, Destiny," she told her.

The blue dragon, Destiny, lowered her head, and Akira scratched it affectionately. Something like a purr rumbled in the dragon's throat and she closed her eyes.

The sound of something scraping made Akira pause and Destiny's eyes shoot open. As Akira snapped her head around, she found Redemption rubbing his belly against a rock.

"Ree!" She sprang towards him.

Redemption froze. His guilt-filled eyes travelled to his rider.

"It itches," he complained.

"Fine." Akira put her hands on her hips. *"I'll just ride Destiny instead."*

"On second thought." Redemption jumped away from the rock faster than a snake could bite. *"I think it suits me quite nicely."* He arched his neck. *"It could be quite attractive in a way, right?"*

"On you? Not in the least." Akira thought dryly.

Destiny chuckled. It came out as a deep rumbling in her throat. Abruptly, she froze where almost simultaneously, both dragons lifted their heads in the air and sniffed the breeze.

Akira noticed the change at once as both dragons tensed; their tails grew rigid.

"What is it?" she couldn't help but ask.

The blue dragon lowered her head; her yellow eyes brimming with worry.

"We should go."

"Destiny?" Akira wasn't about to let it go.

Redemption was still sniffing the air; his nostrils quivering at the scent.

"I smell fire . . ." His tail swished. He seemed oblivious to the look the blue dragon shot him as he continued, *"and blood . . . human blood."*

Before he finished, Akira picked up her sword and pulled herself into the saddle on Redemption's back.

"Ree."

Redemption spread his wings and launched himself into the air.

"Wait!" Destiny followed.

Redemption rose higher into the air. He shot up above the trees with a grace only a dragon could possess. With a thrust of his wings, the meadow they rested on was left far behind.

As the horizon stretched out before her, Akira immediately caught sight of the smoke which poured into the sky. She felt Redemption shiver beneath her.

"I smell death."

Akira didn't reply. Her eyes were glued to the smoke. She could imagine the angry flames that were the cause of it, licking at everything and anything in their path as they mercilessly ate it all. The very thought made images rush through her head—images she didn't want to recall.

Screams echoed in her mind as memories resurfaced and old wounds threatened to open. The sensation of the blistering heat on her skin and the smell of burning flesh filled her thoughts.

Akira's mouth went dry. Her palms grew sweaty as her breath became ragged.

"Run!" the familiar voice yelled in her mind.

"Akira!" She blinked as Redemption's voice pulled her back to the present.

"We're leaving," Destiny declared firmly. The blue dragon had come to hover beside Redemption. She turned away from the fire and headed towards the opposite direction with Redemption following close behind.

As the smoke disappeared from her vision and was replaced with clear sky, a sudden thought hit Akira.

"Isn't that where a village is?"

Neither of her dragons responded.

Realization filled her. *"That's where I bought the saddle!"* Akira twisted in the saddle to stare back at the smoke. *"Is it a raid?"*

"It's none of our concern." Destiny thought grimly as the two dragons continued to fly away.

Akira bit her lip as she turned away.

"But . . . people could be dying."

No response.

She blinked back tears as the memories continued to rattle in the box she had stored them so carefully in.

"No one helped us back then . . ." Her hand tightened on her sword. *"If someone had come . . ."*

She lifted her head.

"We have to help them."

"Don't be ridiculous." Destiny didn't even look back. *"There's nothing we can do."*

Akira stared at her blue dragon's tail in disbelief.

"Nothing?" She turned around to see the smoke was even farther away. *"Did you perhaps . . . smell dragons?"*

No reply from Destiny.

"No . . . only horses and mankind." Redemption thought.

"So no dragons?" Akira's spirits rose. *"Then we can certainly help! It should be easy with the two of you!"*

"There are no dragons, yet," Destiny replied. She continued on her course, showing no signs of changing it. *"They may very well be on their way."*

"In that case, we need to go before they come!"

"Akira." The blue dragon sounded exasperated. *"That's not a good idea."*

"People need our help!"

"People die every day."

"And yet we can help these ones live!"

"We're not going and that's final." Destiny didn't once shoot a glance back.

"You're not my father!"

"And yet he entrusted you to me!"

Akira bit her lip. Her fingers tightened around the saddle. "Don't bring him into this," she whispered. "Any of them."

"Sorry . . ." Destiny's tail dropped somewhat. *"But sometimes it's better to leave things as they are . . ."*

Her dragon's words were lost to her as Akira turned to shoot one last glance at the smoke.

"Run!" the familiar voice from her past screamed in her head again.

"I think it's best if we just go back and lay low until the raiders pass . . ." Destiny was saying.

Shutting Destiny out of her mind, Akira turned her attention to her white dragon.

"Ree?"

"You know . . ." Redemption sounded uncertain. *"She has a point . . ."*

"I won't let others suffer the same fate as I did. Not when we can help. We're going." She knew that in this bond with her dragon, she had the final say.

"So stubborn." Was Redemption's reply. Nevertheless, he didn't hesitate to listen to his rider. Dipping his wings, he turned around. He scarcely made a sound as he stopped following Destiny, who was still having a conversation with Akira who wasn't listening.

"How long do you think till she notices?" the white dragon asked.

"Let's not find out." Akira leaned forward as she stared at the smoke that was visible on the horizon once more.

She swallowed the bitter bile that rose in her throat.

Is this what our village looked like from afar? She couldn't help but wonder. She pushed the question away as soon as it rose.

"Are you sure about this?" Redemption asked softly.

The smoke grew closer.

"Absolutely." Akira's lips formed a thin line of determination. *"Besides, what's the worst that could happen?"*

"I don't know . . ." Redemption replied as he continued on his path. *"A lot?"*

"We'll be fine," Akira said, more so to convince herself. Her heart was racing as the danger ahead drew closer . . .

"Just fine."

If you enjoyed this sample, look for
Dragon of Legend: Destiny
on Amazon.

DRAGON OF LEGEND

A

NEW ERA

ANGELIKA MEYER

CHAPTER I
Academy City

A tall building cut into the early morning sky. Darkness did well to hide its scars from years of battling the elements. For such an old building, it was in surprisingly good shape. Then again, it was built to last. The lights—through old-fashioned slit-like windows—flickered every so often as shadows passed by.

The building looked like the beautiful relic it was. However, at night, it was outdone by the glorious sight at the base of the cliff it stood on. Here, a city stretched as far as the eye could see. Lit up by bright luminescent lights, buildings towered into the sky, challenging the relic that stood in front of them. Billboards flashed the latest trends to tempt anyone who laid eyes on them.

Although it was early, the sound of people bustling around drifted through the air. A few dragons, whose riders were already up, walked through the no-fly streets. Music pounded from small alleyways, and the smell of alcohol lingered in the air from those who partied late. However, that wasn't the case from the top of one of the newest and tallest towers in the city. Here, the music was but a distant pulse, and the air was fresh.

If one looked closely, on top of this particular building, one could see a scaly tail swishing back and forth.

"Ator, your tail," a voice hissed.

The tail swung left before it disappeared from sight.

From where he sat upon his dragon's back, invisible to all, Dominic scanned the city below.

We can't stay here much longer. His dragon warned.

He didn't reply.

You better have a better plan.

The wind picked up.

If Ray finds out—

"I thought you were all in on this."

That was before you went ahead and did your own—

"Stop moving!" Dominic growled.

A patch of aqua-colored scales appeared in sight. A rustle and they disappeared again.

"Honestly, I'm beginning to think you don't understand the meaning of camouflage."

Says the one who's talking out loud.

"There's no one near us," Dominic said.

The wind carries a voice further than you think.

For a while, the two remain silent.

"You're upset."

Worried.

"About Ray? He won't find out." Dominic paused. "And even if he does, it'll be fine. We'll have dealt a large enough blow to the council's ego to appease him." He glanced down. As expected, he could not see so much as a scale of the male dragon under the camouflage sheet that covered them both. It blended in well with its surroundings and was very effective when one held still.

That's not what I'm worried about.

A sigh escaped the rider. "Do share."

They're coming closer.

"What!" Dominic sat up straight.

Can you keep your voice in your head?

He shifted, scanning the area below. *Where are they?*

Close enough that I can sense them.

He groaned.

I told you they wouldn't stop coming after us—especially when we've taken something that means so much to them, Ator lectured.

"They don't even know what it stands for anymore," Dominic snapped. "They don't deserve to keep it in their possession. *We* do."

—*Use thoughts!*

—*If they really value it so highly, perhaps they should have guarded it better.*

Ator stiffened. *Trouble ahead.*

Dominic's eyes latched on to four dragons coming towards them. Each wore blue and black armor that almost completely hid the dragons' true colors. Their riders were dressed in a similar fashion.

"Watchers," Dominic spat in distaste.

Thoughts!

I'm borrowing your vision. Dominic jumped into Ator's mind. He got a closer look at the approaching riders. His eyes narrowed in on the thick tubes strapped to the riders' legs. *Shockers.* He groaned at the discovery.

The dragon shifted. *This is making my scales ripple.*

"Relax," Dominic muttered though he too felt a jolt in the pit of his stomach. It lasted only a moment, as it was drowned out by the excitement brought on by the thought of a possible chase. *They can't see us. The camouflage sheet will keep us invisible.*

Unless it rains, Ator thought dryly.

Way to bring that up. We were just unlucky that time. The sky is clear today. We're fine. Dominic licked his dry lips as he followed the approaching watchers. The way they were heading right toward him was making the hair on the back of his neck stand. It was almost as though the watchers knew where he and his dragon were.

Hey, Dominic, Ator thought as he shifted nervously, his attention glued to the watchers. *What was that Ray was talking about with Celine? You know, about the heat detector thing that the council was working on to get past the camouflage foil?*

It was just a rumor...

The watchers drew closer.

Rumors or not, I don't know how, but they see us, Ator warned.

The watchers pulled their shockers from their sides. They lifted their weapons, aiming right at Dominic and Ator. The ends of the shockers grew an electric blue as they began to charge.

Not good, the aqua dragon warned as a crackling sound reached his ears.

Adrenaline pumped through Dominic's body. He threw the camouflage sheet off to reveal his hooded self. "Go, go, go!" he yelled as four blue balls of electricity were released and came their way.

Ator jumped. He got out of the way just as the balls smashed into the building one after the other. The spot they had been sitting on moments before lit up with blue sparks. Ator dived for the streets, and Dominic leaned as close to his dragon's neck as he could.

You don't think Ray will be too upset about us losing another piece of equipment?

I think your list of things to worry about is in the wrong order, his dragon replied as the wind tore by.

Dominic turned his head. His green eyes caught sight of the four watchers who were in close pursuit. Their shockers crackled as they already began recharging.

"Things might get a bit electrifying!" Dominic yelled over the wind. He turned his head just in time to see the street below. His grip tightened on the saddle a second before his dragon pulled up.

Their speed didn't slow down even a bit as they flew at street level, rising only to avoid crashing into a few dragons and riders walking below. The riders bellowed in anger, shaking fists after both dragon and rider who dared fly recklessly in a no-fly zone.

A smile spread across Dominic's face. The wind would have torn his hood from his head if he didn't clutch it with one hand. A small lock of blond hair peeked out from the side. He leaned further forward.

You're enjoying this, aren't you? Ator accused as he dodged another blue crackling ball shot from behind.

Nope. I'm taking this completely seriously. The grin on Dominic's face said otherwise. *You think they'll let their dragons breathe fire?* he added as an afterthought.

Ator turned a tight corner at full speed. *Doubt it. The law says no fire in the city.*

You never know…With watchers, the council tends to turn a blind eye.

Too many witnesses around. They won't risk it. The dragon turned another corner.

Dominic almost slipped from the saddle. A blue ball passed to their right. It crackled as it smashed into an empty market stall. As the stall collapsed on itself, Dominic guessed that there was going to be one very unhappy stall owner in the morning.

Ator gained height and twisted. His wings brushed the side of a building as he spiraled up it to dodge electric balls and lose his pursuers.

Where to?

The quarries, his rider responded.

Ator took a left. He maneuvered around buildings and dragons as the watchers steadily continued to chase them. Soon, the tall buildings gave way to smaller structures. They had reached the outskirts of the city. Ator turned sharply. Buildings grew shabbier and shabbier, and pretty soon, they became nothing more than bits of wood and roofing sheets gathered by the poor. They had reached the slums.

The smell of open fires drifted through the air. The slowly brightening sky shed some light on the dirty conditions of the residents. There was more activity here than in the city as people were up to start their work and bring in what meager wages they could. Dominic's fingers curled into fists as he scanned the poor living conditions below compared to the inner city.

Ator rolled in the air to avoid another blue ball.

The hair on Dominic's arms stood up as it crackled by.

We're here, his dragon announced.

Dominic's attention flew to the view ahead. The lack of lights in this area made it somewhat darker than the city, yet the rising sun spread enough to show the vast dug-up ground and pits around the area. Dust rose into the sky from the merciless ground that would bake the feet of those who walked on it once the sun rose to its full glory.

Moans from prisoners who worked the pits through night and day drifted through the air. A dragon screamed, making the pit of Dominic's stomach churn. There was no rest for those the council had deemed wicked. It was their sentence to dig up iron for the smelters. It was their fate to work until death, for there was no escape from these pits. Not with the invisible electric field that covered the area and the watchers inside who tormented prisoners.

Dominic wasn't worried about either the field or the watchers below. He and Ator were high enough that they could pass by unharmed. He let his eyes linger on the pits, thoughts of his pursuers momentarily disappearing altogether. His jaw clenched, and his fists tightened, and his fingernails dug into his palm. A lump rose in his throat. *Father...*

As they flew closer, the groaning grew louder. Dominic pushed the urge to help aside. He swallowed hard.

One day, he promised himself. *Soon.*

What now? Ator asked. The sky was getting lighter, and the sun peered from behind the horizon.

Dominic tore his eyes from the quarries of agony. *The abandoned section.*

Ator whirled abruptly, changing their course. They tore towards the area that had been over-mined. All minerals had been stripped from its ground, leaving it a barren waste. It was a desert that spread for miles, leaving no trace of the lush forests that were said to have once covered it. Now, not even insects lived here.

They're catching up, Ator warned as he turned sharply to the right. *I can't concentrate on dodging shockers and getting away all at once,* he muttered as he dove lower.

Why didn't you say that in the first place? Dominic's hand moved under his cloak. His fingers closed around a small tube-like object. He pulled it free from where it had been strapped to his side. *You just get us out of here. I'll take care of any attacks. Just try not to lose me in the process.*

That's a tall order. Ator stretched his neck to gain speed.

Dominic raised the silver tube above his head. "Playtime." He grinned as his thumb pressed the button that was right in the middle of the tube. At once, a metal rod, almost a meter in length, shot out of both ends, making it a long pole.

You enjoy this way too much, Ator remarked as he dived.

Dominic grinned but didn't reply as he felt the hair on the back of his neck rise. As quick as a flash, he twisted his upper body around and swung the pole. He watched in satisfaction as it connected with an approaching blue ball. It knocked the ball right back in the direction it had come from.

No matter how many times he saw it happen, it always fascinated him. The watcher who had shot the ball was hit square in the chest. For a moment, his whole body jerked before he went limp and slid from his dragon's back, dropping his shocker in the process. Feeling that his rider was falling, the dragon dived, going to his aid.

One down. Dominic grinned. *Three to go.* He spun the pole. *Don't you just love how reaper metal repels shockers?*

That's something you better not lose.

I know…It was a gift from my dad. Dominic didn't let the thought linger. He searched the large canyons that lay ahead. They were all made by dragons and humans who had been forced to work throughout the years.

The sun was now steadily climbing above the horizon, lighting up the dusty ground that stretched before the boy, his dragon, and their pursuers.

Dominic turned and deflected another ball of electricity, hitting it back the way it had come. This time, the remaining watchers were ready and dodged it, their dragons twirling gracefully out of its path.

We could use some cover, Dominic suggested.

Reading his mind, Ator descended until he was just above the ground. He was now so low that the dust below rose and swirled about them, hiding them from view. Dominic saw a blue ball pass by some distance away from them.

They're shooting blindly, he noted.

Ator flicked his tail to raise more dust. As they drew closer to the canyon, Dominic turned. He squinted, trying to make out their pursuers. When something to the right caught his attention, he turned his head that way. It looked like there was a large shape flying right next to them.

Oh boy, Dominic muttered.

His eyes widened as he saw a pole like his swinging at him. He raised his own just in time to block the blow that was meant to knock him from the saddle. The attacker drew closer to Ator and his rider and swung his pole once again. Dominic blocked and pushed back, yet the watcher wasn't about to be outdone. The watcher's dragon pushed Ator off course, almost making Dominic lose his seating.

A little help here! Ator grunted.

Dominic didn't reply as he regained his seating and attempted to whack the watcher with his pole. When the pursuer drew back, he felt a moment of relief. The feeling disappeared when he heard a crackle and saw the forming blue light.

Left, Ator warned.

Dominic craned his neck to see a watcher on the other side. He too had his shocker charging. *Splodge! Two at once?*

As the lights on both ends of the weapon intensified, Dominic swallowed. *Any chance you're going to get us out if this one?*

Got it covered. The balls of light were shot. Ator dropped and flipped. Both balls shot past Dominic who watched as each ball passed beneath them and smashed into the watchers on the opposite side.

Now that's how it's done, Ator declared.

One more to go, Dominic agreed.

As they reached the canyon, Ator dove straight down the side of it, aiming for the bottom. With the dust no longer hiding them, Dominic turned to see the other watcher closing in.

Ator twisted, following the canyon's many twists and turns. He flew so rapidly that to Dominic, everything around him passed by in a blur. Realizing that his dragon was widening the gap between them and their pursuer, Dominic pressed the button in the middle of his rod, and the poles on both sides slid inwards. Left holding only a small tube, the rider safely tucked it inside his cloak before he leaned forward. The sun was now fully out, already beating down on the dry earth below with a merciless heat.

The aqua dragon managed to increase the distance from his pursuer to the point that the watcher behind them would lose sight of them when he turned corners and dodged large mounds of dirt. Balls of blue light smashed into walls harmlessly.

Both Dominic and his dragon knew the abandoned quarries like the back of their hands, or in Ator's case, the back of his claws. They had explored them many times.

Are we almost there? Dominic questioned.

Right around the corner.

Dominic leaned as far forward as he could on his dragon's back to aid him. They shot around the corner, a good distance ahead of the uniformed rider behind them. Ator turned his wings vertical to bring him to a skidding halt. He turned in a flash and dove into a dark open hole at the side of the canyon. As its cool interior engulfed them, both dragon and boy craned their necks around just in time to see the watcher and his dragon shoot past. Neither took a second glance at the hole, which at his speed would be invisible.

The dragon and the boy in the cave held their breaths, waiting for the possible return of their pursuer. He didn't come.

"Phew." Dominic grinned as he brushed off the hood covering his head. He closed his eyelids for a moment, enjoying the adrenaline that was still pumping through him from the chase. "That was fun." He blew a strand of his messy blond hair out of his eyes before sliding off his dragon's back and sinking to the floor. He leaned his back against the dirt wall.

They're becoming bolder. Not too long ago, they would have stopped the chase right after the city, Ator mused as he turned. His weight made the small opening shake and dust fall.

"Yeah, yeah, probably just getting tired of us always interfering." Dominic brushed it off.

I'm thinking that they may not have realized yet exactly what we took. The dragon cocked his head to the side. *If they did, we probably would have had more than just four of them on our tails.* Now facing the entrance, Ator peered out cautiously. *You think it's safe?*

Probably. At the speed they were going, they're long gone, Dominic replied as he reached beneath his cloak and felt the long new object he had acquired. A grin spread across his face. "How about we go home?" he asked aloud.

Sounds fine to me. Ator sighed with relief.

Dominic moved over to his dragon and pulled himself onto the creature's back. *Can you believe we did it?*

I don't know if I want to think about it. Ator walked towards the edge of the cave.

I mean we really did it! Dominic's grin widened. *They'll be furious when they find it missing.*

I don't doubt it. Ator's claws curled around the edge.

At least they'll finally realize…

The aqua dragon's muscles bunched.

There's still some of us willing to fight back.

Ator leaped into the open, wings spreading. He soared into the air before turning. The dragon and the boy headed into the day, leaving the city and the groans of the quarries behind.

If you enjoyed this sample, look for
Dragon of Legend: New Era
on Amazon.

COLD
FIRE

SHAYE EASTON

CHAPTER ONE

The moments after it passes are always the coldest.

Not cold in a way I can feel—I've yet to feel the cold once in my entire seventeen years—but cold by comparison. Cold created by the sudden and startling absence of heat. It's an illusion. It's like a trick of the light—you think there's something to it, and just as you're discovering what, just as your hope is building, it's snatched away on the wings of reality.

I have both hands on the rough, damp pavement. Little rocks press into the flesh of my palms. A particularly sharp stone— I suspect it may be glass—has sliced through my skin. My breath comes out of my body in a rush, like a tsunami rolling up from my lungs and spurting out onto the dark ground. I gasp, and the wave floods back in. Out. Then in again.

I am a block away from Southlake High when it hit, when the heat crept into my veins as it does once a day, setting my body on fire. And judging by all the looks I'm getting, it clearly isn't far enough. A particularly loud group of boys pass me, sniggering and howling like a pack of wolves. It's nothing they haven't seen before. I've been here for six months, and I've already cemented my status as the pale girl who doesn't quite wear enough layers to suit the weather, frequently seen doubled over on the ground.

They all stare. One, in particular, won't look away, even after his friends have already moved on. He's dark-haired and dark-eyed, and he lingers behind them, watching me over his shoulder as they continue up the street.

I can't help myself. "What're you looking at?" I snap.

He finally turns away.

I get back on my feet. The knees of my pants are wet and dirty, and I give them a brush with my hands, pretending like I don't notice the whispers of all the students around me. At this point, I'm honestly not sure what they have to whisper about. They've already gossiped their way through the topic of my disease, spread rumours that I'm a witch or a demon or something equally uncreative. *What next?* Am I a vampire now, about to rise up in my black cape and drain the blood of some innocent junior?

The afternoon is heavy around me. The air thick with moisture and dark with clouds. It's raining like it always seems to be when I'm around. The drops are fine and mist-like; they sink into my clothes and collect on my bare arms like glitter. The gloomy weather looks strange here in Corven Lake. It clashes with the cheery shop fronts selling ice cream and beach wear. It doesn't suit the scorched pavements or the tan of this seaside town's inhabitants.

Conversely, it suits me perfectly. I am dark-haired and pale. I am dismal and utterly strange. I am a ghost amongst these people, a half-present spectacle, eternally expecting someone to jump out of a bush and take a snap—*flash*, and my photo will be in the news, below a header in all caps proclaiming: GHOST SIGHTING IN CORVEN LAKE.

I continue down the street, eventually turning onto Corven Drive. It's the predominant road in town, hemmed in by shops on one side and the coastline on the other. If you want to find a tourist, chances are you'll see them on Corven Drive. But in this weather, it's a ghost town.

You wouldn't be able to guess it, but it is in fact early autumn—March—and the leaves have already fled the trees as though they're allergic to the branches. It follows a pattern of uncharacteristic weather that began back in January, when the days took on a slight chill despite it being the middle of the Australian summer. At first, people complained but weren't altogether too concerned. Now we're in the middle of an early winter and I'm the one staring down at the end of the accusatory finger.

It's never spoken aloud, but everyone knows it: it's my fault. The details of my disease are kept as a strict secret, so naturally, they're heavily rumoured. The official story is that I have some rare variation of cancer which causes my body temperature to fluctuate wildly. I'm either so cold my skin burns like dry ice or my blood is so hot that it has me doubled over in pain.

The truth is even more ridiculous. It involves a child, born with an extraordinarily low body temperature. It involves a girl, me, growing and suffering through a daily event termed as a 'heat surge,' in which my body strips heat from the surrounding air to keep my organs functioning.

As a consequence, an unnatural and constant winter soon descends on whichever unfortunate place I choose to reside. Last year it was Perth. This year it's Corven Lake, a sizeable seaside town a few hours south of Sydney, and while no one's been explicitly told it's my fault, it doesn't take much to put two and two together and start spreading rumours. This early winter is what I, and a team of global professionals I've long since fallen out of contact with, lovingly refer to as Side Effect Number One.

After a few blocks, I pause at the corner. Here, I can either go straight ahead for the long way or turn left for the direct route home. Sometimes walking in the rain helps lighten up my mood. When I'm feeling particularly numb, the subtle pressure of the rain against my skin is enough to convince me I'm still alive. But today I'm not feeling much of anything. The rain is too fine. The wind is too soft. My skin is unreceptive to the abnormally early winter air. I take the turn at the corner; I'm heading home.

As a kid, I once leaned on the stove top, unaware it was switched on and heating up beneath me, and melted all the skin off my arm before Mum noticed and screamed at me to move away. We quickly learnt I had a complete and horrifying lack of heat or pain receptors. The winter chill and the summer heat were, and still are, all the same: the feel of a slightly cool, slightly warm room. And if I ever hurt myself, I get all of the pressure and none of the pain. This is Side Effect Number Two.

The back streets of Corven are much like the suburbs of any city: houses, modern and historical and half-and-half, bunched up against each other like boxes packed onto a shelf. A faded Australian flag flaps from a pole in an old man's yard. Out front another, a mailbox hangs open, the flyers and junk mails spewing out, fluttering onto the footpath, torn and damp. In multiple yards, I see gardens of roses, gardenias and tulips sitting squashed under window sills and dying in the cold. Down the street, shivering are frangipani trees with buds yet to blossom. Along the path, gum trees fight against the abnormal weather, their hardy silver leaves holding firmly to their branches. Meanwhile, Australian maples rest barren and still, like giant hands waiting to claw the clouds from the sky.

And amongst it all is the silence, the echo of conversations and laughter of past summers long since faded from the air.

I walk a block. I walk two. After a third, a strange sensation creeps over my body, startling my skin. The hair on my arms rise like sentinels on the lookout for danger. And I must be in danger because my gut churns, my heart pounds and a gasp rockets from the confines of my mouth. I stop dead in my tracks.

It's unlike anything else: this sensation that makes me want to fold in on myself and draws out every tendril of warmth in my bloodstream. Goose bumps dot my arms and the misty rain bites into my skin like shards of glass.

And I realise with a sudden harsh certainty, I'm cold. I lift up my arm and stare at it, alarmed. I'm *truly* cold. It's not a hallucination, nor a phantom feeling—this is the real deal.

When I look up, a man is standing at the other end of the road. But 'man' doesn't quite cut it. Everything from his clothes to his skin and his eyes is tinted an unnatural grey, and he stands out in the gloom like he's cast in a light from a source I can't see.

The cold I felt rolls over me stronger, and I hug my arms to my chest and shiver, a second shocked gasp escaping my throat. I haven't felt the cold since I was an infant, and even that is only the vaguest wisp of a memory. My heart jumps suddenly. *Could I be cured?*

But the second I think it, I know it isn't true. The man is still staring at me, and a deeply buried instinct tells me this has nothing to do with my disease and more to do with my current situation. I try to make out his features but as soon as I focus in on any one element—his nose, the shape of his chin, the set of his brows—they blur. I blink and shake my head. That can't be right.

Sure enough, when I look again, he's blurry and indistinct, a mirage in our quiet, icy desert. He's got a face you forget as soon as you turn away. But I can feel his eyes on me, and I can feel the cold, almost as if he's brought it with him…

I turn on my heels and start heading back the way I came, slowly at first, then faster when I look back and he's still there, still watching me with an unblinking gaze. I start to jog, heart pounding, breath coming quickly in and out. I turn at the corner to take a longer route home, but even once he's out of view, I can still feel his eyes on me.

Stop it, Melissa, I chide. *You're being ridiculous.*

But I'm running now, fear choking up my bloodstream, my instincts screaming at me to move faster, go further. I come to another corner and look back, almost certain that I'll see his blurry grey form at the far end of the street.

That's when I run headfirst into someone rounding the corner. With a yelp, I stumble back, terror snaking through me. But this person isn't grey or blurry. He's dressed in Southlake High's winter uniform: dark pants, white shirt, a navy woollen jumper with the blue and white school emblem. He's wearing a rain jacket over the top and his dark hair is wet and tousled.

He's the same boy I told off for staring at me earlier, but now I'm not feeling so confident. Maybe it's just the residual fear in my bloodstream, but his sudden presence makes me horribly uneasy.

"You might want to slow down a little," he tells me, dark eyes glinting. "The ground is slippery." Except his eyes aren't just dark—they're pitch black.

"I'll take that under advisement," I reply, and my voice shakes. I move past him, continuing hurriedly down the street. When I look over my shoulder, he's watching me go. And despite the fact that the inexplicable cold I felt has worn off, it chills me to the core.

*   *   *

When I reach home, I fumble with the gate, my hands shaking as I lock it behind me. Whatever cold I felt is long gone by now, but its memory has sunk into my bones and refuses to leave. I shiver as I walk up the path, stopping at the front door.

The mat on our doorstep welcomes me home. I grind the dirt on my shoes into the letters. Our current *home* is more of a cold and empty house playing dress ups, pretending to be something that it isn't by hanging family pictures on the walls and turning the television on to fill the silence. Some mornings when I wake up in my room, I catch myself wondering where I am, as if I haven't lived there for six months but only one day—as if all the memories of waking up and getting dressed in that spot are alien, belonging to a different person in a different time. Nothing there is familiar. Nothing there feels like home. My house is a fake, a forgery, and my family is simply going along with the act.

I realise I forgot my keys again and sigh. *Great.* I knock twice.

Mum opens the door, her brown shoulder-length hair lit by the light from inside, creating a golden halo around her face.

There's no smile to welcome me home. Her hard eyes travel disapprovingly over my damp hair and clothing. Beads of rain still cling to my skin and I imagine they glisten like diamonds in the warm light.

"Shoes off before you come inside, please. I don't want you treading mud through the house." I get to work unlacing my sneakers. I've got one off and have set it down by the door when she remarks, "If you're going to insist on walking home, you could at least have the good sense to bring an umbrella."

"That would defeat the purpose."

"Are these walks really necessary?"

"Yes, Mum." I set down the other shoe and look up. "They are."

I step inside and she says, "If all you want to do is get rained on, maybe you should just take a shower."

I have to refrain from snapping at her. "It's not the same."

"Uh-huh."

She doesn't get it, but it's ridiculous of me to expect her to. I'm the unfortunate one out of seven billion who got saddled with this disease, not her.

I head for the stairs. It's only once I'm halfway up that I realise she still hasn't moved from the doorway. She stands silently, eyes trained on the gloom outside the house, and for a moment I fear the grey man has followed me home.

"Mum?" I ask.

"Yeah?"

"What is it?"

"Nothing." She closes the front door with a resonant slam. And it's scary how normal it all seems: a mother who stares at thin air as if she can create something from it with the deadness of her gaze; a daughter who drags winter around like a pet; and a family bond that's cold as ice and just as brittle.

Upstairs, I shower, scrubbing my skin until it's red and raw. At some point along the road, I got this idea into my head that if I just rub hard enough or use enough heat, I'll be able to feel something—I'll be able to cure myself of this disease. But the water remains lukewarm, and like always my skin fails to respond.

My reflection confronts me in the mirror when I hop out. Dark brown hair hangs limp and dripping wet on my shoulders, contrasting starkly with my ghostly pale skin. Eyes rimmed by dark lashes are coloured cloudy blue. Lips too small for my jaw, and almost as pale as my skin, sat beneath a small upturned nose. The mirror is foggy from the steam of my shower and it distorts my features, making them blurry, washed out, and puckered. I rub a hand through the condensation, and in that moment, I swear I see the grey man over my shoulder, staring with hollow eyes.

I jump, spinning around, eyes swinging frantically. He was standing in the open doorway of my shower, but there's no one there. I take a deep breath and try to calm my racing heart. I'm just being paranoid.

Downstairs, my family of three sits in silence for dinner. Across from me, Dad stares unseeingly down at his food, silent and tired. His dark brown hair is shot through with grey, his once-tanned skin is pale and weathered, and his dark blue eyes rest above dark shadows. He's a shell of the father I knew as a kid, before this life stole his vigour. Both my parents work—Mum as a freelance journalist, Dad as a tradesman—but I can tell the years of physical labour and working long hours to support our family have been particularly tough on him.

With a disease like mine, one that slowly freezes my surrounding environment, relocation becomes a yearly event. In the beginning, we attempted to make a life for ourselves in each place we lived in. Then the goodbyes got too difficult, and my disease got worse. Now we float like restless spirits from place to place. We stop to rest each year but we're never present enough to grow roots.

This month marks the halfway point of our stay here in Corven Lake, and the idea of moving again in September is already hanging over our family like a storm cloud. But a year is our deadline. If I stay too long after that, the whole area will become uninhabitable, which means water will freeze in the pipes, plants will wilt and shrivel, the wildlife will have to migrate or freeze, and people will start dying from the cold. If I stay too long after a year, the effects grow irreversible.

For a long while, the clinking of eating utensils, the ticking of the clock, and the distant chatter of the television are the only sounds that fill the house. Family meals seem to be lacking a lot of the *family* these days. We sit and eat at the same table out of tradition and maybe out of hope—a last ditch effort to strengthen the bond of our family.

I finish off my dinner quickly, eager to leave this gloomy void of a dining room behind, and head straight for my room. I take the stairs two at a time and although I know no one can see me, I feel as though every eye in Corven Lake is on my back. Even after I've slammed my bedroom door behind me and drawn the curtains, the feeling still won't ease. It's like every person in town has gathered in my bedroom and is standing over my bed, watching.

I grip the sheets with my hands, skin prickling. *No one knows*, I tell myself. *No one knows this is your fault.*

But even as I try to comfort myself, I know it's a lie. They all know. And one day, Corven Lake is going to become like every other place I've lived in: frozen, dying, and full of hateful eyes haunting my every move.

If you enjoyed this sample, look for
Cold Fire
on Amazon.

ACKNOWLEDGEMENTS

Thank you to Rutchy Marie for finding me on Wattpad and asking me if I would like to publish my book.

To Zena Magto for helping me polish this book and make it amazing.

To my husband for supporting me as I went through this process.

To my daughters for being "good" while I worked on my book.

AUTHOR'S NOTE

Thank you so much for reading *Loved By A Dragon* ! I can't express how grateful I am for reading something that was once just a thought inside my head.

Please feel free to send me an email. Just know that my publisher filters these emails. Good news is always welcome.
sm_merrill@awesomeauthors.org

I'd love to hear your thoughts on the book. Please leave a review on Amazon or Goodreads because I just love reading your comments and getting to know you!

Can't wait to hear from you!

S.M. Merrill

ABOUT THE AUTHOR

Stephanie Merrill lives in Virginia with her husband and two children. She has lived there her entire life. This helped her develop the town of White Valley for her first book, Loved by a Dragon. She loves spending time with her family, exploring the historic sites within driving distance of her home when she is not teaching or writing. Stephanie is an outgoing, inquisitive woman who always wants to know more about the world around her and help make it a better place. Her favorite thing to write about are big beautiful women and the sexy shifter mates who fall in love with them. She writes about these women because growing up she never saw herself reflected in the books she read. She can't wait for others to read her book and escape into a world of forever mates and happily ever afters.

Made in the USA
Monee, IL
13 September 2023

42709764R00164